HAUNTED EARTH

SUPERNATURAL TALES FROM AROUND THE WORLD

GAURAV BHATIA
WRITING AS
JAGDISH SIKAND

Haunted Earth

Supernatural Tales From Around The World

First Edition

This book was professionally typeset on Reedsy.
Find out more at reedsy.com

WIZARD OF WORDS PUBLISHING L.L.C.
745 Barclay Cir
Unit 310
Rochester MI 48307

ISBN: 978-1-5136-8455-0

This book is dedicated to:

my Wife, and my Daughters

my Parents

....and to all those who seek to
draw back the veil.

"Faith begins just beyond the edge of sight."

– Gaurav Bhatia and Jagdish Sikand

May 2, 2021
Rochester, Michigan
The United States of America
Haunted Earth

CONTENTS

FOREWORD

Dear Reader,

As a child, I used to be terrified of horror movies, and I must admit that even now, a particularly suspenseful scene still causes me to avert my eyes from the screen. My wife, a die-hard horror fan finds it quite hilarious and has had many a laugh at my expense.

Horror, in its written form, however, is quite another story (please do excuse the pun). Since I read my first Anne Rice novel at the tender age of twelve (not age appropriate, I know, but back then, the concept was nonexistent in India) I have been fascinated with vampires, werewolves, witches, warlocks and everything else that goes bump in the night. Since then, I have literally devoured horror fiction (again, sorry about the pun) ranging from Lovecraft, Poe, and Stoker, to Rice, King, Koontz and every other notable author in between.

The tales that I have attempted to tell in this book are my own. Some may find similarities with folk tales that they may have heard elsewhere and that is perfectly normal. Mankind shares a common fear of the dark, and therefore when our imagination is fueled by dread of the unseen, the results are similar across the world more often than not. This is the reason why demons have horns in every culture that recognizes their existence.

I have chosen different locales and cultural settings for each story as I feel that doing so has added a dimension to these tales that they would otherwise lack. I realize that this may also have provided the opportunity to some of accusing me of cultural appropriation, and I refuse to provide any defense to such accusations, save the ones below:

1. I have always considered myself a citizen of the world and have refused to limit myself to conform with the identity of any one nation or culture.
2. I have taken great pains to ensure that the settings of my tales are well researched and that any creative liberty that I may have indulged in, remains within reason.

I would also like to take this opportunity to thank **James (Jim) Polley**, of **Toronto Canada**, my friend of many years. Jim not only allowed me to base the lead character in the story titled *The Woman in the Lake* on his own years spent in Japan (thankfully without any supernatural encounters) but he also helped me fine tune the cultural references in use throughout this tale, for which I am grateful. Jim, thank you for your friendship, and long may we raise our cups together.

It's now time to turn this page and meet the characters of my first tale.

Grab a blanket. Light a candle. Shut that window that's been banging all this while.

Are you alone? Are You Sure?

Yours truly,
Jagdish Sikand

DEER DEPARTED

The day dawned crisp and clear, just like any other October morning. A cold wind blew through the trees, triggering a cascade of dry leaves that fell through the air like a waterfall. The ground was covered with a carpet of blazing gold. The sun's rays lit up the horizon with a pink hue that extended to the few clouds scattered across the morning sky—in all, a picture-perfect scene, yet to Jane it all meant nothing.

As she stood sipping her brew and staring outside the kitchen window, her mind couldn't help but wander back to the terrible events of last year. She clearly remembered that October day, almost identical to the one that beckoned outside her window now. It was Halloween—All Hallows Eve. Her son David was excited as only a twelve-year-old can be. Just a few months shy of joining the coveted ranks of teenagers, where any traditions of childhood are scorned upon, David was determined to enjoy to the utmost what he claimed would be his "Last Halloween." Little did Jane know how prophetic those words would soon turn out.

The events of that terrible day were still fresh in her mind. She clearly recalled that it had been a Saturday and that she made pancakes, David's favorite, for breakfast. She had dropped David off at the mall to hang out with his friends and then returned home after buying candy on the way. She remembered her pride at David's pirate costume, that she had spent hours working on, as he walked out to join his friends that evening. She could still call to mind the smell of sizzling steaks she was cooking for dinner when there came that dreadful knock on the door and her world collapsed.

Everything that came after was just a jumble of hazy images and muffled sounds in her mind—her husband John opening the door, the uniforms and flashing lights outside, the snatches of conversation that seemed to come from far away as time slowed to a crawl. "Terribly sorry...," "crossed the street without looking...," "it was dark and the driver didn't see...," "his skull was crushed..." Even as she fell to the floor in a swoon, she knew with the certainty only a mother can possess that her boy was gone forever.

That was the beginning of Jane's free-fall into darkness and despair. Finding reality to be unbearable, Jane decided instead to crawl into that liquor-induced blanket of oblivion that numbs all pain. She stopped taking care of herself, ate little, and slept even less though she was almost always drunk. Her once comely face was now marred with splotchy skin and dark circles under her eyes. Alcohol became both her refuge and her prison, and even the coffee she now sipped contained a generous dose of brandy.

Jane heard footsteps coming down the stairs, and a moment later the front door was opened and then shut with a bang. The truck in the driveway roared to life as John drove off to wherever he went these days to get away from her. Jane couldn't help but feel a momentary pang of remorse. The past year had been hard on John. Not only did he lose his son but apparently he lost his wife as well. When she withdrew from the world, she turned away from John also for, in her mind, the pain, grief, and guilt were hers to bear alone. No matter how hard John tried, she kept shutting him out and finally he had simply stopped trying. She wondered if there was another woman in the picture now and then decided that she didn't care. John was a good man and deserved to be happy.

There were sounds of some commotion outside. She peeked through the window and saw her new neighbors struggling to set up an inflatable dragon in the front yard while their two little boys stood watching with wide-eyed wonder. They seemed like nice people, although Jane had so far neglected to go introduce herself, something hitherto unheard of in the small Alberta town she lived in. She still found it difficult to be around children. Sometimes the sight of kids hurrying to catch the school bus caused her to break down into a fit of crying that lasted for hours and she steadfastly refused to answer the door when children from the neighborhood came selling cookies.

With a start, Jane realized that Halloween was around the corner and her heart filled up with dread at the very thought of costumed trick-or-treaters coming to her doorstep.

Such were the thoughts running through Jane's mind when she noticed the fawn standing in her backyard and looking at the kitchen window. At first, Jane ignored it, fully expecting the fawn to take off once it realized there were humans around, but when she glanced towards it again, the young deer was still there looking in her direction. Curious, Jane leaned closer to the window so as to reveal herself and the deer, now looking directly at her, took a step forward. Intrigued, Jane opened the sliding door and stepped out into her backyard. The cold wind sent a shiver through her body as she wrapped the shawl tightly around her scrawny shoulders.

The fawn, rather than dashing away as any normal deer would have done, stood firm and kept peering intently at her as if it were trying to recognize her. Jane wondered if the animal was sick. It looked to be just about a year old and by all indications in good health. Perhaps it was just dazed or otherwise too scared to react? As Jane tried to make sense of this bold and unusual behavior, the fawn emitted a bleating sound and bounded towards her with a suddenness that caused her to jerk back with a squeal. Afraid that the animal intended to bite her, she clapped her hands and tried to shoo it away but the deer, undeterred, kept trying to come close to her while bleating happily.

Instinct told Jane that the fawn didn't mean her any harm so kneeling down, she allowed the animal to approach. The fawn nuzzled up to her and rubbed his nose against her face while she stroked his satin-smooth skin. She smelt a peculiar odor on the deer, not unpleasant but one which was strangely familiar and caused goosebumps to rise on her skin. Shifting to a sitting position, she put the fawn in her lap where he curled up and promptly fell off to sleep.

Watching the sleeping fawn's chest rise and fall, Jane suddenly felt her motherly instinct, long drowned in drink and sorrow, come roaring back to life. Losing all track of time and oblivious of the wind that kicked up small storms of leaves around her, she sat cradling the fawn in her arms until an involuntary tear escaping from her eye broke into her reverie.

The fawn too woke from its contented sleep, yawned, and then looked up at her expectantly. Jane stood up and rubbed her frozen hands to restore circulation as she made her way towards the kitchen door. She beckoned to the fawn who followed her dutifully into the house. Once inside, the fawn continued with its extremely bizarre behavior by proceeding to explore every nook and corner of the house while Jane followed. It seemed to take a particular interest in photographs in the living room and kept returning to them again and again. Finally, the fawn gingerly picked up a small photograph in its mouth and brought it to Jane. With trembling hands Jane took the photograph from the deer, knowing even before she looked at it that it was a picture of David, taken just a few months before the accident.

Jane felt a shiver through her body even though it was warm in the house. As if pushed by unseen hands, she climbed the stairs to the rooms above and the fawn slowly followed, testing each stair gingerly with its little hooves. The landing at the top of the stairs was covered in darkness and Jane stood there quietly waiting for something to happen, though she was not sure exactly what to expect. After a few minutes, the fawn got impatient and started walking down the hallway while glancing backward as if beckoning her to follow. It then went inside an open doorway and disappeared from Jane's view. Jane's heart began pounding loudly, for somehow she had known which room the deer would go into for it had been David's room before he died.

Jane followed the fawn into the room and saw it sitting on David's old bed. Unsure of what she was witnessing, she decided to test a notion that was quickly forming in her mind. She went to the bedroom closet and rummaged through David's things, withdrawing three objects which she placed before the deer who, without a moment's hesitation, placed his hoof on the object in the middle. A cold shiver ran through Jane's spine for the fawn had chosen David's favorite toy. She repeated the test several times with various items and each time the fawn chose an object that had been particularly dear to David during his life.

Jane was not a superstitious person and even now she fought with herself to curb the irrational hope that threatened to engulf her heart. Surely there was some scientific explanation for all of this? It was inconceivable that somehow her dead son had crossed the void to take birth as deer and had come seeking the mother from his previous life. Jane laughed out loud at the very silliness of the idea and admonished herself for giving in to wishful thinking, even if for a moment. Hope, she reminded herself, was a dangerous thing, for there was no returning from where David had gone and he was lost to her forever. She was hurting badly enough as it was and didn't need to invite more pain that would invariably come from such a foolish flight of fancy.

Deciding that this episode had gone on long enough, Jane got up from the bed, intending to send the deer away so he could go look for his real mother and at that very moment, the fawn turned and lay on his back. Jane stopped short as she stared with wide eyes at the fawn's now exposed belly, for clearly visible on the upper portion of his stomach was a faint crescent mark, identical to the birthmark David had carried all his short years. Jane stared and stared at the mark and touched it to see if it were a figment of her imagination. With sudden tears streaming from her eyes and all doubt vanishing from her mind, she hugged the fawn tightly as an almost unbearable excitement burst through her heart. There was no mistaking the evidence that lay before her very eyes! A miracle had indeed happened and somehow God, whom she had hitherto refused to believe in, had guided David through the valley of death and back into her arms. The fawn, while surprised at the sudden ferocity of affection displayed by Jane, nevertheless was happy to bask in its warm glow.

More time passed by as mother and fawn sat locked in a warm embrace while she whispered loving words into his ears. The fawn responded by alternately licking and rubbing his nose against Jane's face, seemingly content with just being in her arms. Yet as the lengthening evening shadows touched the windows of David's room, the fawn suddenly became restless, and struggling out of Jane's arms, got off the bed and bounded into the hallway and down the stairs. Jane quickly followed and found the deer knocking at the kitchen door with its hooves and looking at her as if asking to be let out. Much as the thought horrified her, Jane somehow understood the fawn's unspoken need to leave. Jane steeled her heart as she opened the kitchen door, the hardest thing she'd ever had to do, and the fawn stepped out, took one backward look at Jane, and vanished into the winter gloom.

Jane couldn't sleep that night. Nervous excitement about the phenomenon she had experienced, mixed with extreme anxiety about the fawn's whereabouts, kept her awake until the small hours of the morning. She heard John come back home around midnight and walk quietly to his bedroom—they had been sleeping separately for a few months now. Dawn couldn't come fast enough for Jane the following morning and as soon as there was sufficient light, she wore a thick jacket and for the first time in many months, left the confines of her home. She assumed that the fawn had entered the garden from a small gap in the wall bordering the woods so she made her way in that direction.

The woods, illuminated in the early morning light, were a cornucopia of sights, smells, and sounds. A mist draped the ground and a blanket of leaves lay on the forest floor, while birds flew among the trees, filling the air with their feathered score. The smell of pine needles mixed with wood smoke filled her lungs as Jane walked through the woods calling softly to the fawn. Suddenly her calls were answered with happy bleats as the fawn materialized out of the mist and came running straight into her open arms. Joy, an emotion Jane had not experienced for a very long time, filled her heart as she and the fawn walked among the trees for hours. Finally, a gnawing hunger, another first in many months, convinced Jane to head back home with the fawn in tow.

Inside the kitchen, Jane struggled with the problem of what to feed the fawn. She tried giving him pieces of bread and lettuce, both of which the fawn refused. He even turned his nose at the two kinds of cereal that Jane put in front of him. She was at her wit's end when suddenly inspiration struck and she quickly mixed batter to make a batch of pancakes with maple syrup and was gratified to see the fawn wolf them down without hesitation. After finishing her breakfast, Jane now pondered on her next challenge, which was sharing this wonderful news with John without appearing crazy. Fortunately, as she discovered, John had already left the house and so she could put off that conversation for later and focus completely on her time with the fawn.

The day went by far more quickly than Jane wanted and with the evening's inevitable approach, the fawn again took his leave. Knowing that he would return the following morning, Jane consoled herself that a temporary separation was perhaps the price nature demanded for this otherwise impossible reunion. She busied herself in making dinner for the first time in almost a year and decided to wait up for John when he came home. She brought out her best dinnerware and set the table. Lighting small candles, she placed them next to the crystal goblets that she filled with red wine. Then she settled down to wait for her husband to return and exhausted from the day's excursions, dozed off after a while.

The sound of the truck in her driveway awoke Jane from her dreamless slumber. She quickly got up from the couch as the front door opened and John stepped in. He stood looking curiously at the romantic setup on the dining table and at her. Jane took a step forward and hugged John tightly and after a slight delay, perhaps to get over his surprise, John hugged her back, albeit without the same passion. Jane held his hand and led him to the table and they sat down to their first meal together in a long time. Jane wanted to find the right opportunity before breaking the news to John so she made small talk while he ate in silence, only nodding his head or shaking it to signal his disagreement with something she said. Finally, they rose and moved over to the living room where John, looking embarrassed, cleared his throat and said "Jane, I have something to tell you." Jane replied in an excited voice "Oh John, I have something to tell you too! You are not going to believe this!" John, ignoring her and looking positively guilty, blurted out "Look Jane, there is no easy way to say this so I will come right to the point. I am leaving! I am leaving you and this bloody town for good. I have met someone else and our plans are made. I have already quit my job and found another one in Toronto and I will be leaving tomorrow. I have the divorce papers signed and ready in my room for you to sign. You can keep the house for now but we will have to eventually sell it. The attorneys can discuss the financial arrangements so you will need to hire a lawyer. I'm sorry, Jane, but that's just the way it is. I wanted to tell you before but could never find the right time to have this conversation. You haven't been yourself in a long time."

Jane felt like she had been slapped in the face. Why this? Why now when suddenly her world was brightening up again? If John had broken the news a couple of days ago, she would've been indifferent to it but things had changed! Her son had returned from the dead and life was going to get better! As Jane's mind furiously tried to make sense of this new development, she saw one small ray of hope—John didn't know about David! He didn't know that their son had returned. Surely once he knew, he would abandon his plans and they would be together as a family.

John was still talking about the divorce when Jane interrupted him. "John, honey, you don't have to leave! Something wonderful has happened. It's David, he has come back. God has sent him back to us!" Now it was John's turn to look stunned. He stared at his wife with an incredulous expression and sputtered "What the hell are you talking about?" In breathless sentences, Jane related her experiences of the past two days to him as he listened with his brows furrowed. Finally, when she finished, John said in a low voice trembling with anger "I knew you were slowly going crazy but this is low even for you, Jane. Making up a story about our dead son to convince me to stay? How dare you? David has come back to life as deer? Do you hear yourself? You need help, Jane! You are crazy!" With those words, John stomped off to his room and slammed the door shut while Jane kept calling his name, but her entreaties went unanswered.

Morning found Jane asleep on the couch, exhausted from crying all night. When she finally awoke, it was past ten o'clock and with a rush of panic she ran to the kitchen door, fully expecting to find the fawn waiting outside but the garden stood empty. After washing her tear-stained face, Jane quickly dressed and left her house heading towards the woods to go search for the fawn. As she walked, Jane remembered that today was Halloween, exactly a year since David died. Out of habit, tears welled up in her eyes but she instantly wiped them away and admonished herself for dwelling on something that was now inconsequential. David had come back to his mother and life was worth living again! So what if John was leaving her? She had gotten her son back and really that was all that mattered. She would find a way to survive. Keeping the house would be a challenge but for the sake of her son, she would fight hard! A stray thought flitted through her mind where she imagined dressing up the fawn as a pirate and she giggled at that image as she entered the forest.

The woods somehow felt different today. Dark clouds in the sky masked the sunlight, causing grey shadows to fall across the trees. The air felt thick and oppressive and the bird song of yesterday had been replaced with a brooding silence. Jane walked on calling to the fawn and each time he failed to respond, the faint feeling of dread that she had felt upon entering the woods grew stronger. Suddenly she stumbled onto a clearing and stopped dead in her tracks, gasping at the grisly scene before her. The fawn lay dead on the ground with an arrow protruding from his midst and his tongue hanging out. Standing near the fawn's body was John with his crossbow in hand. Without looking at her, John said in a quiet voice "I saw him in our backyard this morning. Tried to nail him there but he took off for the woods. Had to chase him down. I did it for you, Jane. I had to do it, for you see, it's not healthy, all the talk about this fawn being David reborn. Here, you can see for yourself, it's just a deer and nothing more. You need to get over this and put your life back together. Are you listening, Jane?"

Jane was listening all right but not to John. Her mind rang with silent, hysterical laughter as she stared into the fawn's glassy eyes and marveled at the irony of fate. A red fog of rage descended upon her eyes as she turned her attention to John who was now bent over the deer's body with his back to her. Picking up a sizable rock lying next to her feet and driven by cold hatred she had never experienced before, Jane crept forward.

Stars had started to appear in the evening sky when Jane finished burying John's body. Once she had gotten over her rage, Jane had given a lot of thought to her next course of action. She would drive John's truck across the provincial line and leave it at a secluded spot, then come back and sign the divorce papers with yesterday's date. She doubted anybody would miss John; he had few friends to begin with and she was sure he had already advertised the fact that he was leaving town for good, even before he told her. His new lover was bound to make a fuss; however, who can really trust a man who leaves his grieving wife for another woman? Who's to say he didn't meet somebody he liked even better and took off with her instead? Jane was sure it'd all work out.

As for David, well, he had found his way back to her once and she knew with the certainty only a mother can possess that he would do so again. November was mating season for deer and Halloween was just a year away.

All she had to do was wait.

VENGEANCE

The visions of her little face staring at me through the rear glass, the horror I felt as the man drove off in my car with my precious Magda still in it, the rage and frustration that I felt towards her abductor but also, and largely towards myself, at my carelessness, all of these remained even after I ended my life. I had jumped off the Mezcala Bridge, drowning myself and my misery into the depths of the Balsas River, floating within its embrace until the river would commit my lifeless body to the Pacific. I had hoped to find peace within death but instead, I found vengeance.

Keep your children close to you, at all times! One slip, a blink of an eye, one single moment of carelessness, and the monsters waiting in the shadows will pounce and snatch them away, as did that evil man who took my little girl. I had picked her from school and was driving home when I remembered that we were out of milk, so I stopped outside the bodega near our home. Magda didn't want to come in and it was hot that day, so hot, so I left her in the car with the engine running for the air conditioning to stay on. I was inside the bodega for only a couple of minutes, but that's all the time that monster needed to get in and drive off with my car, Magda, and my life.

It is true that the police in Mexico are generally corrupt. However, *la policía* in Acapulco de Juárez, where I lived, had figured out how to take corruption to a whole new level. Whereas in other parts of Mexico the police seemed to be working for the criminal element, in Acapulco, especially in the *colonias* outside the tourist areas, the criminals actually worked for the police, who were the real cartel. As a result, crime was rampant in the neighborhood, and law enforcement virtually nonexistent. It was, therefore, no surprise that when I went pleading for help to the police, they brushed me off even though I gave them a clear description of Magda's abductor. Instead of helping me, the police accused me of being negligent. "You are a bad mother," they told me, and could I blame them, when my heart was screaming the very same thing?

Days went by as I suffered in my own personal hell, spending days driving around in a borrowed car, searching for my little Magda, and nights spent trying to cry myself to sleep. Every time the bell rang, I jumped and rushed to the door, hoping to see Magda standing there, and secretly dreading the worst. Our local pastor organized posters with pictures of Magda to be posted everywhere and even managed to round up enough money for a small reward. Friends and parishioners held candlelight vigils as I beseeched God for the safe return of my daughter, but nothing worked. Then, one evening a van screeched to a halt outside my house, dumped the corpse of my daughter at my doorstep, and drove away. The neighborhood rang with my anguished wails as I sat with her broken and violated body in my lap. People came out of their homes to see what was going on and in their faces, I saw only curiosity and accusation. "You are a bad mother," they all seemed to say in unison. Magda wasn't the first girl to have been taken from our neighborhood, and having seen this scene repeat many, many times before, they no longer sympathized; they no longer cared.

With the loss of Magda, I could not go on living. The rage and hate that I felt in my heart were only matched by the sense of futility and helplessness that I felt for not being able to do something about it. Life no longer had a meaning or purpose, and the pain in my soul was getting more unbearable with each passing moment. So I decided to end my life and drove my borrowed car to the middle of Mezcala Bridge. Getting out of the car, I quickly climbed onto the railing, and before anybody could stop me, I jumped. The fall to the river far below took less time than I had imagined and I was not prepared for the force with which I hit the water, almost knocking myself senseless. The water filled up my lungs, causing a few moments of panic and struggle, and then as I began to lose consciousness, a feeling of calm overcame my body and I slowly drifted away...

...Only to find myself standing on the shore of the river, under the bridge, watching a couple of fishermen drag my body out of the water. I wasn't sure what was happening so I walked over to where my body laid, with the two fishermen sitting on the ground and a small crowd of onlookers standing by. "*Hola,*" I called out to them, but nobody seemed to see or hear me. I tapped one person on the shoulder, and then another and another but none seemed to feel my touch. So there I was, dead, and yet not dead—cheated once again by God, trapped between two planes of existence, still wandering the earth with all the guilt, grief, and rage that I had felt in life, and with this added handicap of being invisible and inaudible to the living.

I saw him again, the man who abducted Magda, the monster who ruined my life. After having wandered around the city aimlessly for weeks (I no longer felt tired, hungry, or sleepy), one day I found myself outside the police station on Avenue Adolfo Ruiz Cortines in La Garita. The sandstone pink building that housed the police station was in a better state of maintenance than the other shabby looking structures around it. The building's main door opened onto the roadside where the usual crowd of petitioners and hangers-on were gathered. My gaze fell upon a man who stood near the door talking animatedly with an officer in uniform and had I been alive, I could have said that my breath caught in my throat or that my heart stopped at the sight of him. However, since I was dead, I no longer had the luxury of making such clichéd claims and therefore could only stare at the man, the brief glimpse of whose face as he drove away with my little girl in the backseat had haunted my dreams night after night. The officer said something to the man and they both turned and disappeared inside the police station. I stood there for a moment or two and then followed.

I suppose being invisible does have its advantages. While the guard at the door was clearly only allowing entry to those who had been summoned by an official, I walked right in, unseen and therefore unchallenged. The inside of the station was a dark maze of desks and small cubicles with paint peeling off the walls and a cloying smell of sweat, farts, and stale coffee permeating the air. I stood looking around until I caught sight of the officer I had seen earlier at the door, as he walked towards a cubicle with a couple of bottles of *cerveza* in his hands. I followed him into the cubicle where I found the monster who stole my Magda seated in a visitor's chair next to the officer's desk, looking impatient. The policeman, whose uniform name tag simply said Sánchez, placed a bottle in front of the man and then proceeded to sit down heavily in his own chair.

"This one nearly got out of hand, Miguel," said Officer Sánchez, as he took a deep swig of his cerveza, "I got a call from that *bastardo* Inspector Garcia from the Policía Federal, asking about that woman who jumped. He asked if it had anything to do with the disappearances of young girls in the area." The man-monster whose name was Miguel grimaced and said *"Lo siento, patrón.* I don't know why the *puta* had to go jump off the Mezcala Bridge of all places. That too in full view of other people? There are quieter ways to die." Then with a conspiratorial wink towards officer Sánchez he added: " She could have just asked me; I would have happily obliged, after having my fun with her, that is."

Both men guffawed and Sánchez said, a tinge wistfully, "I know what you mean. She wasn't bad looking either. What a waste."

I stood listening in disbelief, horror, and considerable revulsion, as these poor excuses for human beings sat and casually discussed rape and murder, which of course to them were a normal everyday occurrence. The rage that I had retained even in death threatened to boil over. *"Chinga tu madre,"* I screamed more than once, but of course they could not hear. I stormed and raged around the little cubicle, attacking the two men with my hands, but they felt nothing. I tried to topple objects in the room, but my hands found no purchase on physical surfaces. My rage continued unabated, now joined by deep feelings of frustration and helplessness. Unsure about what I should, or could do next, I just watched and listened to the monstrous duo.

Sánchez's words took on a more serious tone as he said: "Look Miguel, you have your vices and I have mine. Far be it from me to judge someone on how they get their rocks off, but you need to be more careful."

To this Miguel replied: "Come on, Jefe! Don't you worry about those *federale idiotas.* They couldn't solve a crime even if it came and bit them in the *culo.*"

Sánchez shook his head and said, "No, *cabrón.* The Federales may be slow but they are not stupid. There have been too many disappearances of young girls in this area, so I suggest you conduct your depredations elsewhere, for a while." Miguel started to protest again but Sánchez held up his hand, getting angry now. "Stop being a *pinche estúpido,* Miguel. If a pattern starts to emerge, those nosy bastards at the Policía Federal will be all over us, like flies on a pile of steaming shit. You hear me?" he said in a hard voice.

"*Sí, Señor,* I understand. I will be more careful," replied Miguel with a sour face.

Sánchez gave Miguel a long searching look before finally saying: "*Bueno, muy bueno.* See that you do, *pendejo,* for if I get one more phone call from the Policía Federal about this, I will cut off your *cojones* myself." Miguel must have looked sufficiently scared to Sánchez, for he growled "Now get out of here and go earn me some *dinero.*" Miguel left without a word and I followed him as he hurriedly walked away from the police station, cursing Sánchez under his breath. I followed him around all day as he went from one place to another, checking in with members of his little gang, collecting money from his dealers that stood at street corners selling drugs, and generally threatening and intimidating those that crossed him. When the sun went down on the horizon, he made his way to a *comida corrida* food stall that stood in a nondescript street where he dined on tacos and rolled up tortillas that were stuffed with chicken, rice, and beans. After he finished eating, Miguel entered a nearby house and went up the stairs to what was presumably his room. There he proceeded to drink copious amounts of tequila as he watched a small television that stood in a corner of the room, before finally collapsing on his bed in a drunken stupor.

For a long time, I stood by the bedside and watched Miguel sleep, while wishing for some way for me to murder him while he slept. Suddenly another man appeared in the room. To be precise, he simply walked through the door which happened to be closed and locked with a deadbolt. He met my gaze and both of us recognized the other for what we were. "He killed you too?" asked the man.

"No, he raped and murdered my eight-year-old daughter. I took my own life as a result," I replied, somewhat surprised that we could see and hear each other.

The man nodded sadly as he watched the sleeping form of Miguel. "My name is Alejandro," he said, "I used to be his accountant. Even though I counted stacks of money each day, I was only paid a pittance that was barely enough to feed my family, so I started stealing from Miguel. Nothing much, just a small amount that was enough to buy food and clothes for my two young boys."

"What happened?" I asked and Alejandro's face took on a pained expression as he said: "I don't know how the *bastardo* found out but one night he came to my house and tied me up at gunpoint. Then he proceeded to rape my wife in full view of me and the children before cutting her throat. Then he killed both my boys, one after the other, while looking at me with a sadistic smile on his face. Finally, he ended my misery by cutting my throat too."

I could only look at Alejandro with sympathy, and he continued "For three years, I have wandered this city, looking for ways to avenge my family, but to no avail. During this time I have met many other spirits like you and me, trapped in this world until they complete the penance for their sins, or avenge what needs to be avenged. Alas, none had the gift that could help me kill this monster."

"Gift?" I asked in an indignant tone, "What part of this miserable afterlife qualifies as a gift in your opinion?"

Alejandro smiled and said "Ah! I see that you haven't yet discovered yours. Every spirit seems to have a different gift. I have seen some who can move tiny objects with their hands. Others can make themselves visible to the living for the briefest of moments. I have also heard of some spirits that can actually move larger objects, though I have never met any."

"What is your gift?" I asked.

"My gift is to be able to read the thoughts of the living," he replied, "Take Miguel here, for example. I can see that the red urge in his mind that makes him violate little girls is raising its ugly head again. The need that he satisfied with his last victim is slowly growing stronger, and soon it will consume him entirely. That is when he will go hunting again for his next victim."

We had been standing in silence for a few moments when suddenly a flash of bright white light appeared in the room near Alejandro, who looked mightily confused. "I don't understand," he said to an unseen entity, "Why now?" As if he received a response that only he could hear, he nodded his head and a smile appeared on his face. Looking at me, he said, "Finally, I go to join my wife and sons. It's now up to you to avenge all his victims." Before I could respond, Alejandro stepped into the light and vanished, as the light quickly faded, leaving me more confused than ever. I turned around to Miguel, who slept on, completely unaware of the supernatural drama that had unfolded in his room. Finally, I couldn't bear the sight of him anymore and left the dismal room, choosing instead to roam the city at night.

Many a dark street and dark alley I wandered through aimlessly, lost in my thoughts as I pondered on all that Alejandro had told me. In fact, so engrossed was I in my musings that I scarcely noticed the man and a little girl standing by the street corner until I was almost upon them. The man, who was presumably the girl's father and obviously quite drunk, was berating her for being lazy and incompetent and thus being unable to convince the passersby that she begged for money. "You are a stupid, lazy little bitch," screamed the man as he slapped the little girl with a force that sent her staggering and caused her to fall down. I immediately flew into a rage and aimed a punch at the man's head as I screamed *"Bastardo!"* but of course this futile gesture had no effect on the man, and he proceeded to kick the little girl who lay prone on the ground. Unable to hold myself back, I yelled "Stop!" as I tried to grab the man by his shoulder, knowing fully well that he would not feel a thing and that I was powerless to stop him from hurting the child, but then a strange thing happened. The man, who had been in the process of aiming a second kick at his daughter, froze, with his one leg suspended in mid-air. For a long moment, I stood watching him, wondering if he had heard me. Then, placing my hand on his shoulder again, I said: "Apologize to your daughter."

The man looked at his daughter and said *"Lo Siento, niña.* I'm sorry," and I noticed a glassy look in his eyes as he said the words. The little girl sat on the ground, looking up at her father with wide-eyed amazement, whether at his balancing on one leg or his apology, likely the first-ever during her short life, I could not decide. Nonetheless, I was fascinated and decided to repeat the experiment one more time.

"Put your leg down," I commanded and the man obeyed. "Hug your daughter and promise her that you will take care of her and never hurt her again." The man hugged the child and made her the promise. Still not satisfied, I commanded, "Take care of her as if your life depends upon it." The man simply nodded and I released his shoulder.

The glassy look vanished from his eyes and he looked around blinking rapidly and with a confused expression on his face. Then he turned his attention towards his daughter and I waited to see how he would react. The man bent down and after gently scooping the child up in his arms he said "Let's go home, *mija*. You must be hungry. I will buy some food on the way." As he walked away with the little girl still in his arms, there was a smile on her face that would have brought tears to my eyes, had I been alive. It did however help in a small measure to calm the tornado of hate that raged ceaselessly within my heart.

So this was my gift, the power to control people. Strange that while they could never hear my voice or feel my touch, I could still control people if I simply placed my hand on their shoulder.

My immediate thought was to go back to Miguel's room and command him to kill himself, but then I decided against it for two reasons. First, it would have been too simple and that monster deserved to suffer a lot more before he died. More importantly, I knew that Miguel was a product of the corruption that plagued the city, sickening everyone and everything that it touched. If Miguel were to kill himself today, his *capo*, that policeman called Sánchez, would simply replace him in a heartbeat. This city was full of Miguels-in-waiting, and I decided that I had to do something about that as well. So I walked the night again while thinking of what I should do and by the time the first rays of the rising sun fell upon the empty streets, I had decided upon a plan.

I waited outside the house where Miguel had his room and he emerged in short order, dressed in a black shirt and blue jeans. He mounted a motorcycle parked outside the house and as it roared to life, I quickly mounted the passenger seat so as not to be left behind. In this fashion, we rode through the city until we reached the destination that Miguel had in mind, a decrepit warehouse at the edge of the city that stood amidst similar buildings with boarded-up windows and graffiti covering the walls. Miguel dismounted and strode to the warehouse door which was locked. He rapped his knuckles on the door three times in quick succession, and a small panel in the door slid back and shut again. The door swung open and Miguel quickly stepped inside, slamming the door shut behind him, well before I had an opportunity to follow through. That, however, did not stop me and having seen Alejandro pass through a door, I attempted the same and passed right through the warehouse walls, much to my delight.

Inside the warehouse, Miguel stood talking to two heavy-set men with shaved heads and tattoos covering every conceivable part of their bodies. "¡Hola, Gardo! ¡Hola Paco!" he greeted the two men.

"¡*Hola*, Jefe!" they replied in unison.

"Como estas?" asked the man called Paco.

"I've been better," replied Miguel with a sour expression, "That prick Sánchez gave me grief over that woman who jumped off the bridge after we dumped her daughter's body in front of her house. On second thought, we should've just buried the body, instead of returning it so that puta could give her little doll a proper burial. I tell you, no good deed goes unpunished in this fucking city," he added with a smirk.

Gardo and Paco grinned from ear to ear hearing this and it took all my resolve to not command all three of them to kill each other there and then. "So what are the orders for today, Jefe?" asked Gardo.

"Hold on," replied Miguel, "I need to take a piss first. Too much tequila last night." He walked off towards a door at the far end of the warehouse, leaving Gardo and Paco shuffling their feet as they stood looking around.

Both men wore sheaths on their belts with big, ugly-looking knives and I realized that it was time for me to begin Act One of the horror show that Miguel, unbeknownst to him, was going to be starring in. Since both men were standing within touching distance of each other, it was a simple matter for me to place both my hands on their shoulders and command "Cut each other's throats." A glassy look came into both men's eyes as they unsheathed their knives, turned to each other, and then slowly, almost gently pressed the tips of the knives into each other's throats and proceeded to carve ruby red lines into the soft flesh, that almost instantly became gushing rivers of blood. The knives fell from their hands as both Gardo and Pancho fell dying to the floor, making gasping and wheezing sounds as their lifeblood flowed out and away. Within seconds, their legs stopped kicking and it was over. Filled with grim satisfaction at this first act of retribution, I waited for Miguel to return.

"Gardo? Paco? Where are you, *cabróns?*" said Miguel upon exiting the toilet and not seeing his *amigos*. The light in the warehouse was dim, on account of the windows having been boarded up and the floor, therefore, lay covered in shadows. Miguel walked forward, squinting in the low light, frowning. Then he saw the bodies lying on the ground and a curse escaped his lips.

"Mierda!" he swore as he drew a pistol from his pocket and swung it around, looking for any lingering assailants that may be lying in wait. Satisfied that he was alone in the warehouse, he pocketed the pistol and stood examining the corpses of his friends. He noticed the two bloody knives lying on the floor and realized that Gardo and Paco had cut each other's throats. *"Joder!"* he cursed, kicking Paco's corpse and then Gardo's, *"Hijo de puta!"* he spat, naturally assuming that both men had gotten into an argument when he left and ended up murdering each other.

He walked over to a phone that hung on a wall and dialed a number. "*Hola?* This is Miguel, let me speak with Sánchez, quick!" he yelled into the phone. After a moment or two, he spoke again: "Hola? Jefe? This is Miguel. Listen, we have a problem. I just came to the warehouse to see Gardo and Paco but it looks like the *idiotas* got into a fight and killed each other." Sánchez must have given him instructions, for Miguel nodded his head and said "*Sí, Sí,* I understand. You will send a cleanup crew. I am leaving now to go check on the other boys." He hung up and walked over to the corpses for one last look, which is when I raised the curtains on Act Two of Miguel's own personal horror show.

Placing my hand on his shoulder, I whispered into his ear "Pick up the knives." Miguel moved as if in a daze, as he bent down to pick up both the knives. "Now drop them," I whispered again and he sent the knives clattering to the floor. "Forget you ever touched the knives," I commanded and he simply nodded. There was an old and tattered telephone directory that lay next to the phone and I commanded Miguel to look up the number for the Policía Federal. "Call and ask for Inspector Garcia," I commanded, and Miguel complied.

After a few moments, the inspector's voice came from the other end of the line. "*Hola*," he said.

"Confess your evil deeds and make sure you explain officer Sanchez's role in all of them," I said, and Miguel began to spill the beans to Inspector Garcia.

Surprisingly, the retelling of a life full of crimes took less than thirty minutes, and once Miguel finished, I removed my hand from his shoulder and he swung his head around, looking dazed and confused. Then he stomped out of the warehouse, still cursing Gardo and Paco. "Now I'm going to have to do their share of the work too," he grumbled as he mounted his motorcycle. I climbed onto the passenger seat, just in time, for he gunned the bike's throttle and it shot forward onto the dusty road, headed back towards the city.

Miguel visited a lot of gang bangers that day—drug peddlers, cutthroats, and scum of every variety—twenty-seven of them to be exact, all of whom died by his hand, in full view of the passersby, though Miguel, at my command, remembered none of it. As we rode through the city, leaving corpses in our wake, I could almost hear the rumors abuzz in the air around us and knew that it was only a matter of time before someone other than Sánchez would take notice. The dying rays of the sun dropped a curtain on that day, and also on Act Two of the drama that was playing on the stage that I had set. Soon, it would be time for the third, and final act.

Miguel slept fitfully that night. I suppose his subconscious knew that something was terribly wrong and was trying to warn him in his dreams. I stood by and watched, waiting for dawn when the final act of my revenge would begin and the final nail in Miguel and Sánchez's coffins would be hammered in. Unfortunately, patience was a virtue that I lacked, both in life and in death, so I spent the night just as restlessly as Miguel had. Finally, as the golden rays of a new day gently caressed his face, Miguel awoke with a start, leaped out of his bed, and after quickly washing up, went outside and I followed close behind. Judging by the direction in which he was walking, Miguel was headed towards the police station in La Garita. I had known all along that he would run to Sánchez sooner or later and I smiled at the thought of what lay in store for Miguel at the sandstone pink building that he was hurrying towards.

My plan had worked flawlessly up to this point, but things began to go wrong as soon as we neared the police station, where a large commotion was clearly visible. A parade of vans with the words Policía Federal stood parked outside the station, and an army of heavily armed federal agents swarmed all over the building. I knew they had come in response to the tip that Miguel had phoned in yesterday at my command, but I had hoped that he would be inside the station with Sánchez when they arrived. Now forewarned, he instead stood watching the drama unfold from a safe distance. Soon, the federal agents came out with Sánchez and the other policemen, who had been disarmed and were in handcuffs. Sánchez had his head hanging down and as the agents herded the policemen into a waiting van, he stumbled, only to receive a whack on his head from a federal agent. Seeing his *capo* treated this way was the last straw for Miguel, who suddenly bolted in another direction, and in the same instant, I realized what a great fool I had been, for I could have simply commanded Miguel to turn himself in to the *federales*. Now he had run off and disappeared to God knows where, and the opportunity was lost. Dejected, I began scouring through the city looking for him.

Is karma real? I like to think so. It certainly seemed to be the case when two days later, I finally found Miguel lurking beside the same bodega from which he had snatched my Magda. Furtive, unclean, and unshaven, he looked half-mad and I realized that the red fever of lust was upon him again. Before I could get to him, however, history began to repeat itself. A car stopped in front of the bodega. Another mother left her little girl sitting in the back seat, with the engine running, as she ran inside to make a quick purchase. Another anguished scream as the monster drove away while the little girl looked back through the rear window, her eyes wide with terror.

But this time, she was not alone.

As soon as the car stopped and I saw Miguel leering at the little girl inside, I knew what he was going to do, and so I ran towards the car instead and jumped through the door, passing right through its metal body. I did so not a moment too soon, for in the next instant the driver side door opened and Miguel jumped inside and proceeded to drive away, ignoring the screams of the girl's mother who ran shrieking behind the car, as I had done not too long ago, her steps slowing, finally faltering while she watched the car, and her life, quickly become a speck in the distance. I sat in the backseat with the terrified and whimpering girl while Miguel ogled at her through the rearview mirror, telling her about all the vile things he planned to do to her, just as soon as they got to this little place that he had out in the hills.

After driving for about an hour, we left the city behind and started climbing into the mountains. I realized then how Miguel had escaped capture by the federales, who doubtlessly had been hunting him in the city. Miguel must have a place somewhere up in the mountains, where he violated his victims, and to where he was now headed. I decided then and there that I would not let this little girl anywhere near that dreadful place, the spot where this monster had defiled my Magda and countless others.

"Enough!" I screamed as I placed my hand on the little girl's shoulder. "Take your belt off ," I commanded and the girl took off the rope-like belt that she wore around her dress. "Reach forward and put the belt around his neck," I whispered and the girl shot forward and before Miguel knew what was happening, the rope belt was under his chin and pressing against his throat. "Pull!" I yelled, "Pull with all your strength." Despite her young age, the little girl was quite strong and suddenly Miguel found himself being choked from behind, as he struggled to maintain control of the car with one hand, while with the other he tried to get the ever-tightening belt away from his throat. Through the front screen of the car, I saw the road curving to the right and a yawning emptiness beyond that was rushing forward to meet us. Turning to the young girl, I said "Jump" and had she been in her senses, she likely would have hesitated, but she was still in my thrall and therefore needed no second telling. Opening the door, she jumped out onto the ground that rushed by and rolled away from the car. Freed from the belt that had been choking him, Miguel tried to swing the car back onto the road, but it was too late. As the car went over the precipice, its tires finding no purchase in empty air, I looked back through the rear window and saw the little girl get up from the ground, a little bruised and dusty but still in one piece.

The car met the ground with a large boom and the gas tank exploded. Flames engulfed the interior and danced around Miguel who had been knocked unconscious during the crash. Then, as tongues of orange death kissed him and lit him up, Miguel began to scream. I exited the car and walked away from the burning inferno, Miguel's screams music to my ears, until they were abruptly cut off. I turned around and saw him emerge from the car, dazed and confused. Then he saw me, and as our eyes met, the look of pure terror and helplessness on his face finally brought to rest the storm of rage and hate that had lived inside of me for months.

A bright white light appeared in front of me, and within it, I saw the form of a little girl. "Magda?" I whispered and the figure stepped forward as she extended her hand towards me. Grasping it firmly, I stepped into the light, instantly enveloped in its warm embrace.

Then, there was only peace.

MISTFALL

September 14, 1985, 7:14 p.m.
Vitoshka Apartments, uliska Bristritsa Sofia, Bulgaria

The fan lies on the floor, its blades rotating lazily, spreading the debris of dust and plaster that shook loose from the ceiling when the fan fell, while I sit and stare at it with disgust and disbelief. The electrical wires falling from the ceiling remain attached to the fan and I am reminded of the noose that I still wear around my neck. The little stool that I had tried to use as a step up towards my own demise lays on its side near my feet, and I angrily kick it away while cursing the sad state of repairs rampant in apartments lining up the streets of Sofia, making even mundane tasks like hanging one's self nearly impossible.

I hit my head hard during the fall and now it hurts. When my hand touches the sore spot on the back of my skull, it comes away with blood smeared over my fingers. Sighing, I remove the noose from around my neck, throwing it away with as much contempt as I can muster, before getting up from the floor in order to tend to the wound. The irony of the situation isn't lost on me. Here I am now, trying to repair an injury caused by the very act of self-destruction that I had been engaged in just a few moments ago. I briefly contemplate giving death another chance by simply jumping out of my apartment's window, but then realize that I no longer have the stomach for committing suicide, at least not today.

September 15, 1985, 3:00 a.m.
Vitoshka Apartments, uliska Bristritsa Sofia, Bulgaria

Sleep has deserted me! Perhaps it's not such a bad thing, for when I close my eyes, there are no dreams, just the same terrifying nightmare that repeats over and over again. In these visions, I find myself stumbling through the dark (it's always dark here), groping my way through a forest that resembles the one surrounding my native village up in the mountains. Slowly, my eyes adjust to the dim light and I see the silhouette of a woman walking among the trees, moving as if she is sleepwalking. Her form looks familiar and I follow. A fog creeps up and surrounds the forest, obscuring the little visibility that remained. An eerie red glow is visible in the distance and the woman seems to be headed towards it, drawn as if guided by an unseen force. An unearthly growl emanates from the dark and rings from the trees, filling me with dread and despair, yet the woman walks on oblivious to it all. I somehow know she walks towards her death and I try to warn her. I try hard to form words in my mouth, words with which I can wake her up from whatever dream that has taken possession of her mind, but to my horror, I find that I have no voice. I can only watch as she draws closer to the red glow. Then another form steps through the mist and embraces her. I can just make out the tall figure of a man who bends down as if to kiss her, and the woman goes limp in his arms. I watch with horrid fascination and take a step forward, and the stranger looks up at me. Our eyes meet, mine wide with terror, and his black as coal yet smoldering with primal ferocity. Then I notice the teeth! Long, sharp, gleaming white, and dripping with hot red blood, her blood.

This is the point where I usually wake up screaming, my body shaking, drenched with sweat, and my very soul trembling with cold dread.

September 15, 1985, 4:15 p.m.
Vitoshka Apartments, uliska Bristritsa Sofia, Bulgaria

I have slept the day away but fortunately, my slumber was dreamless and undisturbed. I wake up feeling refreshed, living that blissful but fleeting moment between sleep and waking when one remembers nothing and feels nothing except boundless optimism, that is, before memories of misfortunes, current, and past, come flooding back with full force, and the optimism vanishes, replaced by dark despair that gnaws relentlessly at one's very soul.

I sit brooding, lost in melancholic thoughts, thinking of happier times. Thinking of her, Nina, love of my life, the light of my eyes, gone forever, torn from my embrace by cruel fate.

I sit dreading the coming of night, and the nightmare I know it shall bring with it.

Life has no further purpose. Or does it?

September 16, 1985, 3:05 a.m.
Vitoshka Apartments, uliska Bristritsa Sofia, Bulgaria

I wake up screaming from the nightmare. Its potency remains undiminished even with daily repetition, and so it takes a good part of an hour before I am able to get a grip on myself and get out of bed to drink a glass of water.

Something about the nightmare is bothering my subconsciousness. Something was different tonight, though for the life of me I can not remember what.

I rack my brain, even try against my will to relive the terrifying vision, but no matter how hard I try, the answer eludes me.

I sit with a glass of brandy in my hand, beginning my nightly vigil.

Perhaps the morning shall bring better counsel...

September 16, 1985, 7:45 a.m.
Vitoshka Apartments, uliska Bristritsa Sofia, Bulgaria

...and it does!

I wake up with a start and realize that I fell asleep sometime during the remaining hours of the night. The empty bottle of brandy lies near my feet, akin to other bottles that have previously accompanied me during the nightly vigils that began when the news of Nina's death flitted down from the mountains. The letter from her father said it was a wild animal attack, one of several that had taken place recently in my remote village up in the mountains. "Come back home," the letter had said with some urgency. I haven't kept track of dates and days much recently, but the nightmares started around the same time my world ended with receipt of the letter, of that I am certain.

My thoughts are lucid when they should be befuddled on account of the copious amount of brandy I consumed last night. I find myself clear-headed and full of purpose, for the first time in what seems like ages. The only problem is that I have no clue of the reason behind this newfound energy and the purpose my subconscious mind is signaling.

Or maybe I do...my mind dwells on last eve's nightmare for a few more moments. Perhaps because of the neurological cobwebs of despair and self-pity that had hitherto engulfed my mind, and have now suddenly fallen away, I can suddenly see what was different about last night's vision. I recall the memory of the nightmare and once again walk down the terrible path from the very beginning.

A dark forest...the woman walking in the trees...mist that eats everything it touches...terrible growling and my mute attempt to intervene...red glow...tall stranger...the embrace and his deadly kiss...the man's burning eyes, his dripping fangs, dripping with red hot blood...her blood...

...Nina's blood!

A cry escapes my lips as the last scene of last night's mare was finally revealed. In my vision, for the very first time, my gaze had shifted from the stranger's dripping teeth to the woman's face, and to my dismay, it had been the face of my beloved Nina, eyes wide open, frozen in the stillness of death, yet the lips impossibly moving, calling out to me, pleading, saying:

"Avenge me, Aleksander...Avenge me."

"Yes, my love," I respond though it's just me speaking to myself as the only occupant in the room. Nevertheless, I feel energized. Even if not completely full of life, for the great sadness in my heart remains, I feel alive and able to function again.

It will have to do.

September 16, 1985, 3:15 p.m.
Vitoshka Apartments, uliska Bristritsa, Sofia, Bulgaria

I am packed and ready to leave. My landlord stands in the room, already upset that I am vacating the apartment without notice, and now more so at the sight of the damage to the fan and ceiling, resulting from my failed attempt at swinging myself from it towards oblivion. Even though I have compensated him adequately by severely depleting my life's savings, he continues to voice his disgust, until his eyes fall upon the noose that still lies in the corner. Words fail him as understanding dawns in his eyes, and with a cynical smile, I depart the dreary, unpleasant apartment, leaving behind its dreary, unpleasant owner still gaping at the fan, the noose, and the empty air I have just vacated.

I came to Sofia for higher education, as do a lot of young men from my village, in the hope of a better life and to rescue our loved ones, in my case Nina, from the crushing poverty that is our lot in the mountains. Having made no friends in the short months I have been here, there is no one to say goodbye to, and within the hour I find myself on a rickety old bus that soon rattles its way out of the city and begins its climb on treacherous mountain roads, towards my village.

Nina, I will find out what really happened to you. What did happen to you?

September 16, 1985, 7:40 p.m. Somewhere along Route 197 Rhodope Mountains, Bulgaria

I wake up in my seat and find the sky turning dark outside my window. The few passengers that had boarded the bus with me in Sofia have all gotten off at their respective stops and now it's just me and the driver left on the bus. My destination, Kozhari, is a typical Bulgarian high-mountain village situated on a steep rocky relief. The population of this village is less than 300 souls and declines yearly, as young men like me leave for better opportunities that can only be found in larger cities.

"Where are we?" I ask the driver.

"We passed through Trigrad around half an hour ago," he responds gruffly, which means that my village is another 25-45 minutes drive away, depending on the condition of the road that lies ahead.

Kozhari is literally the last stop on Route 197 and buses seldom come this far. The only reason the driver, a Greek by the name of Alyosha, had agreed to drive up here was due to the fact that he already had plans to visit some relatives across the Greek border, which lay another hour's drive down the road—that, plus the sizeable bribe I have given him, in addition to the bus fare. Still, he isn't happy about having to stop in Kozhari, even if for an instant to let me off. I suppose the rumors of recent killings in and around the village have reached his ears too. We drive on in silence.

Thirty-five minutes later, the first signs of the village appear. It is nighttime by now and the village road is deserted. "Get ready," barks Alyosha, and I get up from my seat and move towards the front door of the bus while clutching my luggage.

He brings the bus to a screeching halt near the village center, a sound that I am sure is loud enough to wake the dead. I struggle to depart the bus with my luggage, while Alyosha implores me to be quick. "Hurry! Hurry!" he says in a voice fraught with worry and fear, "the dead ride fast!" he says cryptically. I manage to depart the bus with all my luggage and crossing himself, Alyosha hurriedly closes the door. The bus roars off, once again shattering the silence as it disappears into the mountain night. I am left alone in the dark village square, with a light or two twinkling far in the distance, providing little comfort.

The silence returns swiftly, and I turn and venture down a lane that stands covered in shadows. My parents are long dead and the house I grew up in lies just ahead. Along the way, I notice the other houses in the lane, their windows dark when previously they would have had the lights on at this hour. It's now pitch black, but I grew up here and can find my own house without much difficulty. With no light to see by, I fumble with the lock and finally manage to get the front door open. Thankfully the electricity is still on and when I flick the switch, light and relief flood my childhood home. Exhausted from my long journey, I collapse on my bed and sleep like the dead.

No nightmare plagues my sleep tonight.

September 17, 1985, 8:00 a.m. My Home
Village of Kozhari, Bulgaria

The sun finally rises above the mountain peaks and sends its golden light flooding into my room. My eyes slowly flicker open and for a moment I am unsure of where I am. The surroundings look familiar and yet not. Then I realize that I am back home in Kozhari and I sit up, feeling more refreshed than I have in days.

Mihail Akulov is Nina's father and my deceased *bashta's* best friend since their boyhood. After my parent's death, it was Mihail who took me in and helped me keep my parent's home (now mine) in good repair. His farm lies at the edge of the great forest and I decide to pay him a visit. My house has no provisions for breakfast so I make do with a scratch meal of biscuits that I brought with me from Sofia. These are gone within minutes, and after a quick wash and change of clothes, I step outdoors.

How the village has changed in a few short months since I have been away! While always sparsely populated, it now looks abandoned. The village square, hitherto a beehive of activity and commerce, is almost empty, with only a handful of old men walking or playing a game of backgammon under a tree. I greet them with a smile, but most either ignore me or wave listlessly before turning back to the game.

It is as if the recent deaths in the village have cast a pall of gloom over its residents, turning these usually cheerful folk into shuffling ghosts.

September 17, 1985, 8:35 a.m. The Akulov Farm Village of Kozhari, Bulgaria

Walking amongst the fields in the bright, crisp morning can almost make one forget the horrors that this land has recently witnessed. The melancholy that has surrounded me since Nina's death is dissipated just a tiny bit as I stroll along these familiar paths. Happy memories of time spent here with Nina brings an absentminded smile to my face as I walk towards the Akulov farm. I almost expect to see Nina working in the yard, the terrible news of her death a hoax, a bad dream, a misunderstanding. Then I see Mihail standing by the farm gate, waiting for me.

"You are back," he says, merely stating the fact, for he has always been a man of few words. I simply nod in reply as I walk up to him. We embrace, no further words of greeting necessary, for the bond that we share goes far deeper than civil courtesies. When he pulls away, Mihail's eyes are wet with tears and I feel the same wetness in mine. No words are spoken as Mihail leads me down a path that takes us to the edge of the forest. Right where the path ends, towards its left edge lies a grave. Without Mihail telling me, I know it is Nina's and I get down on my knees next to it.

Nina, my beautiful Nina. Blessed were the days we whiled. Where have you gone, my love?

I can hold back my tears no longer and so the dam breaks. Grief, contagious as always, overwhelms Mihail as well, and he falls on his knees next to me. Long do we weep in silence, until Mihail finally stands up and gently grabs me by my shoulder. Arm in arm, we walk back to the farmhouse, two broken men, lost without the woman who had vanished from our lives like sunshine during a stormy day, leaving the world painted in shades of ugly, dull gray.

September 17, 1985, 10:15 a.m. The Akulov Farm
Village of Kozhari, Bulgaria

We sit drinking coffee in silence at the kitchen table, while I muster the courage to hear what Mihail has to say about the circumstances in which Nina died.

"Tell me what happened?" I finally ask.

"She was attacked by an animal while picking flowers at the edge of the woods one evening," replies Mihail in a quiet voice.

I already know this on account of the letter I had received from Mihail, which bore the terrible news. Back then, my grief had left little room for other feelings, or reason, but now, in a somewhat calmer state of mind, I find myself quite surprised at hearing this. While it is true that the Rhodope mountains are a stronghold of wolves, foxes, and bears, attacks on humans by these wild animals are exceedingly rare and even these may occur only if one were to venture deep into the forest without taking the requisite precautions. "Are you sure?" I ask. "An attack by a wild animal this close to the village is unheard of, at least in recent memory."

Mihail looks at me with an inscrutable expression on his face. and replies: "Nina had gone to pick flowers as was her daily custom since her mother died. It was always the same spot, near where her grave now lies. I was out working in the yard and could see Nina bending down near the edge of the forest collecting flowers. The light was getting low and so I called out to her to hurry home. She replied by saying that she was almost done." At this point, Mihail squeezes his eyes shut as his face takes on a pained expression. It takes him a while before he regains his composure and is able to speak again. "I went about my work for a few more minutes and then looked in her direction again. I found the ground covered with a mist that seemed to have appeared out of nowhere and I could no longer see her. I opened my mouth to call out to her when I heard her scream. Grabbing my ax, I rushed to the spot where I'd last seen Nina." Mihail shudders at the memory and after a short pause, he continues in a voice strained with emotion. "I found her lying on the ground with the empty flower basket laying beside her. Her throat had been torn out." A sob escapes Mihail, "My beautiful Nina! Only a wild beast is capable of something like that!" he exclaims.

I try to shut out the gory images that are beginning to form in my mind but am unsuccessful. The horror of what Mihail just described is also enough to dissuade me from asking any further questions about Nina's death, at least for now.

"You mentioned that there were other deaths?" I ask instead.

Mihail nods sadly and replies. "Nina was the first to be attacked. Not a week had passed since the same thing happened to a lad of seventeen, by the name of Kiril Barkov."

"Kiril? Spas Barkov's son?" I exclaim. "I went to school with the older brother, Andrei. He went off to join the army."

Mihail nods and continues. "Kiril left the village early in the morning to graze his father's sheep. In the evening, the sheep returned to the village but Kiril did not. Fearing that his son was injured and lying helplessly somewhere in the mountains, Spas rounded up the village folk and we went looking for him. We found the poor boy in the pasture where the Barkovs usually graze their sheep, dead with his throat torn out and his corpse pale, almost white from loss of blood."

Mihail shudders at the memory and after a short pause, he continues. "Thinking that a feral wolf was responsible for these attacks, we laid traps in the forest and spent many a night sitting over them, but the beast proved too cunning. Less than a week after Kiril died, while we sat hidden amongst trees in the forest, the beast paid a visit to the village and attacked another young lad who was walking home late at night after visiting a friend. His body was found two steps away from his own front door."

"How do you know it was the same beast that killed this young man?" I ask, even as I know what Mihail's answer would be.

"He too was found with his throat torn out, and not a drop of blood in his body," says Mihail quietly, confirming my worst fears.

"Up to this point, we still believed that these deaths were the work of a feral wolf, albeit an unusually bold one," says Mihail. "We spent many days scouring the forest and shooting every wolf that we spotted and the village residents, especially the young ones, were under strict instructions to only move about in pairs, and to avoid the forest altogether."

"Did it help?" I ask.

Mihail shakes his head. "For two weeks, nothing happened. No one was attacked and we started to believe that the culprit had been bagged amongst the scores of wolves we killed during that time. People started to breathe easier and normal precautions were relaxed. Then, as if trying to make up for lost time, the beast struck again and took five more lives in a span of two days."

"Five victims in two days?" I exclaim, "That does not sound like the work of an animal, even a feral one." Mihail nods his agreement; "It was now that we realized that a great evil was upon us. Something that hides in the shadows, preying on our young, waiting to pounce at the earliest opportunity. We..."

Mihail stops in mid-sentence, as a sudden sound emanates from the attic. It is faint and almost sounds like someone knocking. Mihail looks sharply at the ceiling and then at me. "These damned mice," he growls, "They make quite a racket." I have never heard mice make a knocking sound before, but my mind is too distracted to dwell upon this minor interruption. "You were saying?" I prompt Mihail in order for him to continue.

Instead, Mihail leaps to his feet and declares that he is tired of talking about death and that he has a lot of work around the farm that he can use my help with. Realizing that I could use some exercise and fresh air myself, I follow Mihail out the door.

September 17, 1985, 1:30 p.m. The Akulov Farm
Village of Kozhari, Bulgaria

Time goes by quickly when the hands and mind are busy. I find myself enjoying the labor as I help Mihail around the farm. We take a break to eat lunch outside where he speaks some more about the plight of our village. "A lot of people either bundled off their children to relatives in other places or have moved away altogether," he says with a sigh. "Such is the lot of the mountains. The young die or move away, while the old stay, walking about like ghosts in daylight."

I try to press him for more information, but he refuses to discuss it further. His face has taken on a guarded look, though for what reason I do not know.

September 17, 1985, 4:30 p.m. The Akulov Farm
Village of Kozhari, Bulgaria

The work is finally done, and declining Mihail's offer to have dinner with him, I take my leave, for I want to visit Nina's grave again and stay with her for a while, alone.

I pick up some flowers on the way and I walk the short distance to where Nina lays in eternal sleep. Placing the flowers on her grave, I sit down next to it as I try to come to terms with the fact that she is indeed gone forever.

Time marches on.

September 17, 1985, 6:00 p.m. Nina's grave Village of Kozhari, Bulgaria

A primal alarm in my subconscious breaks me out of my reverie. Millions of years of evolution have ingrained in our minds the notion of safety that daylight brings, a notion so strong that even protections granted by civilization cannot eliminate it.

I estimate that I have about thirty minutes of daylight left, which is just enough for me to make it back home before dark. I take a last look at the peaceful scene around me. Trees preparing to turn color for the approaching autumn, flowers adding some life to Nina's grave, mist floating at the edge of the forest, obscuring all that lies within.

Nina, I will be back soon.

September 17, 1985, 6:35 p.m. Village Square Village of Kozhari, Bulgaria

I have misjudged the timing of the sunset, and as the dark eats away the last remnants of daylight, I sense that my life is in danger. The mist has been following me since I left Nina's grave, creeping across the ground behind me with ever-increasing momentum. Instinct tells me that I must not let the mist overtake me, or all will be lost.

The village square lies deserted, as I half-walk and half-run towards the entrance to the lane that leads to my house. I take a look over my shoulders and am dismayed to see how close the mist follows behind, obscuring everything that it touches. Willing my legs to run faster, I sprint across the square and enter the lane that will take me towards home and safety.

I nearly die of fright when suddenly, a hand reaches out of the dark and grabs my arm in a vice-like grip, just as a lantern is thrust onto my face. "Aleksander Grubov, is that you?," asks a gruff voice, and to my immense relief, I realize that it is Andrei Barkov who holds my arm, with his father Spas standing next to him. Both men are armed with rifles.

"Quick!," hisses Spas, "We need to run for it, there is no time to lose!" We dash down the lane towards my house and once there, I fumble with the lock on the door, while Andrei takes up a defensive position, with his rifle covering the mouth of the lane. "Hurry man!" implores Spas, and I glance towards the direction in which Andrei is pointing his rifle. The mist has just entered the lane and is slowly advancing towards us.

The lock opens and we burst through the door, which Spas immediately closes behind us with a bang, shutting out the night.

September 17, 1985, 7:00 p.m. My Home
Village of Kozhari, Bulgaria

"What is this all about?" I demand as the three of us crouch near the window that looks out to the street.

"Ssshhhhh, keep your voice down," hisses Spas.

By this time, the mist lies thick over the street outside, obscuring the world around. Something moves within the swirling haze and I hear fleeting sounds of laughter that sends chills up my spine.

There is a knock on the door, at first gentle, and then repeated with increasing urgency.

"Who is that?" I whisper.

Both Spas and Andrei cross themselves. "The devil is at the door," replies Spas. "Whatever you do, DO NOT invite him in," he says with some urgency.

The knocking stops and silence reigns for a few moments. Then suddenly a face appears at the window and taps at the glass. I barely recognize its owner as Kiril Barkov, for the face is pasty white, as if devoid of blood and the eyes are as black as coal, and yet smoldering with an unholy light. While looking at us through the window, he purrs in a voice that makes me shiver. "Father, it's cold out here, won't you invite me in?"

"Begone, spawn of the devil!" roars Spas. "You are no son of mine."

The face in the window breaks into a cruel smile and I catch a flash of white, elongated teeth, quite like fangs one sees in the mouths of predators. Now looking at me directly, he taps the glass again and says "Aleksander, sweet Aleksander. Why are you so sad? Come out and play with us. You will never be sad again." I find myself unable to draw my eyes away from Kiril's hypnotic gaze as he continues, "Don't you want to feel happy again? I can reunite you with your lost love. All you have to do is invite me in." The devil tempts me mightily, and he would have likely succeeded had it not been for Spas, who grabs my shoulder as a warning.

The sudden contact breaks the hypnotic spell that I have fallen under and I manage to tear my eyes away. Kiril shrieks with rage and begins banging on the window while promising every manner of prolonged and painful death possible, to the three of us. "Ignore him," says Spas as he and Andrei stand up, "It is as I had hoped. They can not enter a home without the owner's permission."

"They?" I sputter, confused about what exactly it was that I was witnessing, "You mean there are more of them out there?"

Spas look sadly at the specter that continues to rage and rave outside my window and nods his head. "Yes, there are more, and they are always looking to increase their numbers," he replies.

"But what in God's name are they? Your son Kiril is supposed to be dead. Killed by a wolf, or something worse, and yet here he stands outside my window, very much alive."

Hearing this, Spas gives me a searching look and motions that we move away from the window and the awful din outside. I lead the two men to the inner room of my house which serves as both kitchen and bedroom. Here we sit at the table and I pour out the last of the brandy that I have brought with me from Sofia. *"Nazdrave,"* toasts Spas.

"May the dead remain dead," adds Andrei for good measure, before draining his entire cup in one go.

"That thing outside is not my son," says Spas with feeling. I start to protest but he holds up his hand and continues; "He has visited us every night since the day he died, begging for us to let him in. The body may have once belonged to my Kiril, but I assure you that Kiril's soul no longer resides in it, and the will that now animates his corpse belongs to an ancient evil."

"What ancient evil?" I exclaim.

"Vampir," says Spas in a quiet voice, as Andrei spits on the ground.

I am torn between dismissing this superstition outright, as my university education demands that I do, and believing what I have seen with my own eyes but a few moments ago. Ultimately the memory of Kiril's gleaming fangs and soulless eyes are enough to win me over to Spas's side of the argument. "Ok, so there is a Vampir on the loose, preying on the young and turning them into walking corpses," I say while looking at father and son, "Where do we find this Vampir and how do we kill him?"

Andrei looks away but Spas's face takes on an expression that could almost be that of sympathy. "Not him," he says almost apologetically, "Her. For you see, the Vampir is a woman."

I am momentarily confused hearing that the culprit is a woman. Then looking at the commiserating look on Spas's face, understanding finally dawns and my confusion turns to anger. "No!" I yell, "That can't be!"

"I'm afraid it is true," says Spas, "Though God knows I wish it weren't so."

My anger is now at a dangerous level and in a gesture, both desperate and futile, I send the tumblers on the table flying in one wrathful sweep. Andrei, the trained soldier that he is, instantly reacts by attempting to restrain me but Spas waives him off. Mollified, and somewhat ashamed at this uncharacteristic display of bad temper, I sink back into my chair and hold my head in my hands.

"You went to see Mihail?" asks Spas in a gentle voice.

"Yes," I reply through my hands that cover my face, "I was returning from his farm when we ran into each other."

Spas insists on continuing with his questioning. "What did he tell you about Nina's death and everything that has happened since?" I narrate all Mihail had told me, and when I finish, a knowing look passes between father and son.

"What are you not telling me?" I demand.

"I think it is best that you hear the truth from Mihail himself," replies Spas. "When you see him tomorrow, ask him about Nina's mother, ask what happened to her, and also ask him why he buried Nina by himself, before breaking the news to the village."

Try as I might to find out more, Spas remains tight-lipped, saying only that he swore an oath of secrecy and that only Mihail can provide the answers that I seek. He also requests that I allow him and Andrei to spend the remainder of the night under my roof, and knowing that sending them out into the mist would be nothing short of murder, I readily agree.

We talk about old times late into the night and Spas tells me stories about when he, Mihail, and my *bashta* were boys together and the regular trouble they got into. I am surprised to hear this for I never knew that Spas had once been a close friend to my father and Mihail.

I am not sure of the hour when sleep finally overtakes me.

September 18, 1985, 11:00 a.m. My Home Village of Kozhari, Bulgaria

I wake up with a start and instantly realize three things. One, the house is empty except for me, which means Spas and Andrei must have left at first light. Second, I have grossly overslept, and last but not least, despite having slept longer than usual, I feel utterly exhausted, likely on account of the strange events of last evening, whose memory is still fresh in my mind.

I know that I should spring out of bed and rush to the Akulov farm, where I can demand answers from Mihail, but a strange reluctance has come over me. I find myself lacking the will (or perhaps it is courage?) to confront whatever revelations Mihail is supposed to provide me with.

Sighing, I sink back into the bed.

September 18, 1985, 2:00 p.m. My Home
Village of Kozhari, Bulgaria

Finally, I can take it no longer. My curiosity and my dread, both grow ever stronger in equal measure, and the only way out is to confront my fears head-on.

I am going to see Mihail, come hell or high water.

September 18, 1985, 3:00 p.m. The Akulov Farm
Village of Kozhari, Bulgaria

As I stand looking at the farmhouse from the outside, I realize how our thoughts and fears can alter our very perception of reality, and the world around us. The farmhouse lay in front of me, bathed in the same golden sunshine as it had been the day prior, yet what had appeared as a welcoming refuge yesterday, now stands in stark contrast with ominous undertones. I find myself consciously looking for and thereby noticing things that I had failed to observe during my previous visit.

For instance, I notice that the attic windows have been boarded shut, a fact I had missed during my visit yesterday. Nina and I had played in that attic as children and in later years had stolen more than a few kisses up there, and those windows have never once been shut in all that time.

I also notice that there are no flowers growing near the edge of the forest where Mihail claims Nina was attacked and killed. In fact, I can almost certainly attest to the fact that no flowers have ever grown in that spot since my earliest memories of the Akulov farm.

Then there is the choice of location, where Spas has buried Nina. To the unsuspecting eye, the location would bear no concern, but to my eyes that now suspect everything they see, a disturbing fact is immediately evident. Nina's grave lies next to a small path that leads from the Akulov farm and continues past Nina's grave for a few hundred meters. What I missed noticing yesterday is a smaller, almost imperceptible game trail that intersects the main path precisely at the point where Nina's grave lies. In other words, Mihail buried her at a crossroads of sorts, and there is no denying exactly which superstition he was thinking about when he chose that particular spot.

Mihail certainly has a lot to answer for.

September 18, 1985, 3:15 p.m. The Akulov Farm Village of Kozhari, Bulgaria

In response to my insistent knocking, Mihail finally opens the door, looking haggard and hungover. His eyes widen in surprise when he sees me, perhaps because he had expected to never see me as, well, me again after we parted yesterday? I am determined to find out.

He reluctantly invites me inside and we sit at the kitchen table. The atmosphere is tense and so Mihail makes a lame attempt at levity by saying "Come to check on the old man, eh? I could still outrun you in a race any day of the week."

"I doubt that very much," I retort, "Though I will concede that you had me fooled there for a while."

Mihail's eyes narrow and he mutters "What the hell are you going on about?"

"Ah! Now we are getting somewhere," I respond sarcastically, "It is precisely the matter of hell that I have come to talk to you about."

Mihail looks perturbed and says "Have you lost your mind boy? What's the matter with you today?"

"I'll tell you what the matter is," I reply as my voice rises to match my growing anger, "You have been lying to me about Nina, lying to me about everything."

Mihail looks as if struck by lightning. His eyes grow wide with surprise and his mouth is half-open as if unsure whether to utter words or gasp for air that it desperately needs. However, the shock in his eyes is swiftly replaced by a calculating look, which I like even less. Visibly composing himself, he attempts to try a different tact. In a gentle voice, he says "I know what you must be going through, my dear boy. It is normal to feel confused during times like these."

"Oh please stop with the lies, Mihail," I almost spit out the words, "I spoke with Spas last night."

At the mention of Spas, a visible and instantaneous change comes over Mihail. His shoulders slump and all fight seems to leave his body. He sinks heavily into his chair and has a defeated look in his eyes. "Spas? What did he tell you?," asks Mihail in a defeated voice.

"He told me everything," I lie, "And now I want to hear the truth from you." Mihail stares into space without saying anything, so I decide to break down the last of his defenses by driving the knife home. "Mihail, I know you buried Nina in secret, and that too at crossroads. I know that no flowers have ever grown at the spot you claimed Nina was attacked. I also know about the Vampir. Tell me the truth Mihail!"

Mihail buries his face in his hands and begins to sob. I get up from my chair and stand next to him. Placing my hand on his shoulder, I repeat my demand for truth, but in a much gentler tone. Mihail looks up at me with his tear-stained face and finally begins to speak.

"Kezia, Nina's mother, was a *yerli* (Romani Gypsy). I met her in my younger days whilst attending a fair in the Haskovo province. Having fallen in love, we eloped and moved around the country like nomads for a couple of years, but after Nina was born, we decided to return to Kozhari so Nina could have a stable home. At first, my father refused to accept a gypsy as his daughter-in-law, but your *bashta's* entreaties (whom my father loved as a second son) and the sight of little Nina's angelic face finally won him over. Thus we spent many happy years here, and even my parents' eventual passing did not lessen the joy that Kezia and I felt watching Nina grow up."

Mihail pauses for a moment as he smiles absentmindedly at a memory, and then continues. "Alas! Good times, they do not last forever. When Nina was twelve years old, Kezia fell sick. I tried everything possible, including taking her to see doctors in Sofia a few times, but we could not determine what was wrong with her. She got sicker as the days went by and soon it was evident that she was dying. Then one day, at her deathbed, Kezia shared with me a terrible secret. She told me that her family carried a curse in its blood. A curse so terrible, that none who carried the taint of her bloodline could find peace in death. She implored me to do exactly as she instructed, to ensure Nina's safety and mine, once Kezia passed away. At first, I dismissed her words as confused ravings of a fevered mind. However, she continued with her entreaties and managed to somehow convince me to carry out her dying wish. Kezia died the very next day."

Mihail pauses again but this time he begins sobbing and I can see that the words he is going to say next are difficult for him to utter. I wait patiently while keeping my hand on his shoulder for encouragement.

Eventually, Mihail resumes his narrative. "What Kezia had asked me to do upon her death was nothing short of macabre. She told me that unless I cut off the head of her corpse, drove an iron stake through the heart, and buried her at a crossroad, she would rise again from the dead, thirsting for human blood and her first victims would likely be Nina and myself. Such was the curse that she said her family carried, and for generations that is how they had treated their dead. I was heartbroken upon her death, and even though I still dismissed the curse as a gypsy superstition, I had to keep the promise I made to my dying wife, at all costs. So I sought out your *bashta* and Spas, my two best friends in this world, to whom I narrated all that Kezia had told me and swore them to secrecy. At first, my friends were appalled at what I was asking them to do, but they saw how important this was for me, so they agreed to assist. That very night, we visited the site where we had buried Kezia in the morning, dug out the body, and performed the gruesome mutilations that she had asked me to do. We then reburied her decapitated body at the same spot where I buried Nina."

"Wait," I interrupt, "So you are saying that all these years, Nina was placing flowers on an empty grave, while her mother lay buried elsewhere?"

Mihail simply nods his head and then continues "Your *bashta*, God rest his soul, went to his grave thinking that Kezia's dying wish had been nothing more than gypsy nonsense. Spas, on the other hand, seemed to have bought into the whole curse lore, and I could see him watching Nina with growing disquiet. Things came to a head when he approached me one day with his concerns about whether if Nina carried the same curse as her mother, and if so what did we plan to do about it. I grew angry and kicked him out of my house and we have not been on speaking terms since then."

I am shocked to learn all that Mihail had told me thus far, but am also growing impatient for him to tell me what matters most to me, and so I finally blurt out "Mihail, tell me what happened to Nina?"

He looks at me with an inscrutable expression on his face and replies "She died, Aleksander, though not in the jaws of a wild beast, as I had claimed. The same sickness that had claimed her mother snatched her away from me. There was nothing that I could do," he sobs.

"What did you do with her body?" I demand.

Mihail, now on the verge of total breakdown, speaks haltingly as he continues to sob "I knew that I should do the same to Nina's corpse as I had done to her mother's, but I could not get myself to do this terrible butchery to my beautiful child. Your *bashta* was no longer alive, and Spas would not speak with me, so I did the only thing that I could do, I buried her at the crossroads, next to her mother, hoping that it would be enough."

"And was it enough, Mihail?" I ask, already knowing and dreading his answer.

"No!" wails Mihail, "God forgive me but it was not enough. She visited me that very night, and I invited her in, thinking that my precious Nina had returned to me by some miracle. It wasn't until she entered that I realized what a fool I had been. This was not God's miracle, it was instead the devil's treachery! This walking corpse was no longer my sweet Nina, but a vile and evil being."

At this point, Mihail gets up from his chair and falls to his knees, his hands grasped together as if in supplication, though whether he begs for forgiveness from God, or from me, I do not know. "I am a coward," he wails, "She offered to spare my life if I kept her secret, and I, I agreed," he sobs.

"Why did you tell everyone that she had been killed by a wild beast?" I ask.

"She asked me to," replies Mihail, "Just as she asked me to summon you home."

These latest revelations have sent my head spinning, but before I can react, there is a loud thud that could only have come from the attic, and I am reminded of the boarded-up windows that I have thus far neglected to ask Mihail about. Suddenly, an epiphany strikes, and I look at Mihail and say "Who is there in the attic, Mihail? Is she up there?" I start towards the stairs that I know will lead me to the attic door and Mihail attempts to stop me.

"No Aleksander!" he wails, "Stop! You do not understand!" but my rage is too strong for him to overpower, and pushing him off I bound up the stairs and push open the attic door.

"She is not alone!," yells Mihail from downstairs. I hear Mihail's warning, but by then it is too late.

September 18, 1985, 4:30 p.m. The Akulov Farm Village of Kozhari, Bulgaria

The attic door opens and reveals yawning darkness within. Suddenly, strong hands appear from nowhere and grab me, pulling me inside. The door slams shut and the world goes dark. It is pitch black in the attic, on account of the windows being boarded up, and not a speck of light is visible. I am lying on the floor, feeling disoriented and I sense rather than see movement around me. Then a voice hisses next to my ear "Ummmmm, looks like dinner is served." I whip around to grab the speaker but my hands only find empty air. Another voice speaks and it seems that it is coming from inches above my head "He looks tasty! I have been looking forward to this!" Again I leap in the air but find nothing above me. A hand suddenly shoves me from behind and I stumble forward, trip over what seems like a leg, and fall flat on my face. There is tittering all around me, and a third voice speaks with admonishment "Do not hurt him, or she will be angry with us!"

The tittering stops and the first voice hisses "Let her be angry! I am hungry and his blood smells so, so sweet." A chorus of voices chime their agreement in unison and suddenly, powerful hands grab me again, and this time hold me down, immobile and unable to fight back. I know that I have moments left to live, as the creatures prepare to sink their fangs into me and feast on my blood.

Suddenly the attic door bursts open, and in the dim light near the doorframe, I see Mihail standing with his ax raised. He rushes towards the windows and brings the ax down on the wooden planks that have been used to bar them shut. A tiny chunk of sunlight bursts through and I hear the creatures hiss. Another swing of the ax, another piece of wood falls off, and another stream of light enters the attic, this time falling on the unseen hands that hold me down. The owner of the hands screams with pain, and suddenly I am free. "Run, Aleksander!" yells Mihail, "Run!"

I leap to my feet and rush towards the door, just as Mihail brings down his ax a third time, bringing more light into the room, and thereby preventing the creatures from pursuing me. I make it safely out of the attic, but in my haste, I trip over the threshold and fall, hitting my head hard as I roll down the stairs. The last thing I remember before I lose consciousness is Mihail screaming.

September 18, 1985, 5:15 p.m. The Akulov Farm
Village of Kozhari, Bulgaria

I slowly regain consciousness and the world lazily swims back into focus. Groaning, I slowly sit up and touch the side of my head that hurts with throbbing pain. Thankfully, I see no blood on my hands, and looking at the time, I realize that I must have been unconscious for only a few minutes. There is still daylight outside, which means I am safe from the abominations that lie in wait in the attic, at least for a little while.

Suddenly I remember Mihail and his screams. Cursing under my breath, I turn and look towards the attic door, that remains open. "Mihail? Mihail? Are you ok?" I call out, and my efforts are instantly met with jeers and taunts from the creatures within.

"Mihail? Mihail? Are you ok?" they mimic me in a mocking voice, "Why don't you come up here and check on him, Aleksander? Too scared of us, are you?" they taunt.

"Bastards!" I scream with rage. "If you have hurt him, I will make you pay!"

"Hurt him?" they reply, "Not at all! We have taken such good care of him. Here, see for yourself." An object rolls down the stairs and lands at my feet. It is Mihail's severed head, his eyes closed and the mouth opened wide as if screaming a soundless scream. The sight is too much for me and I fall sobbing to my knees. My heart was already broken by Nina's death and now the death of my old friend and mentor has shattered it completely.

The demons in the attic continue their taunts and jeers but I ignore them, as I sit on the floor mourning all that I have lost.

Then I get up to my feet and take one last look around at this once happy place. I know that Mihail keeps kerosene in drums in a shed outside for use around the farm.

There will be no mercy.

September 18, 1985, 6:15 p.m. The Akulov Farm Village of Kozhari, Bulgaria

I have finished dousing the building with kerosene. I especially placed cans of kerosene near the attic door, just out of reach of the fiends inside, and also poured liberal amounts on the stairs and the landing. The demons are well aware of my designs, but since they are trapped inside the attic until nightfall, they are powerless to stop me.

Their screams of fear, rage, and helplessness are music to my ears.

Their false entreaties do absolutely nothing to change my heart. I have no heart left.

I examine my handiwork one last time, then light a match and drop it on to the trail of kerosene that leads from where I stand, and towards the farmhouse.

September 18, 1985, 7:00 p.m. The Akulov Farm Village of Kozhari, Bulgaria

Night has fallen around me, and the farmhouse and everything within continues to burn with a merry blaze. The pitiful screams of the demons in the attic died down a while ago. Soon, the structure too will collapse, obliterating all traces of the evil that was resident within.

In the fire's glow, I notice that a mist has crept up to the edge of the forest, from within. There, it hesitates, as if repulsed by the luminance generated from the fire. I see the figure of a woman within the mist, as it stands watching the burning inferno. Eventually, the figure turns around and retreats, and the mist follows, receding back into the forest.

I follow in pursuit.

September 18, 1985, 7:15 p.m. The Forest Village of Kozhari, Bulgaria

My nightmare has finally come to life.

I find myself stumbling through the dark, groping my way through a forest. Slowly, my eyes adjust to the dim light and I see the silhouette of a woman walking among the trees, moving as if she is sleepwalking. Her form looks familiar and I follow. A fog creeps up and surrounds the forest, obscuring the little visibility that remained. An eerie red glow is visible in the distance and the woman seems to be headed towards it, drawn towards it as if guided by an unseen force.

An unearthly growl emanates from the dark and rings from the trees, filling me with dread and despair, and yet the woman walks on oblivious to it all. I somehow know she walks towards her death and I try to warn her. I try hard to form words in my mouth, words with which I can wake her up from whatever dream that has taken possession of her mind, but to my horror, I find that I have no voice. I can only watch as she draws closer to the red glow.

The figure stops and turns around, and removes her hood.

It is Nina, or at least the face resembles that of my beloved Nina, despite the eyes as dark as coal, and the gleaming fangs protruding from her lips.

In a voice as cold as death, and a smile as cruel as fate, Nina speaks these words of endearment.

"You have come for me, Aleksander! Come closer, and join me, my love. Then there will be no more fear of death, no more pain, and no more sorrow. We shall be together, forever."

The small iron stake that I found in Mihail's shed feels cold in my trembling hand, as I step forward.

Nina, we shall be together, forever.

DON'T LOOK INTO THE MIRROR!

Jacques Dubois, aged seventeen, was going through a low point in his life indeed. First, he had been laid off from his job as a junior clerk at a paper factory, where he had worked for the last three years and had harbored hopes to be promoted to the position of a senior clerk when monsieur Bachand inevitably retired from that position. Then his landlord had evicted him

for failing to pay his rent. Finally, to add insult to injury, Ines, his girlfriend of six months, had dumped him when he could no longer afford to splurge on cafes and theatre. For the last two weeks, he had been staying with a friend, but he knew that he had already overstayed his welcome, and it was time to move on.

Each day he scanned the *La Gazette* newspaper for job adverts and went out to apply in person. Each day he returned home dejected after spending hours in ever-growing lines of the jobless waiting to be considered. The year was 1636, and Paris was only just beginning to recover from the bubonic plague that had ravaged the city five years earlier. The poor and the homeless who had largely abandoned the city during the plague were now returning in even greater numbers, adding more competition for the scarce jobs that were available.

Even though it was a Sunday, Jacques decided to go out and about the city. Ostensibly it was to give his friend Bernard some privacy in the cramped quarters that they shared. Still, the real reason was his wish to avoid the pointed questions about his plans that Bernard's wife Anna was bound to pose at every opportunity. In Jacques's opinion, the chief cause of Anna's behavior was the fact that Bernard did little except mope around the apartment all day while Anna worked at a nearby laundry to pay rent and put food on the table. Now with Jacques as an additional mouth to feed, the pressure on Anna was greater than usual. Granted, Bernard and Anna were almost twice his age, but still, thought Jacques, why couldn't Anna be a bit more respectful, rather than scolding him like a little boy all the time? With a wistful sigh, Jacques left the small apartment that lay in one of the dingy, unnamed streets of faubourg Saint-Victor and came out onto place Maubert. He followed a few more winding streets to reach rue des Grands Augustins, from where he followed the flow of the Seine river in a northwesterly direction, with no particular destination in mind.

Paris of the 17th century was a city of extremes. It was at that time the largest city in Europe, with a population of half a million, matched in size only by London. Under the reign of Louis XIII and with the help of his chief minister, Cardinal de Richelieu, Paris had seen a boom in constructing bridges, monuments, and parks. Cardinal Richelieu had also managed to keep the warring nobles more or less in line; however, his popularity had waned after France's entry the previous year into the Thirty Years' War against the Holy Roman Empire and the Habsburgs, which had brought heavy new taxes and hardships to Parisians. Adding to this growing discontent was the large gap between the rich and the poor that existed in the city at that time.

Jacques walked along the busy rue des Grands Augustins until he reached Pont Neuf that connected the Seine's left bank to its right bank. The river itself was alive with a multitude of boats. The smaller, fancier ones belonged to the ultra-rich inhabitants of the city who mostly resided in Le Marais, close to the place Royale, while the larger boats were of a commercial variety carrying goods or fishing for salmon, which was so abundant and therefore cheap, that it was known as the "fish of the poor." To his right stood Notre Dame in all its gothic glory, with the faithful congregating outside after the service. The city hummed with anticipation, but Jacques was too preoccupied with his thoughts to notice any of this.

As he stood on the old bridge, gazing across the Seine, Jacques considered his options. If any, he had little prospects to land a job soon, given the fact that men far more experienced than he were willing to work for half the wages than was the norm. He had no family to ask for support, and his savings, meager to begin with, had been severely depleted by the demanding Ines and would probably last him another day or two. Thus far, Bernard had braved Anna's jibes and sarcasm and had sheltered Jacques, but that was bound to end soon too. All in all, Jacques had almost reached the bottom. He briefly considered flinging himself into the river and drowning his misery once and for all (he found the pun both ironic and hilarious), but quickly banished the thought from his mind. No matter what, life was a gift, too precious to throw away. He was young and resourceful, and his luck was bound to change sometime.

Slowly Jacques became aware of another presence. He turned to look towards a well-dressed man standing next to him, also staring into the river. Without turning, the stranger said in a soft voice, "It's tempting, isn't it? To jump into the river and close your eyes. In one instant, be rid of this miserable life and all its horrors, forever."

Jacques wasn't sure if the man was speaking to himself or addressing Jacques. Still, he replied anyway, "*Oui* Monsieur, it is tempting indeed, but life has too much to offer for one to waste it on a cowardly suicide."

The stranger now turned towards Jacques and said, "So you believe that life has a purpose? Perhaps so, but have you found yours yet?"

Jacques replied, "Not yet, Monsieur, but I hope to one day."

Hearing this, the stranger smiled and said, "Perhaps you will, my young friend. We shall see."

Jacques was intrigued, both by the man's persona as well as his words. The stranger was tall and quite well dressed, his clothes in stark contrast to the shabby and stained garb that Jacques wore. The stranger had long black hair that was set fashionably around a thin, handsome face and his white teeth gleamed as he spoke. In his hand, the stranger carried a cane topped with a figure of a ballerina, and his eyes were alive with a magnetic intensity that drew Jacques's gaze. With the poor's natural habit, Jacques tried to figure out the social class the man belonged to. He somehow didn't seem to be one of the bourgeoisie, the wealthy middle class of Paris. He certainly was not an aristocrat, for if he were, he would have never addressed a commoner like Jacques. Perhaps a well-paid employee of a wealthy patron? Jacques's question was answered in the next moment when the stranger introduced himself by saying, "Monsieur, I am Armand Bouchard, personal valet to madame Catherine de Lorraine, Marquise of Moy, at your service."

Jacques was pleased with the validation of his shrewd assessment of the man and replied with a grin, "Nice to meet you, Monsieur. I am Jacques Dubois, formerly employed and freshly evicted, at your service, though what help that may be to you, I know not." Armand returned the grin, and with introductions over, the two men stood talking on the bridge.

Jacques was naturally a cautious person and far from having a loose tongue. Yet he couldn't help but open up to this stranger that he had only just met and knew nothing about, save the man's name. There was something in Armand's hypnotic gaze and his manner that gave Jacques hope that perhaps this stranger could somehow save him from becoming destitute. So on and on went Jacques, narrating to Armand every little detail of his life and his recent woes, as the latter listened in patient silence, seldomly interrupting Jacques's monologue with few pointed questions.

In this manner, they stood on the bridge for over two hours, when finally Armand fished out a card from his breast pocket and handed it to Jacques with a flourish. "My young friend, you are quick-witted, honest, and quite likable. I think she will enjoy you very much indeed," said Armand. Jacques was quite puzzled with this statement, and Armand went on to explain, "The mistress I serve, she is quite old, and her estate is quite large. I can always use another helping hand and unfortunately, my previous assistant died recently, so there is a vacancy. Come see me at the address on the card tomorrow at nine a.m. sharp, and we will see if the mistress wants to hire you," finished Armand with another mysterious smile.

Jacques couldn't believe his luck. A chance meeting on a bridge had led to an opportunity to work for a wealthy employer, a marquise no less! He was overwhelmed with both gratitude and trepidation and could only manage to sputter, "Oh, Thank you, Monsieur! But what shall I wear?"

"Why, anything you like, my young friend," said Armand.

"But...But...my clothes are not fit to be in the presence of an aristocrat!" said Jacques as his ears burned with shame.

Armand laughed and said, "Ah! That's no problem. Come by a little earlier than nine, and I will lend you some of poor Louis's clothes. He certainly won't be needing them anymore."

Relieved, Jacques wondered if it would be appropriate to ask about this Louis whose demise had led to Jacques's fortune's betterment. Curiosity, as always, got the better of him, and he asked, "Monsieur, if you don't mind my asking, how did this Louis die?"

"Not at all! You see, poor Louis died of old age," replied Armand with a strange glint in his eyes. After giving Jacques further directions to the marquise's residence, Armand bid him adieu, and they went their separate ways.

"Where were you all day?" hissed Anna as soon as Jacques returned to the apartment. "Do you think this is a *hôtel* where you can wander in and out, whenever you please?" she spat, as Bernard sat in a corner, looking apologetically at Jacques.

Normally Anna's shrewlike behavior would have annoyed Jacques to no end; however, today, he was afloat on dreams of a prosperous future that rose so high, not even Anna's taunts could reach them. "Cheer up, *mon chéri,*" said Jacques with a twinkle in his eye, "I'll be gone tomorrow," he finished with a grin.

"What? How? Where will you go?" exclaimed a concerned Anna, who, despite all indications to the contrary, actually had a good heart and only really taunted Jacques to goad him into action instead of lounging around the apartment all day with Bernard.

Jacques fished out the visiting card given to him by Armand as he narrated the chance meeting on the bridge to Anna and Bernard, who marveled at the ivory-colored paper with gold leaf borders and the seal of the marquise etched in gold ink.

"Mon Dieu!" exclaimed Anna, "This is so amazing! You will work for royalty!" she said with mounting excitement. Over cheap wine, accompanied by hors d'oeuvres that Anna seemed to magically produce despite the paltry budget, the trio discussed Jacques's future plans late into the night. The only thing that gave them some pause was the impending interview with the marquise,

which would decide Jacques' fate. Anna, who in her youth had worked as a maid for a *comté,* spared no effort in coaching Jacques on how to conduct himself and behave in the presence of the aristocracy.

Jacques barely got any sleep that night. Nervous excitement mingled with anxiety kept him awake until the early hours of the morning. Yet when he woke up, he felt refreshed and buoyant with a feeling that today was the day his luck would turn for the better. At Anna's insistence, he took a bath and scrubbed himself clean, and after eating a hasty breakfast while Anna fussed over his hair, he left for the address in Le Marais that was on the card given to him by Armand.

Once again, Jacques walked across Pont Neuf to reach the right bank of the Seine River. However, unlike yesterday, he now noticed the sights, smells, and sounds around him. The busy river traffic, the chatter of pedestrians, the cries of hawkers all seemed to lend energy to his feet as he hurried towards his destination. Jacques crossed the old bridge and made his way to the Hôtel de Ville, where the Provost of the Merchants ran Paris's city administration. From there, he followed Armand's directions to a street called rue des Nonains d'Yerre and shortly before a quarter of nine, found himself standing outside an imposing *château* that was the residence of the Marquise of Moy.

The home of the marquise was significantly larger than the other residences on the street. It was really more a castle than a house, complete with turrets and grand windows. Jacques had approached the château from the rear, where he saw a large garden surrounded by a fieldstone wall, topped with an iron fence. The garden itself was bisected with many rectangular-shaped hedges with stone laid paths crisscrossing among them. A large fountain shaped like a dancing ballerina stood in the middle where these paths met. Jacques made his way to the front of the château by following the building's right-hand side wall. Looking at the château from its side, he could better appreciate the enormity of the structure. This side of the château had rows of arched stone windows going three stories high with wood frames painted in red. The windows were barred with iron rods and covered with curtains. A singular, small red door in the otherwise impenetrable wall provided the only means of ingress or egress from this side of the building. Jacques continued to follow the wall to the front of the château, where he found a large iron gate barring entry. Through the iron gate bars, Jacques could see a cobblestone courtyard and, beyond that, a large red door that was the main entrance to the château.

There'd usually be a footman or two stationed at the gate to announce visitors in wealthy residences such as this, but in this instance, Jacques found the gate deserted. A large bell hung near the gate, and Jacques could see a rope attached to it and stretching all the way to the main building. He gave the bell a tug and heard a deep boom from deep inside the residence. After a few moments, the front door opened and out stepped Armand. He looked across the courtyard and, upon spotting Jacques, motioned the latter to come towards the side of the building where the little red door stood. Jacques retraced his steps to the red door and stood waiting outside. Eventually, there was the sound of a heavy lock being lifted, and the door opened to reveal a smiling Armand.

"My young friend, you are here! I was worried you might've gotten cold feet," he said as he invited Jacques to enter the château with a gesture of his hands. Taking a deep breath to calm his excitement,

Jacques stepped through the red door and into the house of the marquise.

With Armand walking ahead holding a lighted candle, Jacques followed him through a dark, narrow passage with stone walls that led upwards until they exited onto a landing with a winding staircase on one end and three doors on the other. Jacques assumed that these were the servant's quarters, and the little red door was the entrance used by servants when going out on errands. Armand opened one of these doors to reveal a small bedroom. Motioning to a set of clothes that lay neatly folded on the bed, Armand stepped outside while Jacques hurriedly slipped out of his own clothes and into the new ones.

Emerging from the bedroom, he followed Armand up the winding staircase and through a set of heavy doors with ornate wood paneling to find himself in what he rightly guessed to be the grand room of the château.

Looking around the huge room in amazement, Jacques felt as if he had stepped out of the squalor of faubourg Saint-Victor and straight into what could only be a fairy tale. The grand room was not just the biggest room Jacques had ever been in but was also the most richly decorated. Never before had he seen so many beautiful and precious things assembled in one place. The ceiling and walls were ornately painted and decorated with gold leaf. Rare porcelain adorned precious stone desk surfaces that were arranged around baroque style furniture. A grand staircase, complete with red carpet, flowed up towards a circular balcony with marble columns that ran from floor to ceiling. The latter supported a gigantic chandelier of over a hundred candles.

Jacques began to feel dizzy from turning his head up and sideways to get a full view of his surroundings, until Armand tapped him on the shoulder to draw his attention to a screen that was set up in the circular balcony. Jacques could just make out a figure sitting behind the screen, and he could also hear a gasping, wheezing sound coming from behind the screen. "Madame is very old and frail and does not like to be seen by strangers," said Armand to Jacques in a low voice, "I will convey her questions, and you can answer accordingly," he finished. Jacques nodded his understanding, and Armand climbed up the stairs and walked towards the screen, where he proceeded to kneel down beside it.

"Madame, I present to you young Jacques Dubois, of whom I spoke to you about yesterday," said Armand to the figure behind the screen. "He is here to beg your consideration to be hired for Louis's former position." A strange whispering sound emanated from behind the screen as Armand listened attentively, and then, addressing Jacques, he said, "Madame wants to know more about your life. Speak and leave nothing out."

With butterflies fluttering in his stomach, Jacques began to tell his story. Anna's coaching had helped him come up with a narrative beforehand, so he could speak in complete and coherent sentences. He started from his childhood and progressed to his teens. He explained how he had been orphaned when the bubonic plague hit Paris a few years ago. He described his work at the paper factory and his disappointment at being laid off. He spoke of his dreams and aspirations and extolled his virtues, just as Anna had taught him. "I promise that if I am fortunate enough to be considered for this position, I will prove to be a loyal and faithful servant to every command issued by Madame La Moy," he finished by addressing the marquise in the proper manner that Anna had coached him on.

After Jacques completed his narrative, silence reigned in the great hall for a few moments as nothing was heard save the belabored breathing of the figure behind the screen and (in Jacques's mind), the thunderous hammering of his own beating heart. He stood with his head bowed, eyes to the floor, and his hands clasped in front of him in humble supplication.

Then, finally, the strange whispering began anew as Armand listened attentively to whatever it was the figure behind the screen said. A smile crept upon his face as he looked at Jacques, and the latter's hopes rose. "The madame is satisfied with your *présentation* and finds you suitable for the role," said Armand. "Your salary will be 200 livres per year, and you will also receive room and board. I hope that is satisfactory?" asked Armand.

Once again, Jacques found himself at a loss for words. Satisfactory? His last job had paid him eighty livres per year, so the salary offered by the marquise was a king's ransom! He finally found his tongue and managed to sputter, "That...That is most kind. Most kind indeed. *Merci,* Madame and Monsieur."

"Good. You may start tomorrow. The interview is at an end; let me show you out," said Armand as he descended the stairs.

Jacques bowed to the figure behind the screen and quickly followed Armand back the way they had come. He stopped by the door in the servant's quarters to change back into his own clothes, but Armand laughed and said, "No more rags for you, my young friend! Keep the clothes, and I will give you more when you return tomorrow." Armand also tossed a little bag of velvet to Jacques and said, "Here is an advance of fifty livres so you may settle any outstanding debts before you return tomorrow." Then waving away Jacques's profuse words of gratitude, Armand led him to the little red door. Jacques stepped back out into the sunshine as the door behind him closed, and the heavy lock was put back in place.

"You got the job!" screamed Anna with delight, seeing Jacques's new clothes when he returned to the apartment.

"All thanks to you!" said a grinning Jacques. She hugged him, and Bernard slapped him on the back, and in a breathless tone, Jacques described the splendor of the marquise's house as well as the interview.

Anna almost fainted when she heard of the salary Jacques had been offered. "You must work diligently and never give the marquise any reason to complain," said Anna with mock severity.

"Anna, this calls for a celebration. Do you have any food in the house?" asked Bernard.

"Let me check," said Anna as she started towards the cupboard, but Jacques stopped her.

"*Non,* mon cheri, tonight we dine out in style," said Jacques, "They gave me an advance, and the least I can do is take you both out for dinner." Jacques showed them the velvet pouch with fifty livres in it, and that evening the trio went out to a fancy cabaret called Mouton Blanc on rue du Vieux-Colombier.

Anna chose the venue for she had heard from her friends that Parisian notables like La Fontaine, Molière, and Racine were known to frequent this place. They ordered the most expensive dishes and the most expensive wine the cabaret had to offer and had one of the most enjoyable evenings any of them ever remembered having.

Despite consuming what had seemed like gallons of wine the previous night, Jacques awoke early the next morning, full of energy and enthusiasm. Once again, he gulped down his breakfast that consisted of a piece of crusty rye bread and Reblochon, also known as the poor man's cheese. Then bidding Bernard and Anna farewell, he walked at a brisk pace along a now-familiar route until he once again found himself near the garden of the imposing château, which was the home of the marquise. This time he stopped at the red door and knocked a couple of times politely, and eventually, the door opened to reveal Armand standing in the darkness within. "Bonjour Monsieur!" chirped Jacques.

"Ah, my young friend, you are right on time! I appreciate punctuality; it's a virtue seldom seen in our beloved France," said Armand. "Come, let me show you to your quarters, and then we will get to work."

Once again, Jacques followed Armand up the dark passage. When they reached the flight of stairs, Jacques stopped near the door of the room where he had changed his clothes the day before, but Armand continued up the stairs. Turning around, he saw the confused look on Jacques's face and laughed. "No, No, you won't be staying there! The mistress is kind and allows the servants the use of bedrooms on the ground level. Trust me, they are a lot nicer!" said Armand.

Once again, the duo entered the grand room through the heavy double doors, and Armand walked across and entered a corridor connected to the other end of the room. Following Armand down this passageway, Jacques noticed rooms on either side of the corridor with ornately designed doors. Armand stopped in front of one such door and pushed it open as he stepped inside. Jacques followed and found himself in a large bedroom with ornate furniture and drapes of light blue silk that covered a window barred shut with iron rods.

"This is your room, Jacques. Get settled and meet me in the kitchen in exactly half an hour," said Armand as he pointed towards a large clock that stood in the corner. "To get to the kitchen, make a left turn when you leave the room and follow the corridor all the way down." With these words, Armand closed the room's door and left Jacques to take stock of his surroundings.

Jacques's new room was huge by any standard he had ever known. Born and raised in near poverty his entire life, Jacques was used to living with other people in shared spaces that were less than a quarter of this bedroom's size, which he now had all to himself. A large four-poster bed was made out of some exotic wood overlaid with ivory designs and luxurious red and gold curtains made of heavy fabric to enclose the bed on all four sides. Next to the bed, on one side lay an ornately carved wooden desk and chair, and on the other, the large clock made out of redwood with ornate carvings inlaid with gold leaf. There hung a long, oval-shaped mirror with a frame made of some exotic stone that was obsidian black in color on the wall to the left side of the desk. Thrilled as Jacques was with the room, this mirror somehow gave him pause, for it seemed somewhat out of place in the room full of ornate furniture. Curious, Jacques walked over to the mirror to make sure his hair was in place, and his eyes were drawn to the reflection of the wall behind him.

That was the very first time that Jacques saw her portrait!

Jacques saw the portrait of an old woman hanging on the wall behind him in the reflection of the mirror. It was a sideway profile with the woman looking straight ahead with a somber expression. Jacques could see a stately chin, sharp features, and regal nose of the subject. The portrait must have been painted when the woman was at an advanced age, but she must have been quite beautiful in her youth. Suddenly Jacques got a shock, for it seemed that the woman in the portrait moved her head ever so slightly and looked at him. He whipped around to look at the portrait directly but saw only the portrait as it should be, with the woman's sideways profile fixed in eternity. Jacques turned to look at the mirror again, and sure enough, it seemed as if the portrait was looking at him now. "I must be imagining things," muttered Jacques to himself. Suddenly the large clock in the corner chimed loudly, making Jacques almost jump out of his skin. "Mon Dieu! This thing is so loud!" exclaimed Jacques as he opened the bedroom door and made his way to the kitchen.

Jacques found Armand in the kitchen, munching on some ham. Jacques's mouth watered at the smell and sight of the delicacy, and he was delighted when Armand offered him some. "Eat and drink to your heart's content, my young friend," said Armand as he poured the cider into a glass mug and gave it to Jacques. "The work here is simple and will not burden you. You have the freedom of going anywhere in the house except the mistress's room. You must never enter that room, for only I am allowed to do so to tend to her needs." said Armand. His face took on a somber expression as he continued, "Furthermore, the mistress is bedridden so she seldom leaves her room, but even then, the thought of unkempt servants horrifies her. Therefore she requires you to spend at least fifteen minutes in front of the mirror in your room each morning to ensure that you are presentable before you step out."

Jacques found these rules quite odd; however, he had heard about the eccentricities of wealthy people, so he simply said, "Oui Monsieur, I understand and will obey and follow all the rules."

"Understand that these two rules are conditions of your employment. Follow the rules, and you will prosper. Break them, and she has ways of finding out, and you will be back out on the street," said Armand with a hard glint in his eyes. Then his expression softened, and he said, "Come, I will show you around the house and explain your daily duties."

For the remainder of the day, Armand showed Jacques around the massive house. There were two levels in the château with over eighteen bedrooms. There were two kitchens, a large pantry, a beautiful circular library with wooden bookcases stacked on two levels connected by a small circular staircase. There were parlors meant for visiting guests and a large dining hall with the longest table that Jacques had ever seen.

Armand and Jacques were just finishing the tour when there came the sound of a ringing bell. "That's the mistress summoning me," said Armand. "I think this should be enough for today. You may have supper in the kitchen and retire to your room for the rest of the evening if you wish."

Jacques decided that was an excellent idea, and after a scrumptious supper of bread, cheese, and more ham, he retired to his room and, exhausted from his excursion around the house, was soon fast asleep. In fact, his sleep was so deep that he did not hear or sense anything when Armand quietly slipped into his room late at night and stood watching him sleep for a few moments before quietly slipping out again.

The next morning Jacques woke up with a slight headache. When he first opened his eyes, he wasn't sure where he was, and then he suddenly remembered, and a smile broke out on his face. Jacques stifled a giant yawn as he got up, stretched, and peered at the clock. It was a quarter past six in the morning. Jacques opened the door to his room and stepped out into the passageway. The house was silent, and the hallway's oil lamps were no longer alight, leaving the hallway in darkness. Lighting a candle, Jacques found his way to the end of the corridor, where a flight of stairs lay across the kitchen that went to the house's basement. Jacques went down the stairs and found the servant's latrine, which was basically a small tiled room with a small porcelain bowl with a hole in it. Jacques was used to relieving himself like normal people, which was by squatting on the ground. When Armand had introduced this strange device to him yesterday, he had been filled with trepidation. However, now that he was actually sitting on it, he found the process pleasant and less cumbersome than he had imagined. What was more, the device had a trapdoor beneath that opened into the sewers and also had a connection to a water tank. There was a lever in the wall which, when pulled, opened the trapdoor and brought great gushes of water into the bowl, which cleaned away the filth into the sewers. "Will wonders never cease?" thought Jacques as he made his way back up the stairs while still marveling at the rapid advancement of technology.

In his room, Jacques washed his hands and face in a pot he had filled from the kitchen. He then dressed into fresh clothes (he assumed they belonged to his predecessor) that Armand had given him the previous day, and then he turned towards the mirror in keeping with the wishes of his mysterious new mistress. As Jacques was combing his hair, his eyes again wandered to the reflection of the portrait behind him. Once again, Jacques was startled to see the woman in the painting looking at him. Once again, he whipped around but did not find anything out of the ordinary. Muttering to himself, Jacques dutifully preened in front of the mirror for the requisite amount of time before leaving the room to go get breakfast in the kitchen. There he found Armand busy pouring frumenty, a thick porridge made with cracked wheat boiled with milk into a bowl. "I'll take some up for the mistress," said Armand. Pointing towards a basket sitting on the kitchen table, he said, "The baker's boy left these at the door. Help yourself."

As Armand left the kitchen, Jacques poured some of the thick porridge into a bowl and looked into the basket where he found hot bread rolls fresh from the oven. Used to eating hard, stale bread and moldy cheese in the morning, the porridge and bread rolls were akin to a feast for Jacques, and he enjoyed his breakfast considerably.

After he finished eating, he quickly washed up the dishes and then began his daily tasks by sweeping the floors of the grand room. He also dusted the priceless porcelain with the utmost care and wiped clean the stone surfaces. He was tempted to open the curtains to let the sunlight in, but Armand had given strict instructions to keep them closed, citing some strange skin condition that the marquise suffered from that caused her skin to burn if it came in contact with direct sunlight. Jacques then proceeded to clean and sweep the hallways, the kitchen, and the library, where he also put back books that lay stacked in a corner to their rightful spot. At midday, he shared a salad in the kitchen with Armand for lunch, and later they shared a capon that Armand had cooked for their supper. Thus passed Jacques's second day in the service of the marquise.

A week went by with each day passing much as the previous one, when Jacques woke up one morning feeling somewhat lethargic. Being young and energetic and someone who had rarely fallen sick despite having lived in squalid conditions most of his life, this was a novel experience for Jacques. After completing his morning ablutions, he groggily stepped out of his room and set about making himself presentable in front of the mirror. He had by now become used to the phenomenon that made it seem as if the woman in the portrait turned her head to look at him whenever he saw the portrait's reflection in the mirror. In fact, he had convinced himself that it was merely a trick of the light or a figment of his imagination, and deciding to add humor to the ridiculous notion, he would even greet the woman in the portrait by saying, "Bonjour Madame! Did you have a good night's rest?" This was the reason why what happened that particular morning badly frightened him. When he started to comb his hair, he was appalled to find a patch of white in his otherwise raven black hair. His eyes seemed somewhat dull, and his normally radiant skin looked a bit sallow too. Then there was also the visage in the mirror. Today Jacques found her looking at him, but instead of the usual somber expression, the woman's face had a cruel smile, the sight of which sent a chill down his spine. Of course, as always, when he looked at the portrait directly, nothing seemed out of the ordinary, and when he looked back into the mirror, the woman's face had resumed its usual somber expression. Unnerved, Jacques resolved to find out more about the portrait and left his room as he headed towards the kitchen.

"Ah, bonjour Jacque," replied Armand to Jacques's greeting. "*Tout va bien?* You look a bit tired this morning."

"Oui Monsieur, tout va bien," replied Jacques. "I just feel a little less energetic than usual."

"Well, you are a growing lad and what you need is more nourishment," decided Armand. "Here, have some of this pottage that I made with *boeuf* broth. It will give you strength."

The pottage was indeed delicious and made Jacques feel better, and he forgot all about the portrait as he went about his work that day. However, at supper that evening, Armand was in an uncharacteristically conversational mood, perhaps due to the copious amount of wine he was gulping, and the topic of the portrait eventually came up. "There is a portrait in my room of an old lady," began Jacques.

"Ha! I was wondering when you were going to ask me about it," guffawed Armand. "Has she been staring at you lately? Perhaps she desires your youthful looks?" he said with a wink and a conspiratorial grin.

"I'm not sure what the Monsieur means?" said Jacques, scratching his head.

"Oh, don't worry! The mistress's late husband, the Marquis of Moy, was an incorrigible prankster. He got that mirror in your room crafted especially for the purpose of scaring guests that he would put into that room," said Armand. "You see, it has to do with the curve of the mirror's surface that reflects the light. It somehow distorts the reflection of the portrait to make it seem like it is staring at you. Many a poor guest was scared out of his wits, much to the late marquis's amusement," chuckled Armand.

Jacques felt immensely relieved after hearing this explanation. There was no intrigue here, merely a depraved sense of humor of an entitled and long-dead aristocrat. "If the Monsieur does not mind my asking, who is the woman in the portrait"? he asked.

"Not at all, young Jacques, the lady in the picture is the mistress's great-grandmother," replied Armand.

"Oh, that would make the portrait hundreds of years old since the mistress herself seems to be of an advanced age?" said Jacques.

Armand started to open his mouth to speak, but the sound of the bell ringing interrupted him. A look of alarm came over his face as he shot up from his chair and exclaimed, "The mistress needs me!" He scrambled out of the room, leaving Jacques to wash up and retire to his room.

A few more days went by, but Jacques's bouts of lethargy continued unabated. Each morning he found it more and more difficult to get out of bed, and the white patch in his hair seemed to be spreading. He also was looking decidedly older when he looked himself in the mirror, with his once glowing skin now looked more and more sallow. He was also starting to feel pain, hitherto unknown, in various parts of his body. Jacques wondered if he was ill, and one morning he expressed his concerns to Armand, but the latter dismissed them offhand.

"Your birthday is just around the corner, oui? You will turn eighteen? Well, that explains it, young man. It's your changing body playing havoc with your imagination," said Armand.

"But Monsieur, what about my loss of energy? I am feeling worse than I ever have in my life!" exclaimed a perplexed Jacques.

"That's normal too. Look, Jacques, when a boy becomes a man, his body undergoes many changes, and these are never easy. You will feel, see, and hear strange things, but this is just a temporary phase. Why don't you rest in bed for a couple of days? I'm sure you will feel fine," replied Armand.

Jacques found Armand's explanation reasonable, and a chance to rest in bed seemed like a great idea. He nodded his agreement and returned to his room.

For the next couple of days, Jacques rested in bed, leaving his room only to use the lavatory and eat his meals in the kitchen. On the third day, he was decidedly feeling much better, and when he looked at himself in the mirror for the first time in two days, Jacques saw that he was starting to look like his old self again. His skin had regained most of its former glow, and the white in his hair had started to recede considerably. Overjoyed by this seemingly miraculous recovery, Jacques bounded off to the kitchen to tell Armand, but he was not there, which was unusual.

Jacques quickly finished his breakfast and got to work with renewed enthusiasm. He cleaned the dishes in the kitchen, left the bread basket out for the baker's boy to collect the following morning when the latter arrived to deliver fresh bread, and then set about dusting and cleaning the rest of the house.

As a rule, Jacques did not clean the upper level where the marquise's room was located; in fact, he never went anywhere near it. Armand took care of that just as he took care of every other duty related to the care of the marquise. He even emptied her chamber pot twice a day, a task Jacques was thankful to be able to avoid. However, today there was no sign of Armand, and Jacques wondered if he was out running errands. Jacques wanted to show Armand his gratitude for allowing him the much-needed rest and decided to clean the upper level himself. After all, Armand had only forbidden him from entering the marquise's room;

he never actually said anything about the area outside it, so taking his bucket and mop, he started cleaning the passageway in earnest.

Jacques was trying to be really quiet so as not to disturb the marquise, which is perhaps why his approach was not detected, for when he neared the marquise's room, he overheard voices from the inside, one of which was Armand's. Jacques could only catch snippets of the conversation, but he could very well make out the frustrated tone in which Armand was speaking. "But Mistress...the boy was getting suspicious...failing health...I told him a yarn...you must be patient..."

Jacques could not make out the other person's response to Armand's pleading, so he tried to move a little closer to the door and, in the process, almost knocked over the bucket he had been using to mop the floor. At the loud sound, the conversation inside the room ceased abruptly, and after a few moments, the door was flung open, and Armand glared at Jacques with undisguised hostility. "What the devil are you doing here?" he demanded.

"Pardon, Monsieur," stammered Jacques, "I thought you were away running errands, so I thought I would clean this hallway for you to help out."

Armand gave Jacques a hard, searching look and then visibly composed himself. "You have upset the mistress, but I will speak with her and explain that your intentions were noble. Run along now and complete your tasks elsewhere," he said.

"Oui Monsieur," said Jacques as he beat a hasty retreat.

Jacques just couldn't stop berating himself. "You imbecile!" he lamented more than once, "You deserve to be thrown back out on the street!" Such was his dismay at his faux pas from earlier that morning that he totally forgot about the strange conversation that he had partially overheard. When the lunch hour approached, he made his way to the kitchen with great trepidation, fearing the worst. However, Armand, who was busy cooking lunch, only said, "I pleaded with the mistress on your behalf. Luckily for you, she was in a good mood and decided to forgive your transgression."

"That's wonderful, Monsieur!" exclaimed Jacques with immense relief, "I can not thank you enough for all that you have done for me."

"Just be more careful next time, young man," snorted Armand. Then, almost as an afterthought, he added, "One more thing, the mistress was not too happy with your appearance and has mandated that you spend at least thirty minutes in front of the mirror from now on in order to look more presentable." Jacques was far too relieved about not losing his job to care or even wonder about this strange edict, and he simply nodded his agreement.

The next morning, Jacques dutifully spent the requisite thirty minutes preening in front of the mirror and then went about his business with brisk efficiency. He avoided the upper level altogether so as to not give the marquise any reason for complaint. Strangely enough, he was utterly exhausted by lunchtime, and he could, therefore, barely eat the stew that Armand had prepared. Jacques somehow got through the rest of the day by taking frequent rests whenever he could, and by evening he had just enough strength left to drag himself off to bed and fall asleep the minute his head hit the pillow. The thought of dinner did not even occur to him.

When Jacques woke up the following morning, the world looked blurry, and there was an acute pain in both his knees. Somehow he managed to crawl out of bed and shuffle over to the mirror to get dressed, where he was shocked beyond belief as he looked at his reflection. Gone was the youthful face with its smooth skin; it had been replaced with greyish-yellow flesh that was sagging in places with dark circles under the eyes. His hair had turned entirely to white overnight, and his teeth, perfectly healthy the day before, now looked yellow and deformed. His shoulders were hunched as if the weight of advanced age was upon them. "Mon Dieu! What is happening to me?" wondered Jacques. He stood in front of the mirror for a while longer and then walked with great difficulty to the kitchen in the hope of finding Armand, who could perhaps shed more light on this strange ailment that Jacques seemed to be suffering from.

Jacques didn't find Armand in the kitchen. Instead, he saw a note on the table left by Armand, explaining that he had gone out to shop for groceries and that Jacques should go about his duties as usual (and to stay away from the marquise's quarters). Disappointed, Jacques finally paid attention to his rumbling stomach and managed to eat a small piece of bread and cheese. He began his daily chores with some difficulty by starting to dust the precious porcelain objects in the great room. The house stood silent that morning, with the only sound coming from Jacques's exertions as he worked, lost in his thoughts regarding his malady. Suddenly the creaking of a floorboard above his head broke him out of his reverie. He listened attentively as the floorboard creaked again. It seemed as if someone was treading softly across the floor in one of the rooms on the upper level. "Who could that be?" wondered Jacques. Armand had told him on multiple occasions that the marquise herself was bedridden, incapable of walking due to her advanced age, and there were no other occupants in the house save Armand and himself. The floorboards creaked again, and Jacques could tell that the walker was treading softly in order to minimize the sound.

Suddenly an alarming thought came to his mind. What if this were some intruder, going about that very moment robbing the marquise, or worse still, murdering her? With Armand away, there'd be no witnesses, and the crime would be blamed on Jacques. The thought sent a shiver down Jacques's spine and lent a much-needed spurt of energy to his feet as he picked up his mop (presumably to use as a weapon, if required) and silently crept up the stairs.

Jacques stood motionless in the hallway above the great room, quietly listening. "There!" he said to himself as the floorboards creaked again. The sound was definitely coming from the marquise's room. Jacques was convinced that a burglar had somehow slipped into the house and was proceeding to rob the marquise as she lay helpless in her bed. Jacques could only hope that the intruder had not harmed her in any way. Fully aware of his own weakened state, Jacques decided to use the keyhole in the marquise's bedroom door to spy on the intruder before charging in. "I'll have to wait until his back is turned so I can surprise him," thought Jacques as he silently got down on his knees and peered through the keyhole.

Contrary to Jacques's expectation, there was no burglar in the room. In fact, at first, Jacques did not see anybody at all. Through his limited field of vision, he could see a large bed that lay empty. "Where is the marquise?" wondered Jacques. Then a figure walked into view and stood before a chest of drawers that lay next to the bed, with a mirror hung over it. The room was dark, and Jacques could just make out the contours of a woman's body dressed in a black gown. Who was this woman? Was this his mysterious employer? If so, how was she able to walk? Had Armand been lying to Jacques all this time? A hundred questions flooded into Jacques's mind as he continued to survey the scene inside the room through the keyhole.

The figure inside the marquise's room struck a match to light a candle, and the gloom that surrounded her was dissipated for a moment. The illumination enabled Jacques to study the figure's reflection in the mirror, and he saw the face of a beautiful, middle-aged woman. Somehow the face looked strangely familiar to Jacques though he could not recall having met this woman ever before.

Suddenly the woman tilted her head slightly as if listening, and then she looked into the mirror. Jacques was startled as his eyes met those of her reflected face, and it seemed that she was looking directly at the keyhole as if aware of Jacques's presence. A thin, cruel smile crept onto her face, and in a flash, Jacques realized why her face had looked familiar. This was the same woman whose portrait hung in his room, only younger—in fact, much younger. A cold feeling of dread crept over his body as Jacques stood up and shuffled away from the door. He went down the stairs to his room to take a closer look at the portrait that hung there.

Words cannot adequately describe Jacques' confusion and horror as he stood looking at the portrait in his room. Instead of the visage of an old woman that should have been there, the portrait now held the face of the younger woman he had seen only moments ago. It also seemed that the woman in the portrait had decided to give up all attempts at subterfuge and stared directly at Jacques with the now-familiar cruel smile and a malicious expression. Jacques felt dizziness starting to take over and sat down heavily on the bed. "How could this be?" he thought as his tired mind attempted to make sense of what he had witnessed. Jacques realized that there was sorcery afoot and that somehow, the marquise, if indeed the woman upstairs was her, was slowly draining the life force out of Jacques while gaining youth herself in the process.

In a sudden flash, he recognized the instrument of evil that the marquise was using to steal his youth. The mirror! It had to be the mirror in his room, that terrible thing with an edge of obsidian black. The memory of the strange conversation he had overheard two days ago came rushing back to his mind. The more he thought about the marquise's seeming obsession with him looking into the mirror each day and the fact that he had felt better when he didn't for two days, Jacques finally began to see the web of dark magic spun by Armand and the marquise, with him caught within it, as helpless as a fly.

If only Jacques could summon even a small measure of his former strength, he would have taken advantage of Armand's absence and fled that dreadful house. As the matter stood, however, Jacques just did not have the energy to make his way back to his friends and to safety. "How then to summon help?," he wondered, and then an idea came to him.

Jacques knew how to read and write, which is why he had been able to obtain a job as a clerk with his previous employer. He also knew that Anna could do the same, so he made his way to Armand's room as fast as he could in his present condition. He knew that Armand kept papers, pen, and ink on his desk, and Jacques lost no time in scribbling two notes, one addressed to Anna explaining his predicament and the other for the baker requesting that the note meant for Anna be delivered posthaste at the address that he mentioned on the note. He then painfully made his way to the servant's entrance. After collecting the empty bread basket from the kitchen and placing the notes and five livres from the money he still had left, he left the basket in its usual spot. It was fortunate that he did so without delay, for when Jacques returned to the great room, he saw Armand, who must have returned while Jacques was plotting his escape, walking out of the marquise's room and from that point onwards, Armand seemed to keep a close watch on Jacques and followed his every move.

As night fell and dark shadows once again crept into the house, Jacques found it impossible to sleep. During the day, it had taken every ounce of his will to act normal in front of Armand, but somehow Jacques knew that Armand was suspicious of him and was not fooled by this show of nonchalance. Jacques was terrified of being murdered in his sleep by these wicked beings, and yet he was equally terrified of confronting them in his waking moments. He fretted all night regarding the chances of his success in receiving aid. While he was sure that his friends would rush to his rescue once they learned of the danger that threatened his life, what concerned him was the uncertainty about whether his message would even reach them or not. The baker's boy might not realize the purpose of the notes and just toss them after pocketing the money. The baker, too, might do the same instead of involving himself. Worst still, he may report these to Armand, and then Jacques would be in even far greater danger. The worrisome thoughts prevented him from getting rest or sleep, and as dawn broke, he finally resolved that come what may, he will not die without a fight. When he went to the kitchen, despite his lack of appetite, his purpose was to steal one of the knives while Armand wasn't watching, and having successfully done so, he hid the knife on his person. He shuffled about his daily duties to keep up the pretense, knowing fully well that Armand was doing the same.

Meanwhile, over in faubourg Saint-Victor, there was a knock on the door of the small apartment just as Anna finished her breakfast. She opened the door to find a boy of about eight years of age, standing outside with a large grin on his face. "Oui? What do you want?" asked Anna.

The boy continued to grin as he extended his hand in which he clutched a folded piece of paper. As Anna took the paper from him, he turned without a word and ran off. Puzzled, Anna closed the door and opened the folded piece of paper. As she started to read, her expression changed from puzzlement to incredulity and then to alarm. "Bernard!" she screamed, "Come quick! Jacques is in trouble; we need to go!"

As they rushed out of the apartment, Anna showed Jacques' note to Bernard, who could neither read nor write, and explained its contents. Incredible as Jacques's story sounded, Anna could well make out the undertones of desperation in his plea for help and was convinced that he was indeed in danger of some kind.

In 17th century France, law enforcement was conducted by the Maréchaussée, which had been merged with the constabulary more than two hundred years ago, making it the oldest law enforcement body of any kind in France. Unfortunately, what had once been an efficient and noble force had now become a most corrupt and inept institution. Still, it was all the Parisians had, and so Anna and Bernard half walked and half-ran until they reached the Notre Dame cathedral where constables could usually be found lounging outside. They saw a constable who was a giant of a man standing outside the cathedral and rushed up to him and began to narrate their tale, as Anna tried to show him the note she had received from Jacques. However, the big brute grunted something unintelligible and just stared at them, and Anna realized that the oafish fellow was likely illiterate. She looked around with mounting desperation until she spotted another constable in the distance and dragged a still talking Bernard by the hand; she ran in that direction.

This other constable turned out to be a pleasant-looking fellow with a neat little mustache. "Madame! Please! Relax and take a deep breath," he said as Anna started blurting out her story to him. Composing herself, Anna narrated the tale for a third time that day, with Bernard nodding his head as the constable listened patiently.

He took the note from Anna, read it carefully twice, and then calmly put it in his pocket. However, when he looked back up at Anna and Bernard, the expression on his face had hardened. "How dare you?" he hissed. "How dare you accuse an esteemed member of the aristocracy with this nonsensical tale of mirrors and black magic?"

"But Monsieur! You must believe me!" cried Anna, "We know Jacques, he would never make up a story like this. I understand this sounds unbelievable, but whatever the reason, his life is indeed in danger."

The constable spat on the ground and growled, "Common filth, you think you can swindle someone as high born as the Marquise of Moy with this scandalous accusation? I should arrest you just for making false claims and wasting my time."

Anna was getting angry now. "If you won't help us, then give me that letter back so I can find someone who will listen and do their job," she spat back.

The constable's face went red, and he said in a low menacing voice, "What sort of work do the both of you do?"

"I work in a laundry," said Anna haughtily as Bernard kept quiet with his eyes to the ground.

"Ah!" said the constable as understanding dawned in his eyes while he stared at Bernard. "The Monsieur lives off his woman, does he? The Monsieur is unemployed, is he?" said the constable sarcastically. "I'm afraid it's off to the poorhouse for the Monsieur if he doesn't get his wench under control."

The implied threat in the Constable's words was not lost on Bernard or Anna, and the very thought of Bernard being dragged off to Paris's notorious prisons for the unemployed deflated her fighting spirit. "Come away, Anna," said Bernard in a quiet voice, "There is nothing more that we can do." With hearts full of sorrow and heads hanging in dejection, Anna and Bernard walked away from the constable and went back to their apartment, praying that the good Lord would watch over their friend. Still, unbeknownst to them, God too, it seemed, had abandoned Jacques.

At the house of the marquise, there was a loud banging at the servant's entrance. Jacques, who had been waiting in anticipation for help to arrive, rushed as fast as he could to open the door and felt his heart leap with joy at the sight of a constable with a neat little mustache standing outside. "Monsieur!" he croaked, "I can't tell you how glad I am to see you!"

The constable smiled at him and said, "You must be Jacques."

"Oui, Monsieur and I must tell you about..." Jacques started to say but was cut off in mid-sentence as a hand clasped his shoulder with an iron-like grip and

Armand stepped to the door from behind and pushed Jacques aside.

"Ah! Pierre, what brings you here?" said Armand to the constable.

"Pardon my intrusion Monsieur Armand, but may we please speak in private?" said the constable. Armand motioned angrily to Jacques to go back upstairs, and the latter started walking back while wondering at the constable's deferential attitude towards Armand. Things were not going as Jacques had imagined. In his eager anticipation, Jacques had envisioned an army of constables, urged on by Anna and Bernard, bursting through the front door to rescue him and arrest Armand and the marquise. Instead, a single constable had shown up, who also happened to be an acquaintance of Armand. Jacques stopped midway in the passage where he couldn't be seen from the door and stood listening.

The constable spoke with Armand in a hushed tone, and Jacques could not make out the words, but when the constable handed Armand a piece of paper, Jacques could clearly see that it was his note to Anna, and his heart again filled up with cold fear and dread. Armand folded the note and put it in his pocket, and handed the constable a few livres. The latter saluted smartly and turned away as Armand started to close the door. Jacques knew that time was now running out for him. Fear lent speed to his weakened body as he rushed back up the stairs and to his room. He shut the door and stood looking at the mirror while avoiding its reflection as he racked his brains for a plan. What could he do? Armand was sure to tell the marquise that Jacques had become aware of their diabolic design, and the only possible course of action for the evil duo would be to kill Jacques and dispose of his body.

"Think Jacques, think!" he said desperately to himself, and then inspiration struck. Whatever dark magic Armand and the marquise were weaving, the mirror seemed to play a central role in it. If he broke the mirror (it was glass after all), would that not destroy their power? Hopefully, the mirror's destruction would also restore Jacques to his youth and vigor, and he would be more than a match for Armand in physical combat that was likely to follow. With these thoughts, Jacques picked up the chair that lay in his room, and mustering the little strength left in his body, he threw it at the mirror.

The chair hit the mirror with a loud crash and a force that would have shattered any other mirror to pieces, but in this case, the chair simply rebounded off the mirror and hit Jacques with a force that knocked him senseless. How long he was unconscious is not known, but when he came to, he found himself looking at his own reflection in the still intact mirror, and he realized that Armand was holding him upright with one hand as he forced Jacques's head with the other towards the mirror. Jacques tried to shut his eyes but found to his horror that his eyelids had been stitched to his forehead, and he could no longer close them.

A woman was humming merrily in the room, and eventually, the marquise came into view behind Jacques. She twirled around gracefully like a ballerina as she made her way to Jacques's side. Bringing her face close to Jacques', she purred, "Oh, you poor child, stop fighting the inevitable. You are giving up your life for a noble cause, as have many before you."

"Who are you people?" sputtered an increasingly feeble Jacques.

The woman laughed merrily as she resumed her dancing and said "Why, I am the Marquise of Moy, of course!

Armand here comes from a long line of loyal servants. In fact, I was there when his great-grandfather was but an infant."

Jacques sensed that he was now very close to death, and slipping his hand into his pocket, he searched for the knife that he had stolen from the kitchen, but his hand found only empty space within his pocket.

"Looking for this?" said Armand as he released Jacques's head and brandished the stolen knife in his hand. Throwing the knife on the floor, Jacques once again forced Jacques's head towards the mirror as the latter seemed to give up all hope and become resigned to his fate.

Even with his blurring vision, Jacques could see the rapid change in both the dancing woman and him in the mirror. Moments ago, he had looked like a man in his sixties while she had looked middle-aged. Now he looked as if close to ninety years of age while she was looking more and more like a woman in her early twenties. "You are a monster!" he managed to croak.

The woman seemed to be offended by this remark. Stopping her frolic, she rushed once again to Jacques's side and spoke in a voice full of injury. "Monster!" she cried, "No, Monsieur, you are mistaken. I am no monster. I will tell you who the real monster is. It is no other than Nature herself, for she hunts us from the day we are born. She robs us of our beauty, our strength, our very lives." Then the marquise's expression became wistful as her beautiful face took on a haunted look. "Do you think I enjoy taking the lives of others? No, Monsieur, this change you see is, alas, not permanent. I am cursed to take the life of another, again and again, so I may live," she said softly. "Tell me, Jacques, is it a crime to want to live? Does the beast in the forest commit a sin when it hunts so it may sustain itself? Are we really any different, the beast of the forest and I?"

Jacques tried to speak, but his voice came out in wheezing gasps. Hearing this, the marquise, who by now was decidedly looking like a girl in her teens, signaled to Armand, who gently laid Jacques down on the floor. Taking Jacques's head in her lap, she said, "Hush, it's time to say goodbye, mon cheri. Your suffering in this world is coming to an end."

With those words, the Marquise of Moy gently kissed Jacques on his forehead, and he finally fell into a sleep from which there would be no waking.

IT DRAWS THEM TO YOU

Frank's funeral was beautiful indeed, beautiful and sad. The pastor gave a sermon about eternal life after death and the promise of being reunited with our loved ones in heaven. Frank's best friend Eddie gave a eulogy that moved everyone to tears, though there were some smiles too at his mentions of the capers that he and Frank had been through in school, while in college, and then later during their stints in the Army. The organ player churned out one haunting melody after another, surrounded by beautiful flower arrangements that brought splashes of color against the grey backdrop of stormy clouds and rain pelting the large windows. There was a small break in the deluge and the pastor took advantage of it by quickly moving the procession outside so Frank could finally be laid to rest. Then, suddenly it was all over and for the first time in my forty years of marriage, I was left alone, truly alone.

Frank was the love of my life. We had met in college in Virginia during our sophomore year and had been together since. Frank joined the Army right after college and we were married shortly thereafter just so I could go with him wherever in the world he was posted. The Vietnam War had ended by then and the present day flames of conflict that threaten to engulf the world were at that time little more than smoldering embers, so we had a great time during Frank's postings in Germany, Korea, the Philippines, and elsewhere. When he finally retired from the Army, Frank and I built a small home for ourselves in Northern Virginia. We grew vegetables in the garden, caught fish in the river, and took long walks among the forests of oak and pine trees that surrounded our little slice of paradise. My only regret in life is my inability to bear children, but Frank never let me feel even a moment of sadness due to that fact. "We have each other; that is enough," he had often said to me. Now, my best friend in the whole wide world was gone and I had nothing to fill my hours with, except the memories.

God they hurt, the memories! Memories of our time together. Memories associated with every small thing. Our daily routines, sitting near the kitchen window sipping our morning coffee, the lazy afternoons spent picnicking in the forest as we watched the varying shades of autumn adorning the trees while holding hands, our bodies pressed against each other for warmth. Frank in that silly hat that he insisted on wearing each time we went fishing. Our evenings spent listening to old records and drinking wine. Frank washing the dishes after dinner while he sang and looked at me with a smile that would still melt my heart after all these years. Everywhere I turned, every little thing I did, a memory of Frank came flooding in my mind and each time this was followed by a sense of immense loss. The fact that slowly the house was losing his essence made matters even worse. My grief knew no bounds.

Family and friends tried to help, but eventually gave up after I kept pushing them away. I didn't need their sympathy. I needed my Frank and nothing else would ever suffice. I needed to feel close to him again, to feel his presence, so I started spending more and more time hanging out in the cemetery where he was buried. Each morning I packed some food, filled a thermos with coffee, and after stopping to pick flowers that had been Frank's favorite, I drove to the cemetery. After placing the flowers on his grave, I would often sit and read aloud a book I brought along, just as I had read to him in the hospital during his final days. I would take long walks along paths that circled the cemetery, returning each time to his grave. In this manner, I passed many hours and many weeks. I'd like to mention that while doing this brought me no peace, it helped fill the long and empty hours that I otherwise found myself unable to bear, and it helped me feel a little closer to Frank.

One such day, as the evening shadows lengthened and I sat lost in my thoughts near Frank's grave, I noticed a man standing a few feet away and observing me. "Hello," I said and he walked over.

"Hello, my name is Chris Hemsway," he introduced himself.

"I'm Laura Pratt," I replied. I noticed that he was dressed for a funeral, in all black, and out of curiosity I asked "Are you here for the wake?" while motioning towards the church that stood within the confines of the cemetery and where I could see a lot of people gathered. Chris simply nodded and I noticed the wistful expression on his face. "Did you lose someone close to you?" I inquired and again he simply nodded sadly. "I'm very sorry for your loss," I said, "I lost my husband a few months ago and I know how much it hurts to lose someone."

"Is that his grave?" he asked while pointing towards Frank's tombstone.

"Yes it is," I replied.

Chris nodded his understanding and said "I'm sorry to have intruded" and started to walk away.

I said, "Oh no, it's quite alright. You weren't intruding. It's actually nice to talk to someone after such a while." Chris stayed and we chatted for another half an hour or so. I learned that Chris had been a traveling salesman who had visited more than half the countries in the world, including some that I had lived in with Frank. We spoke of foreign places that we both knew of and compared notes. It was almost dark by the time I decided it was time to head back home. "It was very nice to meet you, Chris," I said, "I visit Frank every day. I find that it helps. Maybe I will see you around."

"It was nice to meet you too Laura, and yes I will be around," replied Chris. Bidding him goodbye, I walked back to my car and drove off home.

It rained incessantly the next day so it wasn't until early afternoon that I was able to make it to the cemetery. The ground was wet but I had brought a sheet with me on which to sit on. Settling near Frank's grave, I began my daily ritual of reading aloud to him. The sun slowly descended into the horizon as time went by, and just as twilight's fingers were starting to softly caress the land, I spotted Chris walking towards me in the company of another woman. "Hi Laura!" he greeted me.

"Hi Chris!" I responded, happy to see him.

He introduced his companion by saying "Laura, this is Ascension. I met her here yesterday after you left." I said hello to Ascension who responded to my greeting with a polite nod of her head. I was quite taken in by her looks for she was very tall, with smooth, satin-like black skin and a regal nose placed in perfect symmetry to her large hazel-colored eyes. Ascension was absolutely gorgeous and even at my age, that gave me a small tinge of jealousy.

The thing that struck me as odd was the way both Chris and his lady companion were dressed. Ascension wore a flowing white dress, which seemed to me as an unusual choice for someone in mourning. Chris on the other hand still wore the raven black clothes from yesterday, as if he never went home to change. Before I could say anything, however, fat drops of rain started to fall from the sky and quickly turned into a deluge. I realized that I had not brought an umbrella with me and within seconds I was well on my way to being drenched to the bone. "Oh Lord!" I cried as I quickly collected my things. "I have to run. It was nice meeting you Ascension, and it was nice seeing you again, Chris." Without waiting for their response, I sprinted to my car, and as I drove off, I looked in the rear mirror and saw them both standing near Frank's grave, seemingly impervious to the rain as they watched me drive away.

I returned the next day to the cemetery and spent an uneventful day beside Frank's grave. Once again, as the failing light of the sun heralded the evening hour, I spotted Ascension walking towards me, with a little girl of ten, maybe twelve years of age. Ascension was dressed in the same flowing white dress from yesterday while the little girl was dressed in a black frock. Of Chris, there was no sign. "Hello there!" I greeted the pair. "Chris didn't come today?"

Ascension smiled mysteriously at me and spoke for the first time "He finally went home, Laura." I didn't know quite what to make of this cryptic statement, so I instead inquired about the little girl.

"She is lost," said Ascension. "I need to guide her home as well." Her voice was rich and sweet, like warm honey lazily trickling from the dipper.

I realized that I had never asked Chris where he lived. "Oh, I was hoping to see him since we didn't get a chance to talk much yesterday," I said, feeling somewhat disappointed.

"You will, sweetie, someday you will," said Ascension, again smiling that mysterious smile. Then looking at the little girl who stood silently next to her, Ascension said "Laura, I have to take little Sarah home, but I want to show you something first, will you come with me?"

"Sure, where do we need to go?" I asked.

"Not far, just to there," replied Ascension as she pointed towards the church and we started walking towards it. I noticed that there was another wake in progress, and when we reached the door to the church, both Ascension and Sarah stopped outside. "Go on in, Laura," said Ascension, "See, observe, and know. We will be waiting for you outside." I was greatly mystified but went in anyway.

The wake was well underway as I walked down the aisle. I saw the pastor on the small stage, I noticed the relatives sitting in the pews, I observed the young couple sitting at the very front sobbing quietly, and then I saw the photograph set on the table near the casket, that of a young girl smiling. In a daze, I walked over to the casket and peered inside and there she was, little Sarah, dressed in the same black frock that I had seen her in, minutes ago, her skin the color of pasty white, her face serene and her hands clasped together in supplication. I was stunned and confused beyond words. Quickly turning around, I rushed outside where I saw Ascension standing with little Sarah, waiting for me. I stared at them, unsure of what to say.

"Do you understand now?" asked Ascension in a gentle voice. I could only nod, for I was at a loss for words. Ascension continued to look at me, this time her smile more kind than mysterious, and finally I managed to ask "and Chris...?"

Ascension simply nodded in her reply and her previous statement about "Chris having finally gone home" began to make sense to me. I noticed that there were people milling about near the church's entrance, quite certainly here for the wake, and yet none of them seemed to be paying any attention to Sarah, who stood there, visible to me as clear as the day. "Can they not see you?" I asked and Sarah sadly shook her head. "Then why can I...?" I started to ask.

Ascension responded by saying "Laura, grief is the most powerful emotion we possess. It burns away all other emotions and desires, leaving the soul pure and clean. The greater the grief, the more one's soul shimmers and as it is, your soul shines the brightest amongst all the living gathered in this place. That's what attracts us to you." I did not know quite how to respond, and could only nod.

Suddenly Ascension cocked her ear to the side as if listening to something, then turning towards Sarah, she said "It's time, darling." Turning back towards me she smiled and said "Go live your life Laura, and be secure in the knowledge that when it's your time to come home, Frank will be waiting for you on the other side."

With those words, Ascension and Sarah turned around and walked hand in hand until they slowly became transparent, and then as I watched, they disappeared altogether. I stood rooted to the spot for a while, trying to fully comprehend all that had just happened.

Then for the first time in what seemed like ages, I smiled.

MANEATER

Northwest of the Nepal border with India and below the permanent snow lines of the Himalayas, there lies the cold windswept region known as Kumaon. Ruled over the centuries by a succession of dynasties ranging from Katyuri, Chand Rajas, Gurkhas, and lately the British, Kumaon is a maze of mountains and a part of the Himalayan range, some of which are among the loftiest known. While its upper reaches are only visited by herders who graze sheep and goats there during the short summers, its lower elevations that lie between

3,500 and 8,000 feet boast of a temperate climate that encourages year-round settlement. The hills are covered with forests of pine, cedar, and rhododendron, their thick marching lines broken intermittently by small terraced farms and isolated villages that dot the hillside. The people of this enchanting land are simple folk engaged mostly in farming and raising livestock.

The surrounding forests once used to be filled with herds of deer and wild boar and were also home to many a Himalayan black bear, leopard, as well as that most majestic of felines, the tiger. Unfortunately, the ceaseless deforestation and reckless overhunting of the last few decades has significantly decimated the forest and its inhabitants. It has not only caused major land degradation and erosion but has also brought man and beast into open conflict as never before. I'm afraid that if the government does not soon begin to prioritize nature over the nationwide hunger for timber, the majestic beauty of this land and its inhabitants of all stripes may soon be lost forever.

But I have begun this tale badly, for what I should have started with are the events of that summer of long ago that brought me to Kumaon in the first place. The year was 1896 and it was a great time for a young British expat to explore the wonders of India. I, Josh Harding, was then merely twenty-five years of age and had been living in India for a little under seven years. Having arrived from England with my father's expedition (he was a renowned archeologist), I so fell in love with this most magical of lands and its people that I decided to stay put after the expedition returned to England. My mother had passed away many years ago and my father had always led a nomadic lifestyle that left little room for parenting, so my decision to stay on in India was met with only the most cursory of protests.

However, prior to returning to England, my father saw to it that I would receive a good education and find meaningful work instead of whiling away my time in frivolous pursuits. This is how I came to work as an apprentice engineer under the august supervision of T.W. Ashhurst, Esquire, who was then the chief engineer on the Agra Water Supply project. This is also where I first met Raj, another apprentice engineer working on Ashhurst's team.

Sardar Rajbir Singh Bahadur (Raj for short) was one of the most remarkable people that I have ever met. He was the scion of a wealthy Sikh family in Punjab, who had been educated almost entirely in England due to his family's connections and considerable means. Standing six feet tall, Raj was handsome and well-built, with an athletic streak. He excelled at every sport he played, was a crack shot and an avid hunter. Since he practically grew up in England, he spoke fluent English and had lost the inhibition and subservient attitude that many Indians at that time displayed towards the British. He could go toe to toe with the best that the British establishment in the Presidency of Agra could offer, whether it be in cricket, polo, rugby, or hunting. This, of course, irked some of the old blowhards in the establishment to no end, and they often took their revenge by pressing upon Raj the most difficult of assignments. To their dismay, however, Raj had also proven himself to be a brilliant engineer who always found a solution to the convoluted problems set before him. While a majority of the British grey beards detested Raj simply on principle, he was indeed quite popular amongst the younger expats. His quick wit, charming manners, and impeccable sense of dressing had also made him quite the favorite amongst the fairer sex of the British society in Agra. Above all, he was my best friend and the brother that I never had.

Raj and I could not have been more different in our physical and mental outlook. He was solidly built where I was slender. He was brash where I was soft-spoken and deferential. He would run towards a burning fire while I was more inclined to run in the opposite direction. Yet despite these differences, we found common ground in our great love for the land that we both called home.

We soon became inseparable, and together we explored locales that stretched from the backstreets of Agra to the ramparts of the red fort in Delhi and everything in between. We shared a particular love for nature, and whenever work and weather permitted it, we spent hours and sometimes days wandering the forests around Agra. Being an avid hunter, Raj would never miss the chance to engage in a spot of shooting while I, even though being the proud owner of a Heym Model 89B double rifle (my father's parting gift to me), rather preferred to shoot animals with my camera instead. Often joining us in these adventures was my two-year-old mastiff, Shadow, a gift from Raj's father during my latest visit to the Bahadurs' ancestral home. Thus we spent many wonderful evenings in the jungle, cooking game bagged by Raj over the campfire, as he narrated Shikar yarns from his considerable repertoire, tales which never lost their vigor even with the frequent retelling.

So the glorious months flew by until there came the fateful day when our boss, T.W. Ashhurst, was transferred to the public works department in the Kumaon district. Water supply in the hills was a chronic problem year round. The British Government had plans to collect water from springs and ravines and direct it to reservoirs by cutting channels into rocks and lining them up with concrete—a task that sounded far easier than it actually was, which is why Ashhurst decided to take his best engineers, which included Raj and I, with him to Kumaon.

The next few weeks were spent in preparation for the team to decamp to Kumaon. Travel in India at that time was slow and arduous due to the scarcity of roads and other means of modern transportation. The Delhi Junction railway station, built over thirty years ago, only connected the region to Calcutta via broad gauge track and to Ajmer via meter gauge track. The tracks connecting to Agra would not be laid for another nine years and therefore of necessity, our group traveled on horseback while the coolies rode bullock carts laden with our luggage, equipment, and household items. Our destination was the small hill town of Almora which lay 25 km east of the Ranikhet Cantonment and was the district headquarters of the Kumaon region. The plan was to build the main reservoir in Almora and replicate the process in other strategic points in the region. The long journey from Agra to Almora took a little over three weeks to complete and we reached our destination in the middle of June.

I will not bore you with the mundane details of our work in Almora except for the fact that the work was arduous as we surveyed the land around Almora and slowly made our way westwards, while mapping the likely routes for cutting the channels in the rocks. As if our work wasn't hard enough due to the rugged terrain, sudden and torrential rain, and the landslides it invariably caused, greatly added to our misery. The only silver lining in the clouds (do excuse the pun) was the breathtaking views and the abundance of flora and fauna that we witnessed each day. Thus we passed three long months in Kumaon, toiling during the day and braving the elements in tents and temporary huts at night, for queen and country it was said, though I very much doubted that her majesty either knew or cared about our labors.

If one were to track our progress on a map, they would draw an almost straight line from Ranikhet all the way to the tiny hamlet of Karanprayag in the north, with Dwarahal, Parkot, and Chamola as waypoints along the way. At Karanprayag, which sits at the confluence of the Alaknanda and the Pindari Rivers, we turned westwards and mainly followed the left bank of the Alaknanda in a South Westerly direction. Thus passing through the hamlets of Tilani, Rudraprayag, Srinagar (not to be confused with its namesake city in Kashmir) and Dhungi, and having covered little over 700 km across one of the most difficult and rugged terrains in India, we finally arrived at the village of Pauri which was at that time the only significant settlement in the area.

Ashurst decided that the team needed some time off after all the hard work we'd put in and declared a one week vacation. Raj, who apparently had spent some time in the area with his father (the latter owning a timber contracting business among many others), immediately set upon planning a hunting trip for the two of us. "You are in for a treat, old cock!" chirped Raj, "There is a *dak* bungalow that lies a few hours' walk from here and the guard there knows me well. It's fairly secluded and a hunter's paradise!" Dak bungalows were rudimentary structures built by the British throughout the hills to provide way stations for the fledgling Indian postal service where mail carriers could rest and store mail. These also doubled as "vacation spots" for the *sahibs* looking for a spot of shooting in the hills.

"That sounds like a capital idea, Raj" said I, and soon we were off, accompanied by Shadow who had come along with us from Agara and had braved the toils of the past months with hardly a whimper.

We had started for our destination early in the morning and a forced march across beautiful hills laden with deodar, oak, rhododendron and surai trees brought us to our objective shortly before three p.m. The dak bungalow at Khrisu lay at an elevation of 5,900 feet and was a small, two-room affair built on the edge of a hill that offered breathtaking views of the Himalayas and the valley below. Birju the caretaker indeed knew Raj well and even though we did not have official permission to put up at the bungalow, Raj's charm and a small *baksheesh* ensured that we had a place to stay. Life in the hills was hard and Birju, who himself had only just returned from Pauri that morning with supplies, was grateful for the extra income. The food provisions that we had brought with us also added greatly to his meager store.

We set down our bags inside, and after a bath taken in the open and hot tea graciously provided by Birju, we felt ready to explore our surroundings. There was a steep forest path that started from a banyan tree growing near the bungalow and went all the way down to the valley. We explored the valley for some time as we slowly made our way westwards to another spot that Raj wanted to show me. On the hill adjacent to the one that bungalow was built upon, but at a lower elevation, there stood an ancient stone shrine known to the locals as the Daungadera Mahadev temple. Its devotees were followers of Lord Shiva, the destroyer. The shrine itself consisted of a simple stone structure that housed the deity, and the temple premises also boasted of a small pool fed by rainwater. It was early September, when days are hot and humid in Kumaon, and we had worked up quite a sweat during our trek, so laying down our clothes, rifles, and backpacks at the edge of the pool, we waded in for a much-needed swim.

After splashing in the water for a few minutes, Raj and I were both startled by a deep growl that emanated from Shadow, who had plopped down at the edge of the pool to keep watch over our belongings. The temple had been built by clearing a small space in the forest, and therefore stood with its back to the hill and the forest growing on three sides. The part of the forest facing the temple lay merely six feet away from the pool's farthest edge and had a large amount of undergrowth. It was at this undergrowth that Shadow was now directing his attention as he stood growling with his teeth bared.

It was apparent to us that Shadow's canine senses had detected some danger that we could not yet see so we quickly made our way to the middle of the pool which seemed to be the safest spot at the moment. We stood in this fashion for a few long, tense moments while an eerie silence reigned all around us, broken intermittently by Shadow who had gone from growling to occasionally whimpering as he stood cowering with his tail between his legs.

Then all of a sudden things began to happen at once. The silence was broken by a "*coooie*" from the hill above the temple, and at the same time a low growl emanated from the undergrowth, followed by some agitation in the bushes that grew on the slope leading down to the valley, and then silence reigned again.

Modern means of communication were almost nonexistent in the hills, so the locals communicated by means of yelling greetings and messages from one hilltop to the next (as sound carries a great distance across mountains). In this fashion, important messages could travel a great distance in an amazingly short amount of time.

The "*coooie*" was repeated, and this time we were able to determine its source as we spotted two men standing on the hill directly above and to the left of the temple. One of the men yelled that a *baagh* (tiger) had been watching us from the undergrowth but had now gone down the valley, so it was safe for us to come out of the pool. Putting our clothes back on and gathering our rifles and backpacks, we made our way up the hill towards the two men, but not before showering poor Shadow with many pats on the head for having warned us just in time of the tiger's presence.

Upon reaching the two men, we were greeted by the question of whether we were mad or suicidal, for did we not know that there was an *aadamkhor* (maneater) on the loose who had already claimed three lives in the past week alone? Upon hearing that we had only just arrived in the area and doubtlessly impressed by the rifles we had slung over our shoulders, the two men invited us to their village that lay a few minutes' walk further up the hill. Along the way, they explained that the temple premises were visible from the village and an alarm had gone up when somebody spotted Raj and I frolicking in the temple pool. We were grateful to these men for the great personal risk that they had undertaken by leaving the confines of the village in order to warn us.

The village of Kothagi from which the men hailed was a small hamlet with about fifty residents. When we reached the village, we found the residents in a state of abject terror. Sitting in the village courtyard and hearing the villagers' tales of woe, we gathered that a tiger had appeared out of nowhere about a week ago and had carried off the headman's daughter-in-law who had been cutting leaves off a tree that grew at the edge of the village proper. Another woman working nearby had seen what happened and the village men had immediately set out to rescue the poor victim, armed with drums, *laathis* (bamboo sticks) and an ancient blunderbuss owned by the village headman. They followed the blood trail from the scene of the attack to some bushes about 500 yards away from where the tiger had taken its kill. Doubtlessly the din made by the drums and loud voices unnerved the tiger, who had just started on his meal, and with a terrible roar the beast jumped out from the bushes and ran for the safety of the dense forest that lay just a few feet away.

The group of would-be rescuers had, in the meantime, turned and fled in the opposite direction. Upon reaching the village, the air was thick with accusations as to who had bolted first, with a majority of the fingers pointed at the headman who, apart from owning the only firearm in the group, also had a personal duty to avenge the death of his daughter-in-law. Thankfully, cooler heads prevailed and the group returned to the scene, albeit with far more caution this time around, and successfully recovered the mostly intact corpse of the poor woman.

The tiger, deprived of its prize, lost no time in securing another victim that very night. An old widower who lived in a hut at the edge of the village ventured out to answer nature's call, and the waiting tiger pounced on him as the man squatted on the ground. This time there were no witnesses to the tragedy and the tiger, having carried his victim into bushes a few feet away from the hut, proceeded to feast without interruption.

When the widower did not show up for the customary morning village gathering, it was assumed that he was getting lazy in his old age and a lad was dispatched to fetch him. The lad came running back in short order and breathlessly described the great splashes of blood outside the widower's hut. Once again a party of men ventured out to the rescue and subsequently found what remained of the widower in the bushes. On the ground outside the widower's hut they found signs of a struggle and saw, for the first time, the pugmarks of a large male tiger.

Just two days after this incident, the village *pujari* (priest) who tended to the shrine we had visited was attacked and carried off by the maneater. This attack was peculiar for the fact that it happened in broad daylight, in the presence of a dozen other men, and in an open area. The beast simply burst through the bushes, ignored the men scattered around the temple and after grabbing the priest, proceeded to walk calmly into the jungle with the priest screaming for help. The men stood rooted to the spot in terror as they listened to the entreaties of the still screaming priest fade into the distance, and then as if a spell was broken, they ran helter-skelter back towards the village. Since that day, people stopped leaving the confines of the village, and the unsanitary condition in the village indicated that they were also not willing to venture far for their daily ablutions.

It was now well past six p.m. and the daylight was fading fast. With a maneater on the prowl, a trek back to the bungalow in the dark would have been a certain way to commit suicide for one or perhaps both of us. When we had walked from Pauri that morning, we had unknowingly ventured into maneater country, and I shuddered to think of the many spots along the way where the maneater could have ambushed us but had failed to do so. We had also indeed been fortunate at the temple where the tiger had doubtlessly been waiting for an opportunity to bag another victim. We had gotten lucky twice that day, but trying our luck a third time would have been tantamount to tempting fate.

That said, there was absolutely no way that we could spend the night in one of the filthy huts which stank of human excrement and would become unbearable when the doors and windows were fastened for the night. Our only option was the old widower's hut that lay abandoned after the demise of its erstwhile occupant. It was here that we elected to spend the night, and after partaking the scratch meal that the villagers graciously provided, Raj, Shadow and I saw ourselves safely shut inside the small hut by seven p.m. The night went by uneventfully except around ten p.m. when Shadow gave a deep growl that caused us to wake up with a start and grab our rifles. A few tense minutes went by, after which Shadow relaxed, signaling that whatever danger he had alerted us to had passed.

It had rained the previous night, and when we stepped out of the hut the next morning, we saw fresh imprints of a large male tiger outside the hut. The maneater had doubtlessly paid us a visit the night before while on the prowl for his next victim. The pugmarks led away from the village and down the path that led to the temple. Bidding the villagers a hasty goodbye, we hurried down the path with the utmost caution, steering clear of any obstructions in the path that could conceal sudden and painful death in the form of a hungry maneater. We of course had Shadow to rely upon, who walked slowly ahead of us sniffing the air, as if aware of the danger that we faced.

Soon we reached the temple and made our way across to the path that led further down into the valley. So far we had seen neither hide nor hair of the tiger, and the forest sounds around us did not betray the presence of a predator. Raj, who had far more experience than I in hunting tigers, was keeping an ear out for the telltale signs of the jungle folk, that would alert us to the presence of a tiger. In this fashion, we soon reached the valley and regained the path that led us back towards the bungalow.

Suddenly Raj, who was walking in front of me stopped and let out a curse. Looking over his shoulder, I saw what had grabbed his attention, for in the mud there lay clear imprints of the tiger's pugmarks, going in the direction of the bungalow.

Birju! In our preoccupation with the events at the village, we had completely forgotten that Birju was alone at the bungalow, and having just arrived from Pauri himself, would likely be unaware of the maneater's presence in the area. With a sick feeling in our stomachs, we threw caution to the wind and raced full speed up the path towards the bungalow. When we arrived, we found no sign of Birju, and the lack of any marks on the ground gave us some hope that perhaps he was alright and had gone to the well to fetch water. We therefore set off towards the well that lay about a hundred feet away from the bungalow, hidden from view by thick Himalayan knotweed that grew in profusion in the area.

However, when we reached the well, our hopes were dashed to pieces for we saw the water bucket laying on its side and great splashes of blood on the ground and on the walls of the water well. There were signs of a struggle etched into the mud as well as the large paw prints of the maneater. We cast about for more signs and were soon able to piece together the tragedy that had unfolded here the night before. Birju had come to the well to draw water and the tiger had lain in a patch of knotweed, observing him from a few feet away. Just as Birju had knelt to drop the bucket in the well, the tiger had pounced on him. Given the profusion of blood on the ground and the bloody trail that led on from the well, it was clear that the tiger had killed poor Birju before carrying his body away.

We followed the gruesome trail from the well while taking every precaution against a sudden attack. Even though tigers never kill in excess of their requirements, the maneater, upon learning that it was being pursued, could decide to turn the tables on its would-be slayers. Thus we eventually reached a ravine that lay a distance of half a kilometer from the bungalow where we found what little remained of Birju. The tiger must have been very hungry indeed, for it had eaten all of the lower portions of the body and most of the upper portion as well. Only a part of his chest and his hands were left. Also spared was his head that stared at us with sightless eyes. I couldn't help but let loose a torrent of vomit at the macabre scene while Raj, made of sterner stuff than I, only stared sadly at the pitiful thing laying there. Stripped of all clothing and human dignity, the unfortunate Birju had been reduced to a lump of flesh that bore little resemblance to the man with twinkling eyes and easy laugh he had once been.

I will not further distress the readers of this tale by describing the horror of what we witnessed any more than I already have. Let it be sufficient to say that even at that moment I knew with certainty that the horrific scene would be cause for nightmares for years to come. Birju was sadly beyond our help, and the question that lay before us was, what we were going to do about it?

We had two options. One was to decamp from the area and return to Pauri. The tiger had had his fill so the journey through the forests would be relatively safe, provided we took every precaution along the way. However, doing so would leave the people of the locality to the tender mercies of the maneater until some help arrived from the Kumaon government. It was certain that many lives would be lost in the meanwhile.

The second option then was to somehow kill the tiger and put an end to its depredations. However, our chances of success were low given the fact that neither of us had any experience in hunting maneaters and the pursuit could easily prove fatal for either or both of us. Looking at Raj I could see that a similar struggle raged in his mind and as our eyes met, a silent understanding passed between us. We simply could not allow the further loss of human life and so the second option was the only real choice that we had.

Having made up our minds, our next step was to figure out how we would carry out our mission. Maneating tigers were rare in Kumaon, and Raj and I certainly did not have any experience in hunting them. However, in Raj's opinion, a man-eating tiger was still just a tiger and could therefore be killed using the usual methods that were used to hunt tigers.

In that India of long ago, there were mainly three methods that were used to hunt felines of all kinds. The first and safest method was to hunt them while seated on the back of an elephant. The second method was to determine where the beast was hiding and then use a strategically deployed column of men, called a *beat,* who would bang their drums and cut off all but one possible escape route for the feline, thereby driving the animal to where the hunter would be waiting for it. We obviously did not have access to elephants or a sufficient number of men to set up a beat, so the only option left to us was the third one which basically involves sitting over a kill, and waiting for the tiger to make an appearance.

Here another problem presented itself. Sitting over a kill usually involves building a *machaan*, a makeshift platform tied to branches of a tree, with a camouflage of leaves so that the hunter may remain hidden. Feline predators in general and tigers, in particular, are extremely wary when returning to a kill, perhaps due to long experience with being shot at by hunters who regularly choose this method. Unfortunately, there were no suitable trees in the immediate vicinity, with the nearest tree big enough to hold a machaan being almost 500 yards away. The tiger would likely return to the kill at night when visibility would be quite poor, and therefore taking a shot at it from anything further than a hundred yards would not be advisable. Raj finally came up with a plan which, typical of him, was dangerous, foolhardy, and yet perhaps the only real option available to us at that time.

I want you to imagine the ravine as a narrow strip of rough terrain that lay between the sheer rock face of a hill about 1,200 feet high and a smaller ridge on the other side, and perhaps 200 feet in length. The tiger had brought his kill to a point that lay almost in the center of this ridge. There was a small ledge near the ravine side of the kill which was about ten feet from the ground and roughly four feet from the top of the ridge. Raj suggested that I sit on this ledge which I could reach by simply lowering myself down the side of the ridge. Sitting on the ledge, the kill would be about fifty yards to my left, a more than adequate distance to shoot a tiger, even at night time. There was also a large boulder that lay several feet away further down the ravine, and Raj decided to climb on this boulder and lie in wait. His theory was that the tiger could approach the kill from either side of the ravine, and whichever of us it passed first would take a shot, while the other would be ready with a follow-up shot in case the first shot failed to stop the tiger in his tracks.

I immediately objected to this plan due to several reasons, the chief of which was the grave danger that Raj would be placing himself in. I pointed out that if Raj could climb a boulder then, well, so could the tiger and for that matter, it was also no great feat for a tiger to jump down four feet onto a ledge either. Secondly, I absolutely hated the idea for us to be separated in the dark, unable to come to each other's aid should the need arise. We argued about this throughout the day and by the afternoon, Raj had finally convinced me that this was indeed the only viable option we had. I did, however, manage to convince Raj to take his shotgun instead of his rifle, as he would be firing from much closer range than me and a shotgun would be far more effective in such a scenario. Once decided on our methods, we grabbed a few hours of sleep, and at around six p.m. that evening we left Shadow behind at the bungalow, as much for his own safety as ours, and left for the ravine. Just around seven p.m. that evening as the light began to fade, Raj and I positioned ourselves on the boulder and ledge respectively.

Only those who have experienced a jungle night in the hills of India can attest to the paradox that it really is beautiful, yet at the same time, awful. As the sun slowly dips below the horizon, the coming twilight triggers a sudden transformation.

The creatures of the day quickly finish their business and hurry home, while the creatures of the night slowly wake up and stretch in anticipation of the approaching night. The joyous bird song of daytime slowly fades away as the more haunting melodies of their nocturnal counterparts begin. Then comes the sudden and total period of darkness that is unique to the Indian hills. A blackness so complete that one cannot even see his own hands. This dark period is when the predators are at their most active, a fact that may call unbidden to the minds of the uninitiated all sorts of morbid thoughts. Fortunately, there are limits to even nature's cruelty and this gloom is eventually replaced with the stars that slowly start to appear in the night sky, bathing the land with their soft glow.

Sitting on the ledge and witnessing this phenomenon firsthand, I too was somehow preoccupied with the morbid thoughts that raced through my mind. What madness had caused Raj and I to place ourselves at the mercies of the maneater? At that moment I felt totally and utterly alone, far from civilization and powerless against a force of nature that I had no control over. If something was to happen to me or Raj, there would be no witnesses and no human agency to render assistance.

Fortunately, with the appearance of the stars, this feeling passed and I instead focused my faculties on the task at hand. My eyes scanned the ground for the tiniest of movement just as my ears strained to pick up the slightest of sounds that would betray the presence of the tiger. Long practice in the jungles had enabled Raj and me to maintain complete silence, but we knew how much more silent the tiger's own coming would be, and that our very lives depended upon our remaining undetected.

Scarcely had this thought crossed my mind that a feeling of impending doom came over me, just as the hair on the back of my neck stood up. An inner sense screamed at me that my life was in grave danger and in a flash I realized what had happened! The maneater had arrived in the ravine and had somehow become aware of my presence. Backtracking out of the ravine, it had gone up the ridge and was perhaps even now peering down at me from over the top of the ridge while it prepared to spring. I knew that any sudden movement would very likely launch the charge that was coming, so I slowly extended my arm to grab the barrel of my rifle, and pushing down on the butt with my other hand, began to raise the barrel ever so slowly to point it towards the ledge instead. I had completed the motion only halfway when there was a low growl from somewhere above me, followed by the sounds of stealthy movement in the bushes that grew a few meters away from the edge. The feeling of imminent danger left me and the same sense that had warned me about the presence of the tiger now told me that the tiger had moved away from the immediate vicinity.

Breathing a sigh of relief, I now pondered over a new problem that had presented itself. The tiger already knew where I was and having been foiled in his plan to bag me at the ledge, he might either leave the area entirely or he may lie in wait for us on the path to the bungalow. Both options were not palatable, for if the tiger left the area, there was no telling when we may be able to track it down again, and how many human lives would be lost in the meanwhile.

On the other hand, the path to the bungalow twisted and turned through boulders and dense vegetation that offered the tiger almost unlimited opportunities to set up an ambush. I knew with certainty that if we allowed the tiger to meet us on the way on his own terms, one or both of us would not reach the bungalow that night. So I decided on the only course of action that was left open to me, which was to meet the tiger on my own terms. I wondered if I should call out to Raj and explain my plan, but then decided against it, for I was sure that Raj too had heard the tiger growl and move away, and seeing me descend from the ledge, would guess what my plan was. Secondly, I did not want the tiger to hear me speak and suspect the presence of another human, which may cause the tiger to lose his nerve and leave the vicinity.

Slinging the rifle over my shoulder, I gently lowered myself from the ledge until my legs were dangling in the air. I measure six feet and two inches from tip to toe, and with my arms stretched to the maximum, the drop from the ledge was less than two feet. Still, during those few moments before my feet hit the ground, I was plagued with terrible thoughts of the tiger seizing me from below or my falling and breaking my ankle or even worse still, my rifle slipping and getting damaged, all of which would put me at the maneater's mercy. Thankfully none of these happened and I made it safely to the ground. Taking the rifle off my shoulders, I undid the safety and with the rifle at the ready, I slowly started walking towards the boulder that Raj was on while keeping a sharp lookout behind me. I prayed that Raj would guess my plan and if the tiger attempted to attack me from the front, he would be able to shoot it without injuring me in the process.

I had walked forward a few paces when suddenly the silence of the night was broken by a terrible scream. In a flash of epiphany, I realized that the tiger had turned the tables on us. The cunning beast had re-entered the ravine from the opposite end, and as he approached the boulder that Raj lay upon, he had detected Raj's presence and had reached up and grabbed Raj's leg to pull him down. I threw caution to the wind and ran towards the boulder, hoping that I wasn't too late.

As I came abreast of the boulder, my torchlight picked up a terrible scene. Raj lay on the ground with his right left badly mangled while the tiger, having released Raj's leg, was now trying to bite him in the neck. The only thing that had saved Raj was his shotgun that he had somehow retained control of as he fell. His hands must have come up in defensive action and the tiger, therefore, found the stock of the shotgun where Raj's neck should have been.

With not a moment to lose, I fired both barrels from the hip at the tiger. The recoil almost tore the rifle out of my hands just as the tiger gave a mighty roar and somersaulted into the air. Landing on his feet, he then miraculously ran off into the gloom in the direction he had come from. Quickly reloading the rifle with my last two cartridges just in case the tiger came back, I ran over to Raj who lay on the ground writhing in agony. His leg was a mess of torn flesh and blood as the tiger's teeth had cut all the way to the bone. Raj was losing blood rapidly and something had to be done, and quickly, or he would die of severe blood loss. I took my shirt off and cut it to shreds using my knife. Creating a tourniquet with these, I managed to stem the blood flow for the time being; however, I knew we had to get the wounds cleaned soon before they got infected. For that, we needed to get back to the bungalow, and therein lay our biggest peril.

Raj was unable to walk with one leg mangled, let alone manage a firearm. I would have to support him and carry the rifle while keeping a sharp lookout ahead, behind, and on either side, as we made our way through a path where the maneater held all the advantage for an ambush. My plan to bag the maneater had gone horribly wrong, and having seemingly missed hitting the tiger at such a close range, I was more miffed than I cared to admit. Staying at the ravine until daylight was not an option, for Raj's wounds would surely get infected by then and there was a high chance of gangrene setting in. As was fast becoming a pattern that day, the only option left open to us was also the most dangerous one.

However, not all news was bad, for when I surveyed the ground where the tiger had conducted his acrobatics, I saw to my joy a great splash of blood and a tuft of tiger hair. One of my bullets had doubtlessly hit the tiger, and judging by the amount of blood I saw, the bullet must have gone clean through which would explain why the tiger was able to run away. The second bullet must have clipped the hair off another body part without causing any damage, which was regrettable. However, realizing that the tiger was wounded, I very foolishly surmised that it must have turned tail and slunk off to its lair, and hence it would be safe to return to the bungalow. Thankfully I still decided to exercise every caution along the way on the off chance that the tiger had not retreated and as it turned out, it was fortunate that I did so.

Raj's shotgun had an attachment for a flashlight, which my rifle did not, so I decided to take the shotgun and come back for the rifle later. Attaching my flashlight to the clamp on the barrel, I held the shotgun in one hand with a finger on the trigger, directing the light beam in sweeping arcs, while with the other hand I supported most of Raj's weight so we could walk together. In this fashion, we began our journey away from that dreadful place on a dark path, while watching out for lurking death in the form of a hungry maneater.

Few can truly imagine the strain on the nerves that one feels when walking through a dark forest with only the light of a small torch for guidance, and where anything less than staying completely alert means the difference between life and death. Since I had to bear most of Raj's weight and at the same time scan every bush, rock, or tree that we would pass by, the progress of necessity was slow. Providence showed us yet another kindness that night by letting the wind blow in the direction we were traveling. Tigers, you see, have no sense of smell.

However, they know that other animals do; therefore, they use the wind direction to mask their presence. So if one is walking with the wind, the danger lies ahead and on either side. If one is walking against the wind, the danger lies behind. By walking with the wind, we were at least sure to keep the maneater from attacking us from behind in case it was still on the prowl. During all this, Raj made an immense effort to bear the sheer agony he must have felt and with clenched teeth he too silently kept a lookout all around.

As we were passing a patch of dense undergrowth, there was an agitation in the bushes that sent our hearts hammering in our chests. I almost fired the shotgun into the foliage but thankfully did not, for the bushes parted and out trotted a familiar shape. Shadow! Dear God, was ever a man happier to see his canine friend than we were at that moment in time? The unexpected appearance of Shadow, who had somehow managed to get out of the bungalow and had come looking for us, had mended our fortunes considerably and as Shadow walked ahead with his head swiveling left and right, we followed. In this fashion, we progressed faster than we otherwise would have and soon we were at the water well near the bungalow.

The sight of the water well brought to surface a thought that had been nagging my subconscious since we started from the ravine. The maneater had thus far proven himself to be somewhat a creature of habit. The fact that he had lain in wait near the temple where he had previously secured a victim and the fact that he had revisited the same hut where he had nabbed the widower a few days prior clearly showed the animal to be both cunning and tenacious. Having killed Birju at the well just a day before, wouldn't the beast now also consider this locale as a spot from which victims could be procured easily?

Scarcely had this thought registered in my mind when Shadow suddenly stopped in his tracks and let out a blood curdling growl while looking towards the same clump of Himalayan knotweed where the tiger had lain in wait for Birju the night before. The tiger who, contrary to my earlier presumption, had indeed been lying in wait for us, realized that his presence had been betrayed and decided to charge at us. With a loud roar, the maneater burst through the knotweed which lay a mere five feet away from where we stood, no great distance for a tiger and certainly not enough time for me to aim and fire the shotgun. Reality seemed to slow down as we saw that horrible, snarling visage of death bear down upon us, but at that moment the tiger, whose attention was fixed on Raj and I, seemed to have forgotten the presence of the fourth actor in this deadly drama.

The tiger had just launched his charge when he was met with a formidable opponent in the form of Shadow who crashed into the tiger and locked his massive jaws onto the tiger's neck. With a mighty roar, the tiger fell back into the bushes, with Shadow still latched onto him. Knowing that Shadow was no match for the tiger and greatly concerned for the well being of my canine friend, I half dragged, half carried Raj to the well where I laid him down with his back against the wall. I then turned with my shotgun pointed towards the wildly shaking foliage where the tiger and Shadow had disappeared. Suddenly there was a loud yelp and then complete silence. Tears formed in my eyes as I realized that my faithful friend had made the ultimate sacrifice in our defense. Silence reigned all around us and of the tiger there was no sign, though I knew with certainty that he was still there, watching and waiting in the dark.

The safety of the bungalow lay a mere hundred feet away, but it might as well have been a hundred miles afar at that moment, for to walk towards it with our backs to the well would have been an invitation to certain death. We were stuck in a deadly game of cat and mouse, with the cat displaying a most definitive appetite for our flesh. I had no choice but to sit down with Raj with my back against the well wall, which at least provided protection against an attack from the rear. By this time, Raj had become almost unconscious from exhaustion and the unbearable pain in his mangled leg. I don't know how long we sat like that but it seemed like an entire age had passed before fate decided to play yet another cruel trick on us.

Lightning lit up the sky as fat droplets of rain descended upon us. The shower quickly turned into a deluge and within seconds we were soaking wet. The opportunity that the maneater had been waiting for had finally arrived, for the elements were all in his favor and none in ours. Dark clouds had eliminated the precious little starlight that we had before. The incessant rain made visibility poor and masked any and all sounds around us. The tiger of course was not hampered by any of these in the least, and all I could do was to helplessly peer into the curtain of water before me as I moved the barrel of my shotgun from left to right. The feeble light of the torch was one small comfort that I had but soon that too started to flicker and so I turned it off to preserve the charge.

Suddenly the same inner sense that had previously saved my life on the ledge started screaming that the maneater was near and was advancing on me. I could not see anything in the pitch dark that laid all around us, and though I knew with certainty that our lives were in grave danger, I did not know from which direction the tiger was approaching or indeed how close he was to us. Deciding to risk what little battery was left in it, I switched on the torch and was met with the sight of the tiger, less than ten feet away, crawling towards us on his belly. As the light shone in his eyes, the tiger's face devolved into a hideous snarl as he gathered on his haunches, preparing to launch a charge that would bring him upon us in two bounds. However, the tables had now turned, for this time I was prepared and taking careful aim, I pulled the trigger, only to hear the click that signified the one rookie mistake that has sent many sportsmen before me to an early grave.

I had exchanged my rifle for Raj's shotgun in the ravine and it was a weapon that I was not too familiar with. I never thought of releasing the safety on the weapon and now the the gun had failed to fire just when I needed it the most.

The time it has taken you to read the above paragraph is more than the time it would have taken for the tiger to reach me had he launched his charge, which he had in fact proceeded to do at the sound of the click. However there rose suddenly a vicious barking that seemed to come from all directions at once and the tiger stopped in his tracks and half turned to look back towards the bushes, expecting another attack from his canine nemesis. At that moment, I fumbled with the gun, found the safety switch, turned it off, aimed the gun at the tiger, and let loose both barrels. The tiger simply jerked, turned towards me with surprise written all over his face and then, mercifully sank to the ground, dead.

Closing my eyes, I sat shivering as much from the wet chill as from relief that washed all over me. Then wondering about the barking, I hobbled over to the bushes where I had last seen Shadow and found his poor mangled body with the throat torn out. I knelt down by his body for a few moments, saying a silent prayer for my fallen friend and then walked over to Raj who had been barely conscious during the climax of our ordeal. I helped Raj to the bungalow where I proceeded to bathe and treat his wounds by liberally applying the stock of potassium permanganate we had bought with us.

The next few days are a blur in my memory. Having heard the gunshots of the previous evening reverberate through the valley, the villagers of Kothagi arrived the next morning to check on us and were overjoyed to find their nemesis, the tiger, laying dead. He turned out to be a large male tiger (as we knew from his pugmarks), well past his prime, who had taken to killing human beings for no apparent reason. Maybe he felt old age creeping up on him and his natural prey become harder and harder to catch, or perhaps he found human flesh to be far more favorable to his rotting teeth, I do not know.

With my ministrations and the care provided by the grateful folks of Kothagi, Raj's leg healed just enough for us to mount him on a mountain pony that the villagers lent to us, which allowed us to make our way to Pauri where professional medical care helped him regain the use of his leg, though he would always walk with a slight limp. As for me, much was made out of our adventure with me somehow being elevated to the status of a hero for bringing to book such an evil nemesis that dared to feast on human flesh. I tried to explain at every opportunity that the tiger was not some diabolical villain but an animal that was simply trying to survive. I tried to reason that in the tiger's eye, the taking of human life was no crime; it was merely his dinner and the only law he had broken was the law of men for which he had paid with his life. Needless to say, none of this made any impact on the public sentiment and with each retelling of the story, the tiger became bigger in size, his victims increased manifold, and my heroics as the "Great White Hunter" more popular.

Perhaps if they knew the small part in this story that I left out, they too would wonder about my so-called hunting prowess. I never told anyone about the barking that checked the tiger's final charge. At that time I had assumed that Shadow was merely injured and it was he who had barked, but subsequent examination of his body showed that the tiger had killed him by tearing his throat out and there is simply no way he could have barked or even stayed alive after that. What then was the source of the barking? Was there another dog around that night or did my faithful companion somehow reach across the veil to render one last service to his master? All I know is that if the tiger's attack had not been checked due to the dog barking, I would not be alive to tell this tale today.

CAPTAIN'S PASS

The world that we live in is full of mysteries. That which we can see and explain through the scientific lens is hailed as a discovery or breakthrough, but that which cannot be explained thus is dismissed as the stuff of superstitions and fairy tales. It is said that faith begins just beyond the edge of sight and every now and then, our otherwise ordered lives cross paths with a phenomenon of the unseen universe that forces us to reconsider our own worldview. This is the story of a couple called Hugh and Kristina Bonneville, who experienced just such an encounter with the unknown.

Hugh and Kristina met at an office party a year ago and it was a classic case of love at first sight. The fact that they shared an almost insane passion for travel only fueled their burning desire for each other and after a courtship of a mere eight months, they decided to get married. If such a thing was possible, their future plans focused more on where they would travel to for their honeymoon rather than the actual wedding itself, and after carefully considering all options, they finally decided to visit Georgia (in the former Soviet Union). Kristina's father had been stationed there during his stint in the army, and Kristina grew up hearing his stories about the country.

Two days after the wedding, the Bonnevilles caught a flight from London Gatwick to Tbilisi, the capital city of Georgia. They had pored over maps of the region and scoured through travel blogs, and finally decided to explore the remote mountain villages in the eastern part of the country in a region called the Telavi district. They had also hired a local tour guide who lived in Tbilisi but originally hailed from Telavi and knew the area well.

The flight to Tbilisi took a little under five hours, and after clearing immigration and collecting their luggage, the Bonnevilles stepped out of the airport into bright May sunshine which is spring season in Georgia. Their guide, Viktor Burduli, was a cheerful and talkative sort who spoke passable English. Viktor took charge of the Bonneville's luggage and guided them to the rental vehicle, a Range Rover, that he had procured at the Bonnevilles' request.

Hugh drove while Kristina dozed in the passenger seat next to him, and Viktor provided directions from the rear. Their ultimate objective was the mountain village of Omalo which lies on the northern slopes of the Greater Caucasus Mountain Range. The plan was to drive towards Omalo, do some sightseeing along the way, and spend the night at the first waypoint along the way, which was the village of Pshaveli that lies roughly 120 km northeast of Tbilisi. "Where to, mate?" asked Hugh.

"First I take you to Dzveli Shuamta, very old and beautiful place, you like for sure," replied Viktor.

"Lead the way!" said Hugh as he followed Viktor's directions to their destination.

The drive to Dzveli Shuamta took them up a steep road that curves around the Tsivgombori Mountain until it reaches the monastery parking lot. There were only a couple of other cars parked and the Bonnevilles followed Viktor through a large wooden gate into the monastery premises. Dzveli Shuamta lies in a clearing among a dense forest with woods on three sides and a wall on the fourth. The complex has a large church with a triple-nave basilica and two other smaller, cross-domed churches. Viktor explained that while the smaller churches were built in the 7th century, the larger church dated back to the 5th century, making it one of the oldest churches in Georgia. "Dzveli means old and Shuamta means among the mountains in our language," explained Viktor. As the Bonnevilles proceeded to explore the monastery, they noticed fragments of frescos and inscriptions made in the old Georgian Asomtavruli alphabet on the walls of the churches. They also noticed clay jars of all shapes and sizes arranged in various spots across the monastery grounds, and Viktor explained that these were used to make wine in ancient times.

As Hugh and Kristina took pictures and selfies at Dzveli Shuamta, they noticed that while a handful of people were visiting the larger church, there did not seem to be anybody in charge. Viktor confirmed that indeed, Dzveli Shuamta did not have any resident nuns or monks, to which Hugh quipped "Then how do they keep the donation box from getting stolen?"

Viktor smiled and said, "Not to worry, the angels look after box."

The Bonnevilles laughed and followed Viktor inside the large church where they saw an improvised altar with several icons and offerings left by the faithful. "Road to Omalo dangerous, you please put offering to angels for protection!" urged Viktor.

Hugh was about to say something on the lines of "We are not that kind of gullible tourists," but Kristina nudged him with a look that promptly shut him up and he said instead "We'd be happy to!" Hugh wondered why Kristina was allowing them to be taken in for what was obviously a tourist scam but held his tongue.

Much later, when they discussed all that transpired afterward, she told him that there had been something in Viktor's voice and expression that had prompted her to go along with it. At Viktor's suggestion, the Bonnevilles dropped a few quid into the donation box and also, much to Hugh's regret, left at the altar a bar of chocolate that Hugh had long held designs on. As they walked back to the Rover, Hugh couldn't help but take a parting shot. "I hope the angels brush their teeth at night after all the candy they eat," he said. Viktor gave him a knowing look and kept silent as they drove off from the monastery.

Peshaveli turned out to be a delightful little village of fewer than 1500 souls nestled in a valley in the Kakheti region, which is famous for its rolling vineyards and golden hills. The village itself was comprised of buildings, some old and ramshackle and some newer, that stood far apart from each other against the backdrop of surrounding hills. Viktor had made reservations for the Bonnevilles at the best hotel in town, Babaneuris Marani, which was shaped like a fort, complete with turrets and arched windows. Viktor himself had plans to stay with a cousin in the village, so after making sure the Bonnevilles were settled comfortably, he took his leave. Hugh and Kristina ate a simple but delicious dinner provided by the hotel, and exhausted from their travels, were soon fast asleep.

The next morning, Viktor joined the Bonnevilles on the terrace of the hotel where they sipped coffee and took in the breathtaking views of the surrounding hills that were aglow in the light of a golden dawn. After finishing breakfast, the trio resumed their journey to Omalo. From Pshaveli, the road to Omalo got more and more rugged. With the coming of spring, the winter chill was slowly disappearing; however, there was still a good chance of rain and fog in the high mountain passes that they would encounter on the way. The most dreaded of these was Abano Pass, an extremely narrow mountain road that is 84.5 km in length and which lies at an elevation of 9,350 feet above sea level, making it the highest drivable mountain pass in the Caucasus. The Bonnevilles knew from their research that this road could be extremely dangerous and slippery due to mud and frequent patches of ice, and in many places, the road is bordered by a drop of more than a thousand feet, unprotected by guardrails. This was the main reason the Bonnevilles had requested Viktor to rent a Range Rover, a vehicle Hugh was very familiar with and which could handle the rough terrain that lay ahead.

With Hugh again at the wheel, they drove past beautiful scenery consisting of rivers, pine forests, and alpine meadows. The hills were dotted with many little villages and also a multitude of crumbling tower fortresses built upon the hills that Viktor called *koshkebi.* Viktor explained that these structures were centuries-old and had been used for communication between the villages during times of invasions or other catastrophes. In every village that they passed through, Hugh and Kristina also noticed strange piles of stones that were arranged in a variety of ritual designs. According to Viktor, these were stone shrines called *khati* where the family's guardian angels were supposed to reside. He also mentioned that these shrines were often decorated with the horns of sacrificed goats or sheep and white stones. There also seemed to be an unusual number of eagles flying high in the sky. When Kristina commented on the same, Viktor narrated a local belief that guardian angels often take the form of an eagle.

The meandering route through the villages eventually bought them close to the Abano pass. As they rounded a bend in the road, they were met with the eerily beautiful sight of a large Christian cross atop a hill with a smaller cross planted next to it. The Bonnevilles knew about this spot from their research, and after parking the Rover on the side of the road, the trio walked up the hillside to where the cross stood. As they stood admiring the cross, Hugh spotted an old man standing a few feet away and observing them. Hugh waved at the man, who walked over to the group. He was of medium height and dressed in strange attire which the Bonnevilles, again from their research, recognized to be the traditional Tush clothing. The old man addressed the Bonnevilles in a language they did not understand; however, Viktor thankfully was there to translate.

"Madlobas gikhdit dzvel adgilze shetavazebistvis," said the old man.

"He says thank you for gifts you leave in ancient place," translated Viktor.

The old man spoke again and said *"Prtkhilad iq'avit k'ap'it'ani."*

"He says to beware the captain," said Viktor. The Bonnevilles were greatly intrigued. The old man's reference to the "gifts left at the ancient place" could only mean the offerings they made at Dzveli Shuamta the day before. They were, however, curious as to how the old man knew, as they had not seen him at the monastery. They were also curious about the ominous-sounding warning about this mysterious captain. At Hugh's request, Viktor attempted to ask the old man more questions, but the latter only smiled and proceeded to walk away.

Greatly puzzled, Viktor and the Bonnevilles started back down the hill towards the Rover. Hugh turned back to catch a last glimpse of the old man, but he seemed to have disappeared into thin air. Shaking his head, Hugh walked on as an eagle screeched high above.

The road now started to get increasingly treacherous as it rose among steep cliffs. Often, Hugh had to slow to a crawl to navigate a particularly hazardous ice patch. While there was no oncoming traffic, the very thought of having to pass another vehicle on that narrow road, with their wheels almost hanging off the precipice, sent shivers down Hugh's spine. Soon enough the fog started to blanket the road in earnest and the cliffs around them melted into a grey nothingness, as visibility dropped down to less than a few feet. Hugh had to be especially careful around the turns in the road to avoid driving off into the void.

As they steadily climbed higher into the pass, the fog became thicker and thicker, until finally Hugh could only see a couple of feet ahead and was forced to slow the vehicle down to a crawl. Suddenly he saw brake lights and could barely make out three cars stopped ahead, apparently waiting for the fog to lift. Hugh stopped the Rover behind this procession and the three of them discussed whether to turn back or wait it out.

Suddenly there was a tapping on Hugh's window, and they saw a silhouette standing outside in the fog, holding a lantern. Hugh could barely make out the figure of a man wearing what appeared to be an olive-colored overcoat. The figure walked on towards the cars ahead, tapping on the driver's window of each car until he reached the first car in line. He then proceeded to wave his lantern as if to show them the way through the fog.

The cars ahead started to crawl forward as they followed the directions of the man with the lantern. Hugh also slowly edged the Rover forward to follow the procession. The world outside was covered with thick fog through which nothing could be seen, and the occupants of the Rover felt enveloped in a cozy sense of warmth and security that brought about a dreaminess to the whole scene. The man with the lantern slowly walked ahead of the cars while gesturing to the drivers to follow by swinging his lantern. After a few meters, the man suddenly veered to the left and disappeared into the fog. After a moment's hesitation, the driver of the first car followed and also disappeared from view. The drivers of the second and third cars followed suit and Hugh saw their brake lights disappear into the fog as well. Hugh assumed that there was a turn in the narrow road that the lantern bearer was helping the drivers navigate and he released the brake to allow the Rover to slowly roll forward and follow the cars ahead. Suddenly an eagle materialized from the fog and landed on the hood of the Rover. Startled, Hugh hit the brakes as the eagle, staring at the occupants through the windshield, proceeded to emit a loud screech.

The eagle's screech seemed to snap the trio out of their dream-like state. The warm and fuzzy feeling they had felt only moments ago dissipated and was replaced by cold fear and dread. Their vehicle was now almost at the spot where the other cars had turned left, but a strange sense of foreboding had taken over Hugh as he sat in the idling Rover, reluctant to act.

Suddenly the mysterious figure materialized again from the fog and began motioning to them urgently. The eagle screeched again, turning its head at the man in the fog and back at Hugh again as if trying to communicate something. The mysterious figure started to approach the Rover, but the eagle turned towards it and while emitting loud screeches, flapped its wings in a threatening manner, which caused the figure to stop in his tracks with a jerk. In this tiny moment, the figure's overcoat flapped open and the gold epaulet with four stars on his uniform became visible. Victor exclaimed *"Ghmerto chemo! es aris k'ap'it'ani,"* which meant "My God! It's the captain," though neither Hugh nor Kristina needed the translation to realize that the man in the fog bore the rank of an army captain, just as the ominous warning of the old man came flooding back to their minds.

As Kristina began to sob and Viktor started to pray in a trembling voice, Hugh was torn with indecision. Was this just a misunderstanding and the man in the fog was simply trying to help, or was he really some evil menace that first the old man and now the eagle had warned them about, absurd as the notion appeared to be? There were only two directions in which Hugh could drive, either left or right. Backing up in the fog-covered road would have been suicide but so would have been making a wrong turn. Trust the figure and turn left or trust the eagle and turn right? Never before in his life had Hugh felt so helpless. As if sensing Hugh's weakness, the mysterious figure in the fog once again started towards the Rover. This time, however, the eagle didn't just flap its wings but instead launched a full-scale assault on the figure which caused it to hastily step back and melt into the fog, as the eagle returned to its perch on the hood of the Rover.

Suddenly Kristina exclaimed, "Road! I can see the road." "W-W-Where?" stammered Hugh. "To right! Go to right!" screeched Viktor from the rear. Hugh saw that the fog had somewhat lifted and he could barely make out the outline of the road curving to the right. Looking at Kristina who nodded her silent agreement, Hugh turned the steering to the right and took his foot off the brake as the Range Rover started to move forward slowly into the thick fog. It must have been mere seconds but to the occupants, it seemed like an eternity had passed, when suddenly all the light and colors of the world returned with a flash, as the Rover emerged from the fog with the road stretching out in front of its occupants. Looking back, they could clearly see the precipice, with a sheer drop of more than a thousand feet that they would have fallen into, had they driven left instead. The fog still hung thick over the spot they had just emerged from, and Hugh thought he saw in it the mysterious figure standing and watching them before it retreated and disappeared. The eagle too gave a final screech and took off into the air, never to return.

As they sat in the Rover, shivering from both relief and residual fear, the trio tried to make sense of what they had witnessed. "What the hell just happened?" Hugh wondered aloud. "Those poor people!" sobbed

Kristina, thinking about the unfortunate occupants in the cars that had been ahead of them. "I thought it was just old woman's tale," whispered Victor while staring at nothing in particular. The Bonnevilles turned around to Viktor who haltingly narrated a tale. "When I was little, my old *bebia* (grandmother) tell scary story from the great war. A truck full of soldiers driven by their *opitseri* (officer) got stuck in fog at Abano pass. The driver, an opitseri (officer) took wrong turn and truck fall down cliff. My bebia say the ghost of truck driver now look for more victims in fog. She always force my *babua* (grandfather) and my *mama* (father) to make offering at Dzveli Shuamta before they travel this road. Nowadays people not believe but I always still put offering in memory of my bebia," he finished with a shudder. "Well now we know why so many accidents happen around here!" said Hugh quietly, as he silently thanked the guardian angel that had watched over them.

It was a grateful but much-subdued trio that continued their journey to Omala.

THE WITCH NEXT DOOR

Less than thirteen miles from where National Highway 66 enters the Kozhikode district in the state of Kerala, there lies the small and idyllic village of Koodathayi. Its population, which is almost evenly split between the male and female genders, stands a little over 12,000 strong as per the last census conducted by

the Government of India. The majority of the village residents are followers of the Mohammedan faith; however, there is also a sizeable minority presence, chief of which are the Christians.

Highway 66 runs from north to south, with the northern stretch connecting Koodathayi to Mangalore, Goa, and Mumbai, while the southern stretch connects it to Cochin and Trivandrum. The nearest town is Thamarassery that lies in the east less than three miles away and is home to the regional police headquarters and other government offices.

The strange events that I am about to relate took place in this otherwise peaceful village in the summer of 1959. My name is Aabid Kunju and I am a doctor by profession. At the time of these events, I was a bachelor at age thirty and was teaching at the Calicut Medical College. There happened to be a little too many vacation days to my credit and I was told by the dean that I should use these up soon lest they expire. I therefore decided to take time off from work and visit my maternal uncle, Ismail Paniparambil, who stayed in Koodathayi. Boarding a bus at eight a.m. at the Kozhikode bus terminal, I found myself deposited around noon at a point by the roadside where a small dirt road led into Koodathayi. The fact that it took me four hours to travel a mere thirty km from Kozhikode should give you an idea of the dismal condition of road travel in India during those times.

My uncle's house was about an hour's walk from the highway, so slinging my bag across my shoulders, I started walking briskly in the direction of the village. The hot summer sun bore down on me as I strode along the dirt path which was flanked on both sides by coconut and jackfruit trees. Flowers grew in profusion by the wayside, lending color to the unbroken sea of green, as did the thatched huts that peeked out from amongst the foliage. To pass the time I turned to botany, which is a hobby of mine, and tried to name the trees and flowers that I saw along the path. A species of plants that are called *Nerium indicum* in Latin and *Arali* in the local dialect particularly caught my interest. These plants, for some reason, grow in abundance around Koodathayi and have exceedingly beautiful flowers similar to dogbane. They are quite resilient and grow as herbs, shrubs, trees, and even as climbers. The stem and leaves of the plant produce a milky sap which is extremely poisonous and can cause severe brain damage and cardiac arrest if consumed in sufficient quantities. However, the plant is also of much medicinal value as it is used for the treatment of scabies.

After walking for nearly an hour, I finally reached the junction where the dirt path merged into Kodencherry road. The St. Mary's Orthodox church stood on one side of the road and the Joi Joi toddy shop stood on the other. This spot also marked the beginning of the village proper. I had visited Koodathayi during many a summer vacation of my youth and was glad to see that these old landmarks still stood firm. My uncle's house was just a few hundred meters down the road next to the rice mill that he owned and I soon arrived there in a sweat. My uncle, whom I had informed of my pending arrival via telegram, was waiting for me at the gate and after helping me settle in my room, he left to see about lunch as I prepared to take a much-needed bath.

A shower and change of clothes made a new man of me and I went downstairs to join my uncle at the dining table. My aunt placed a large mound of mouth-watering chicken biryani in front of me and insisted that I eat all of it, so it was some time before I pushed my plate away with a sigh after doing due justice to the food. We then retired to the veranda where we sat in the shade sipping coffee and chatting about this and that. I sensed that both my uncle and aunt were somewhat distracted as they frequently kept looking at the house next door. Upon my inquiring if there was something wrong, they glanced at each other and my uncle, clearing his throat, said "Look Aabid, you are only visiting for a few days so don't worry about it. As it stands, even we are not sure what to make of these strange things occurring so let it be and enjoy your vacation." My uncle's words only served to double my curiosity and I, therefore, kept pressing him on the subject until he relented and narrated the following tale.

Next to my uncle's house stood a large pastel pink colored villa with an iron fence running all around it. A little plate on the gate bore the name of Cyril Kurian, who was the patriarch of the family. I knew the Kurians well from my previous visits to my uncle's home. They were a wealthy and affable bunch comprising of old man Cyril, his wife Aamani, and their two sons Luke and Joshua who were born roughly ten years apart. Luke and I were of similar age and had played together during my summer vacations in Koodathayi. We had gotten along well but had eventually fallen out of touch once I went off to medical school after matriculation.

The Kurian family had been enjoying a quiet and prosperous life when they suddenly fell victim to misfortune. The trouble started when Luke, who had been away to Mangalore to tend to a business matter, returned with a new bride in tow. He claimed that he had met his wife Juliet (known as Jolly to her friends) in Mangalore where she was studying at the Kasturba Medical College. It was love at first sight for the couple and their whirlwind romance lasted for all but three days, after which they decided to get married immediately. Luke was sure his parents would approve of this match and would forgive him for not seeking their permission first while Juliet, being an orphan with no family, did not have to worry about any such formalities. The wedding was a simple church affair in Mangalore with only a couple of Luke's local acquaintances in attendance. Curiously enough, none of Juliet's classmates showed up for the ceremony.

Contrary to Luke's hopes, his mother Aamani hated Juliet at first sight. While it is normal for mothers to view their sons' better halves with some skepticism, Aamani's animosity towards Juliet was quite unusual and by all indications unwarranted. She made no secret of the fact that she thought Juliet to be a gold-digging fraud and a most unsuitable match for her cherished boy. The fact that Jolly was Kannadiga (from the state of Karnataka) and not Malayali (native of Kerala) only added fuel to the fire that burnt in Aamani's heart. This caused quite a bit of tension between mother and son and within the family in general. Throughout all this, "Jolly" proceeded to win the hearts of the rest of her new family and neighbors. She was soft-spoken, respectful (even to her mother-in-law despite the latter's harangues) and always offered to help anyone who needed it. She attended church regularly and soon became famous for the rum cakes that she baked and freely distributed after the service on Sundays. From all accounts, these cakes were indeed so delicious that people around the village started buying them in boxfuls and Jolly soon had a thriving home business going. Even Aamani, who had always been partial to rum cake, conceded this as the one and perhaps only redeeming quality in her daughter-in-law, though her cold behavior towards Jolly continued unabated.

Things continued in this fashion for a few months, when people started to notice a strange change in Aamani. She had always been a robust woman with a sharp wit and boundless energy but lately, she seemed plagued with fatigue and lowered mental faculties. She started lying in her bed all day, something that was contrary to her nature, and her responses to conversations became quite listless. She started eating less and less and dark circles formed under her eyes as her once glowing complexion took on a sickly pallor. It got to a point where she was unable to sit up for more than a few minutes and her speech became garbled. Alarmed at this drastic change in his wife, Cyril sought help from any and all doctors in the immediate vicinity, but nothing worked, as Aamani's situation continued to worsen. Finally, Cyril decided to take her to a hospital in Kozhikode for treatment, so leaving Luke and Jolly to look after the house, Cyril and his younger son bundled Aamani in the car and drove off in haste.

Aamani started to get better at the hospital. Though the doctors could not figure out what ailed her, it seemed that being away from home was proving good for Aamani, for there was a noticeable improvement in her condition within a week. The pallor left her skin as her vitality slowly returned. Her faculties improved to the point where her speech was coherent and she also regained her appetite. All in all, Aamani started feeling her old self again after a two-week sojourn at the hospital. The doctors, aware of Aamani's displeasure with Luke and Juliet's union, attributed her symptoms to depression, and after prescribing her medication, declared her fit and ready to return home.

Once back in Koodathayi however, Aamani's recovery was short-lived. Within a couple of days of returning, Aamani's condition started to deteriorate at an alarming pace. In fact, so rapid was her decline that where previously it had taken a few months for her to become bedridden, this time around she reached a similar stage in a matter of days. Finally one day, she started complaining of acute pain in her forearms and chest and Luke ran off to fetch Dr. Thomas, the village doctor. By the time they returned, Aamani had become unresponsive and Dr. Thomas, upon examination, declared her dead. The cause of death listed by the doctor on the death certificate was a heart attack.

This sudden loss of Aamani broke Cyril's heart and he was never the same again. A few days after her death he too began to experience similar symptoms of declining health and mental faculties but refused to visit the hospital or consult with doctors. He turned over the entire management of his business to Luke and turned a deaf ear to the entreaties of his sons to seek medical help. Jolly took over the responsibility of his care as she had previously done for Aamani but Cyril's health kept declining and he soon followed his wife into the grave. The cause of death listed on the death certificate was, again, a heart attack.

Due to the frequency of these deaths and the similarity of their cause, tongues soon began to wag. The village rumor mill was working overtime and there were two dominant schools of thought. The first attributed these deaths to the work of a supernatural agency while the second speculated that it was a conspiracy perpetrated by human actors. However, both factions concurred that there was murder afoot and that all signs pointed to the newest member of the Kurian clan. The fact that both Cyril and Aamani had been in the prime of life and healthy by all accounts prior to Jolly's arrival only served to confirm people's suspicions. Even the reading of Cyril's will that left everything to Luke and Joshua, with absolutely nothing in Jolly's name, did little to make people think otherwise. It is important to note that not everybody suspected Jolly at that time. There were some folk, mostly Christians that attended church with Jolly, who defended her against her detractors.

This is how matters stood, as narrated by my uncle when I arrived in Koodathayi that summer. He again warned me to mind my own business and just to get him off my case, I promised that I wouldn't get involved unless I absolutely needed to, a play on words that he scowled at but accepted for the moment. I did, however, tell him my plan to visit Luke in order to give him my condolences, to which he acquiesced. That very afternoon I walked over to the Kurian's house and knocked on the door which was opened by Luke. Though I had not seen him for many years, I was startled by Luke's gaunt appearance. His face was lined by worry and even though we were similar in age, Luke's slumped shoulders and greying hair made him look much older. He failed to recognize me until I told him my name and even then it took him a few moments to realize who I was. Then he smiled and invited me in.

Inside the house, I met Luke's younger brother Joshua (called Josh by everyone), who had grown a lot since I last saw him. He was turning out to be a handsome lad but his face held a haunted look and there seemed to be deep fear in his eyes. I also met for the first time Jolly, Luke's enigmatic wife, about whom my uncle had already given me an earful. She was a beautiful woman with long silky hair and a dusky complexion. Her oval face was perfect in its symmetry, with finely defined features and a regal nose. However, it was the smoldering eyes that were perhaps her most striking feature. They burnt with intelligence and an animal-like intensity that caused shivers to run down my spine. I could see why Luke had fallen head over heels in love with her for, given the opportunity, I likely would have done the same.

As if reading my mind, Jolly gave me a knowing smile and offered me coffee, which I declined. I gave the Kurians my condolences for the untimely deaths of their parents and we made small talk for a while. All this time I noticed Jolly looking at me with a curious expression, as if trying to evaluate me on parameters that were known only to her. I also noticed that Joshua seemed somewhat agitated and kept looking at me with beseeching eyes and a meaningful expression that I was unable to decipher. Luke remained oblivious to it all and sat despondently during my visit. Finally, I took my leave after signaling to Joshua with my eyes and once outside the iron gate, stood waiting next to the fence, hoping that Joshua had understood my cue.

Sure enough, a few minutes later Joshua came out of the house, and upon seeing me, his face broke into a smile. *"Chettan"* he exclaimed, which means elder brother in the local dialect and what he has always called me since we have known each other. "I can't tell you how good it is to see you Chettan! I have been hoping to talk to someone but you saw how Luke is acting these days and I don't trust anybody else in the village for they are all in league with HER." The last word he spoke with such vehemence that it took me by surprise! "Who are you talking about Josh?" I asked. "HER" repeated Josh, "The *mohini* who has come to live in my house and has killed Achan and Amma and is now after Luke and me." He could only have been referring to Jolly and I was curious as to why he felt that way. I was also puzzled about Josh's use of the word *mohini* for it literally means female demon and is used by the superstitious across India to describe fiends that hunt for human victims at night in the guise of a beautiful woman.

"Have you seen or heard anything Josh?" I asked. "It's important for you to speak out if you have," I said as I held his shoulders with my hands. Joshua indeed started to speak but stopped mid-sentence as he looked towards the house and the expression on his face changed to one of fear and loathing. I followed his gaze to the balcony that runs all around the top level of the Kurian home. Standing there and watching us intently was Jolly.

"Meet me behind the church tonight, Chettan," whispered Josh, before slinking off back into the house. As I turned to head towards my uncle's home, I couldn't help but glance again at the balcony. Jolly was still standing there looking at me with a mysterious smile on her face and unknown to me, that smile penetrated my heart like cupid's arrow.

All evening I could do nothing else except think of Jolly. The sight of her standing on the balcony kept replaying in my mind while the memory of that smile kept pulling at strings, hitherto unknown, in my heart. Just as it was getting dark, I left my uncle's house again and walked down the Kodenchery road to St. Mary's Orthodox church. Koodathai was not as well developed then as it is today, so there were no streetlights. However, there was a full moon that bathed the countryside in its soft glow, and I therefore had no difficulty in finding my way. Joshua had not yet arrived so deciding to wait for him, I sat on the steps of the church, watching the sparse village traffic go by. Eventually, the owner of the toddy shop that stood across the road came over to chat. He was a Hindu gentleman by the name of Adoor Ravindran and knew my uncle well. We made small talk for a few minutes after which the conversation inevitably shifted to the subject of the Kurian family. "What to say to you sir?" bemoaned Adoor. "That woman is evil I tell you. Not only did she kill Cyril and his wife but she is also trying to ruin me."

I was surprised at this new allegation against Jolly and asked Adoor what he meant by that. "Before she came, I used to sell lots of toddy sir. Now most of my customers prefer her rum cake to my toddy," said Adoor. "I ask you, how is it fair that my family has sold good toddy here for generations and then this wench comes out of nowhere and steals my best customers? Alas, my son may never get to take my place behind the counter, for if this continues I may soon need to close my shop," he finished with a sigh. I wanted to tell Adoor that perhaps selling toddy was not the best career choice for his son anyway, but I refrained from doing so as I did not want to hurt his feelings. Finishing his tale of woe, Adoor returned to his shop and just then I spotted Joshua coming down the road towards the church, with many a backward glance as if to make sure he wasn't being followed.

Joshua and I walked towards the back of the church that faced the cemetery. We sat on a bench and watched the tombstones bathed in moonlight as hundreds of fireflies danced all around us. Joshua looked sadly for a few minutes towards the cemetery where the recent graves of his parents lay, as I sat with him in sympathetic silence. Eventually, he spoke in a quiet voice laden with sadness, "We were a happy family, Chettan, before Luke dragged that monster into our home." I responded by saying "I can understand your pain, Josh, but tell me why you think Jolly has anything to do with the deaths of your parents?" to which Joshua replied, "I don't even know where to begin. My parents were healthy with no history of heart disease. Then Jolly came to live with us and things got bad. Amma hated her and suspected that Jolly had ensnared poor Luke for our family's fortune," he continued. "Jolly knew this and she also knew that as long as Amma and Aachan were alive, she would never get her grubby hands on our money so this she-demon used her black magic to kill my parents and now she is trying to kill Luke and me," he finished with tears now starting to run down his face.

I consoled Joshua for a few minutes as we sat there on the bench. The countryside around was awash in a pale light, lending an eerie quality to the whole scene. I said to Joshua "Listen, I do agree that there is something fishy about the whole affair, but you are a sensible and educated fellow. How can you believe in superstitious nonsense like black magic?"

Joshua gave a wistful smile and said "Please believe me. There have been strange things going on in our house..."

"Tell me more," I asked.

"Well, take for instance her nightly disappearances. Every night she leaves the house and is gone for a couple of hours to God knows where. I even tried following her one day and saw her go into the forest at the edge of the village where she disappeared before my very eyes!" said Josh. "Then upon returning, she walks around the house mumbling in some weird language and making strange gestures with her hands. This all started a few days after Amma died," explained Joshua.

"Have you spoken to anybody else about this?" I asked.

"Of course I have!" exclaimed Joshua, "but no one wants to believe me because I am young," he said bitterly. "The first person I obviously spoke with was Luke but he got really agitated and did not want to hear a single word against his wife. Next, I went to see Constable Joseph but that fat slob just laughed in my face while stuffing his mouth with that infernal rum cake as I watched. Did you know Jolly gives him a full box of that stuff each month, for free?" He continued, "Then I went to Dr. Thomas who was equally dismissive of what I had to say, though he had the good sense to not flaunt the free rum cake that he too receives each month from Jolly. I guess we should thank God for small mercies!" said Joshua with a wry smile. "Finally, I went to see

Father Timothy at the church. He was certainly more sympathetic but ultimately of no help, for he asked me to let things be and believe in the power of prayer. Tell me Chettan, how can I do that? Does the lamb pray when he sees the she-wolf approaching with her fangs bared?" asked Joshua. Not being of the Christian faith myself, I was unable to comment on the theological veracity of catechism embedded in Joshua's question. Instead, I sat in silence, mulling over all that Joshua had just told me.

Constable Joseph was Koodathayi's lone representative of the law. He was also fat, lazy, and corrupt to boot. His investigative prowess was limited to chasing down stolen chickens and the occasional stray cow, so his shrugging off Joshua's concerns was exactly the reaction one could expect of him. Even Father Timothy's response was understandable, him being a man of faith. What concerned me, however, was the apathy thus far displayed by Dr. Thomas. He was a practitioner of medicine and had sworn an oath to apply all possible measures for the benefit of the sick and to keep them from harm and injustice. Why then did he pass off the deaths of Cyril and Aamani as a simple heart attack? To the best of my knowledge, beyond a cursory examination, he had made no attempts to establish the true cause of death in either case, something he should have done given the suspicious circumstances in which these occurred. I was also perturbed by the frequent references to Jolly's seemingly notorious rum cakes and wondered if they somehow played a role in this mystery. I am not sure whether it was the desire to rid a distressed young man of his morbid fear or a hidden and admittedly selfish hope to somehow exonerate Jolly, but despite my promise to Uncle Ismail, I assured Joshua that I would look into the matter and decided to pay Dr. Thomas a visit the next day. As we walked away from the church, Josh's face lost some of its haunted appearance, though his eyes still held signs of dread that stemmed from the conviction that he too would somehow share the terrible fate that befell his parents.

The next morning as I left my uncle's house, I stole a furtive glance towards the Kurian's balcony and felt disappointed for not finding Jolly there. Driven by something deep in my subconscious mind, I couldn't but help walk a few more steps until I stood in front of the Kurian house. Here my efforts were rewarded, for I found Jolly watering the plants in her garden as I stood helplessly rooted on the other side of the gate, watching her graceful movements. Eventually, she turned in my direction and upon spotting me, she again gave me that knowing and mysterious smile that sent a deep thrill through my body, just as my ears burned hot with shame for having been discovered and perhaps also due to the feelings that the sight of her brought to my mind.

Admonishing myself, I departed the spot in haste and walked down the Kodencherry Road in the direction opposite to that of the church. The road at this point also served as the village main street and was lined with small houses, shops, and temporary stalls with thatched roofs. Dr. Thomas's clinic was on this street next to a dry goods store and was open. Since there were no patients waiting to be seen at this early hour, Dr. Thomas, who also knew my uncle well, greeted me and invited me into his office. We sat down and talked shop for a few minutes, after which I explained the purpose of my visit. "I see the rumors have made their way as far as Kozhikode," quipped the doctor. "I tell you Dr. Kunju, these illiterate village bumpkins have nothing better to do than to malign a good, God-fearing Christian woman," he said in a frustrated voice.

I replied, "That may be so, Dr. Thomas, but wouldn't you agree that these deaths do seem somewhat suspicious? Both the deceased had no known history of heart disease and yet both died of the same cause one after the other. Also, what about Joshua? He is a sensible and educated guy and he too firmly believes that there is something fishy about his parents' deaths. I personally am also of the opinion that these deaths were not due to natural causes as you have stated."

Hearing this, Dr. Thomas's friendly demeanor seemed to vanish. "Are you questioning my professional judgment, Dr. Kunju?" he bristled.

"Not at all!" I exclaimed in an effort to pacify him, "I'm merely curious if you had in fact noticed any strange symptoms in either Aamani or Cyril prior to their deaths."

The doctor gave me a searching look and said "I may be a village doctor but I'm not a complete idiot. I know where you are going with this and if you must know, both Aamani and Cyril complained of nausea, excessive vomiting, and irregular heart rhythm, symptoms that, as you are well aware, are consistent with poisoning. When Aamani died, I had no reason to suspect foul play; however, with Cyril's death, I did harbor suspicions so I took some blood samples and had them tested at a lab in Kozhikode."

This was certainly news to me and I couldn't help but exclaim "What were the results?"

Dr. Thomas gave a cynical smile and said "They were clear. The lab could not find any traces of poison whatsoever."

I replied, "If they weren't poisoned, what then do you think is the reason for the similarities in symptoms and the rapid deterioration that both the deceased suffered?"

Dr. Thomas looked at me with a condescending expression on his face. "It was just coincidence. I'm sure you have heard that people die of natural causes all the time. Could be bad genes, previously undiagnosed health issues, or plain bad luck. Such cases are not exactly unknown in medical science as I'm sure you've learned in school," he said sarcastically. With that, the doctor got up from his chair to signal the end of my visit and while escorting me out, he couldn't help but take a parting shot. "I've been practicing medicine since you were in diapers, son. You should know better than to question the judgment of your elders."

Knowing that the old man was annoyed by my meddling in what he considered his "turf," I decided to let it go. Besides, having hit a dead wall with the doctor, I needed a fresh line of thought to consider.

That both Aamani and Cyril had been slowly poisoned to death, I had no doubt. The symptoms described by Dr. Thomas also backed up my conclusion. However, I was still stumped by the lack of a possible motive. What did Jolly stand to gain from murdering her in-laws? In fact, the culprit was far more likely to be either Luke or Joshua, for they stood to gain the most with their parents dead. I was also perplexed by the doctor's revelation that Cyril's toxicology report had found no traces of poison in his blood. What sort of poison kills slowly and yet remains undetected even to the trained eye? I kicked these thoughts around in my head as I walked back to my uncle's house.

Halfway there, I spotted Joshua rushing towards me with his arms flailing wildly. With great effort, I managed to get him to take a breath and tell me what was wrong. In a panic-stricken voice, he exclaimed, "It's Luke! He is dying the same way Amma and Aachan did!" Regrettably, I had not brought my medical instruments from Kozhikode so out of sheer necessity, we both ran back towards the clinic in order to fetch Dr. Thomas. However, by the time the three of us made it back to the Kurian house, the sound of Jolly's wailing and the throng of people outside told us that Luke's sufferings were finally over.

Joshua fell to the ground sobbing and Dr. Thomas and I helped him get up and gently led him into the house where we were met with a pitiful scene. Jolly sat in the living room cradling Luke's lifeless body and wailing in grief. Luke's face was contorted with anguish as if he had suffered great pain prior to his death. Upon seeing his brother's body, madness seemed to take hold of Joshua as he ran to Jolly and grabbed her by the hair with one hand and her throat with the other, while he yelled, "You killed him! Just as you killed my parents, you witch! I will kill you!" It was with some effort that we extricated Jolly from Josh's grasp and while Dr. Thomas led the sobbing Jolly away, I sat down with Josh and tried to calm him down. However, here my efforts failed completely, for the cold fury that raged in Josh's heart just wouldn't subside and he kept swearing his intentions to avenge the deaths of his parents and brother.

Mercifully, at that moment Dr. Thomas came back stating that he had given a mild sedative to Jolly, and Father Timothy also arrived along with my aunt and uncle, so leaving Josh in their collective care, I escaped that dreadful room and stepped out into the garden for some fresh air.

The Kurian's garden was beautiful and well-tended to. The grass was lush and green and birds chirped as they flew among the mango and jackfruit trees that grew in the garden. Flowers of many varieties were in full bloom and as I stood taking in the peaceful scene that lay in stark contrast to the one inside the Kurian home, my gaze fell upon the back wall of the garden where there were brightly colored flowers growing in the corner. At first, owing to the distracted state of my mind, I stood simply admiring their beauty but then my heart skipped a beat, for I suddenly recognized these gorgeous blossoms for what they were! The Arali flower, *Nerium indicum* in Latin, whose consumption in small amounts cause excessive vomiting, irregular heartbeat, and severe brain damage and which, when taken in sufficient quantities, could cause cardiac arrest. The various pieces of the puzzle slowly began to fall in place as I stared at death growing in the Kurian's garden!

The heart often refuses to believe what the mind knows to be true. This was exactly the predicament I now found myself in, for it was obvious what had happened. Jolly had been feeding Aamani and Cyril small doses of the sap of the Arali flower growing in the Kurian's garden, causing a slow decline in their physical and mental health until she finished them off with a lethal dose that brought about cardiac arrest. Yet my besotted heart had difficulty believing that a person as comely as Jolly could be capable of cold-blooded murder. On the face of it the plan was as brilliant as it was diabolical. With her medical training, Jolly knew exactly the kind of damage the sap of the Arali flower would do and she was also aware that unless one was specifically looking for traces of the sap, it would not show up in a normal toxicology report that generally focused on poisons like arsenic, cyanide and the like.

I also began to suspect that the village's mass addiction to Jolly's rum cakes was due to a secret ingredient that was made up of one or more opiates. It was a smart way to keep public opinion on her side, should the need ever arise. Brilliant plan indeed, and yet somehow I was reluctant to accept that Jolly was capable of executing it.

However, I was pragmatic enough to realize that my judgment was somewhat impaired due to my feelings for Jolly and if I were to solve this mystery, I needed an unbiased opinion. I immediately thought of Raghupati (Raghu) Padmanabhan, a native of Kozhikode and my childhood friend, who had progressed in the ranks of the state police and was incidentally now posted in Thamarassery as an Inspector. I decided to pay Raghu a visit and brief him on the situation. Apart from his impartial viewpoint, I also wanted Raghu's backup in case my theory proved to be true. The thought of pursuing murderous criminals with the dubious assistance of that Fat Constable Joseph hardly inspired confidence, and Raghu's solid presence in such a scenario would be very welcome. Hence, borrowing my uncle's motorcycle, I made the journey to Thamarassery in little under twenty minutes.

The police station of Thamarassery stood diagonally opposite to the district courthouse and did double duty as the regional police headquarters. After parking the motorcycle I went in and presented myself to the head constable, whom I found with his nose buried in a large, important-looking register. Upon explaining the reason for my visit, the head constable, without once looking up, replied with the same bored tone of officialdom the world over that "Inspector Sahib was very busy and did not have time to meet with every Tom, Dick, and Harry that walked in from the street and that I should try my luck tomorrow or maybe the day after." However once I told him that Inspector Raghu was my childhood friend, the head constable's attitude went through a rapid and astonishing change. Leaping to his feet, he gave me a smart salute and with a sheepish grin asked me "why I had not said so before?" and to "please, kindly sit down" and to "kindly not mention this regrettable error to Raghu Sahib," all in a single sentence. He then ran to what was presumably Raghu's office to announce my arrival, even as he sent another constable running to fetch tea and samosas for "Raghu Sahib's distinguished guest."

A few minutes after the head constable's departure, I heard heavy footsteps coming down the corridor, and eventually, Raghu strode into the room, with the head constable in tow, and proceeded to grab me in a bear hug. Standing six feet and four inches tall and weighing roughly two hundred and fifty pounds, Raghu was a giant of a man. His colossal proportions, coupled with his smart uniform, tended to strike fear and awe in the hearts of the guilty and innocent alike. Yet those like me, who knew Raghu personally, could vouch that a kinder and more helpful person had never walked this earth. He was fiercely loyal to his friends and I can not count how many times he saved my bacon by driving away would-be thrashers in our school days of long ago. With a boyish grin extending from one end of his face to the other, Raghu took my hand and led me to his office while a constable followed with a tray of tea, samosas, and other such tidbits.

Sitting in his office, we sipped tea as I related the events to date to Raghu, who listened in patient silence. When I finished, he asked a couple of questions and then sat for a few more minutes, deep in thought. Then he suddenly sprang to his feet and exclaimed, "Come on Kunju! There is not a moment to lose!" as he dashed out of the office while yelling at the head constable to bring the jeep about and to also bring another constable along. Soon we were on our way back to Koodathayi as Raghu drove the police jeep at breakneck speed with its siren blaring and I sat next to him holding on for dear life. The head constable, apparently used to his boss's reckless driving, sat in relative comfort in the back while the other constable followed the jeep on my motorcycle. Along the way, Raghu explained the reason for his hurry. He wanted to make sure that Dr. Thomas did not sign Luke's death certificate before a post mortem was conducted. He also stated his intention to seek permission so he could exhume the bodies of Cyril and Aamani and have a forensic analysis performed on their bodily fluids. Above all, his chief worry was the grave danger that threatened Josh's life and he said something that alarmed me to no end. Apparently under state law, if Joshua were to die, all the Kurian property and wealth would automatically transfer to Jolly for being the sole surviving heir to Luke. With the siren clearing the way, the return journey to Koodathayi only took a little over ten minutes.

Back at the Kurian house, we discovered that we had arrived not a moment too soon, for Dr. Thomas was indeed busy filling out Luke's death certificate. Seeing me there with the police, he got really annoyed and made no secret of what he thought of meddlesome, young know-it-alls but with the police on the scene, his protests were futile. Besides, I believe he was more than a little intimidated by Raghu's immense form briskly strutting about and ordering the constables to arrange for Luke's body to be taken to Thamarassery for post mortem.

I saw Josh standing in a corner, blankly watching the drama while of Jolly there was no sign and I assumed that she was still sedated. I took Josh to a corner and gently explained to him my theory about how his family died and also Raghu's concerns as he listened with a grim expression on his face. Finally, he simply said "Amma had planted that flower bush a couple of years ago. She didn't know it would become the death of her and her family," as he put his hands over his face and starting weeping. Consoling him as much as I could, I walked over to Raghu, who by this time had commandeered both the dining table and Dr. Thomas's stationery and was busy writing a letter to the district court to request permission to exhume the bodies of Cyril and Aamani. By the time he finished, the constables had returned with transportation to take Luke's body to Thamarassery and Raghu handed the letter to the head constable with instructions to deliver it personally to the magistrate.

By this time Fat Joseph, upon learning of his boss's presence in the village, had also turned up, but the poor sod was not prepared for the public tongue lashing that he received from Raghu for dereliction of duty, failure to spot a crime going on under his fat nose and general conduct unbecoming a policeman. Then with dire warnings of being drummed out of the police should he fail again, Raghu tasked Joseph with watching over Joshua and not letting the latter out of his sight. Looking back, this was a momentary lapse of judgment on Raghu's part that would soon prove immensely consequential.

Having taken care of the arrangements, Raghu, myself, and a now composed Joshua huddled together in a conference to discuss our next course of action. Raghu was of the opinion that he should arrest Jolly on suspicion of murder and then seek judicial remand so she would stay locked up, unable to create further mischief while the police investigated this case thoroughly. I differed in opinion saying that there was no concrete evidence against Jolly yet so instead of arresting her, the police should take her into protective custody which would have the same net result but without tipping our hand. Ultimately it was Joshua who presented the idea that Raghu and I both jumped at and which in hindsight was a huge mistake on our part.

Joshua said he was convinced that Jolly had committed these murders at the behest of someone who could only be her lover and with whom she met every night in the woods. He suggested that we follow Jolly when she left the house that night to meet up with her partner in crime and then nab the duo during their tryst. The plan was simple and workable but Raghu, to Josh's disappointment, absolutely refused to let him participate. Ignoring Joshua's protests, Raghu made it clear that under no circumstances was Joshua to leave the house after dark, and again he ordered Constable Joseph to keep a strict eye on the lad. Joshua seemed to accept this with a resigned look and retreated to his room, followed closely by the much chastised Joseph.

Our plans made, we now removed ourselves from the scene and went to the only hotel in the village for a much-needed repast. Finishing our meals, we went back to my uncle's house where we briefed my uncle and aunt on the events of the day. My uncle was not happy with my involvement but he nevertheless agreed with our strategy. After packing torches and a few other things we might need for our night's adventure, Raghu and I decided to take a nap and so we retired to my room in short order. It was just getting dark when my uncle woke us up.

After washing our faces and quickly gulping down the coffee that my aunt provided, we sat on the veranda at a point from which we could see Josh's room but ourselves were not visible to anyone on the road. After about twenty minutes of waiting, we saw flashes of light in quick succession coming from Josh's room which was our prearranged signal to confirm that Jolly was on the move. Quietly slipping out of the gate into the night, we walked on the road in darkness towards the direction of the forest. Soon we could make out Jolly's silhouette walking at a brisk pace in front of us and we stealthily followed her down the road. Soon the houses and shops along the road were replaced by fields as we neared the edge of the forest. Jolly kept walking towards the tree line and then suddenly seemed to vanish into thin air.

Half walking and half running, we quickly reached the spot where we had seen Jolly disappear. Switching on his torch, Raghu started to cast about in the grass, and eventually, he found what he was looking for. Motioning to me silently, Raghu started following a small trail that began at the very edge of the forest and continued eastwards, almost hidden in dense undergrowth. Every now and then he had to stop and shine his torch around in order to pick up the trail again which wound through the dark forest in a serpentine fashion.

We walked silently so as not to alert Jolly of our presence and eventually the trail led us to a small clearing where we came upon a seemingly bizarre scene. A circle made up of lighted candles had been formed in the clearing with a stone altar situated in the middle. On top of this altar lay an object, which by the dim light of the candles, we could just make out to be a statue, though we could not clearly see its features. Kneeling on the ground with their hands clasped together in prayer and their backs towards us were the hooded figures of a man and a woman. They were chanting something in a low voice and we could not make out the words. The dancing shadows cast in the candlelight lent a mystical aura to the whole scene. Raghu and I looked at each other and nodded in silent agreement that we should wait and watch what happened next. So we stood quietly at the edge of the clearing, observing the strange ritual being performed by the mysterious duo.

Eventually, the female raised her hands to the heavens as if in supplication, and at that instant, a figure rushed past us with a roar and was upon her before Raghu and I had time to react. The woman emitted a scream and fell to the ground while her attacker now advanced menacingly at the male robed figure who sat cowering with his arms wrapped around his head in self-defense.

Freed from our momentary paralysis, Raghu and I finally sprang into action. Raghu grabbed the attacker from behind by pinning his arms as I relieved him of an evil-looking knife that the attacker held in his hand. I noticed blood dripping off the knife as Raghu shined his torch on the attacker's face, and we were shocked to see that it was Joshua. His eyes glinted with madness and his face was a kaleidoscope of emotions ranging from fear, anger, and triumph. Then the male figure slowly got up from the ground and threw back his hood and we saw that it was none other than Father Timothy. He slowly walked over to the woman lying motionless on the ground and I joined him there as he bent down to pull back her cowl. A great sadness took hold of me as I saw the comely face of Jolly with her face contorted in pain and her lifeless eyes, staring into eternity.

"What have you done, my child?" said Father Timothy in a sad voice, as tears streamed down his face.

"I avenged my family! She was consorting with the devil! See? See all this?" screamed Joshua as he motioned with his head towards the altar. "She was...," he began again but stopped mid-sentence as recognition hit all three of us would-be flatfoots, for the object on the altar was no effigy of satan or instrument of black magic but a simple statue of The Madonna holding baby Jesus in her arms. Joshua looked around, blinking wildly in apparent confusion and I confess that I was equally confused.

Finally, it was Raghu who spoke to the weeping priest, "Father, I think it is time you fill us in on what was going on here," he said in a gentle voice. Wiping his tears, Father Timothy looked at us with a wistful expression and began to speak.

"Aamani was a good woman, but she could be quite dominating and possessive, especially when it came to her sons," said Father Timothy. "She had high hopes of marrying Luke to a girl from a wealthy family that she knew and so when Luke married Jolly instead and without her permission, Aamani took it as a personal insult and never forgave Jolly for stealing her son from her," he continued. "Her anger and resentment got so bad that she consulted a *tantrik* (witch doctor) in Thamarassery who apparently gave her a spell of dark magic that was supposed to remove all love and affection for Jolly from Luke's heart. Aamani performed the spell secretly in her house on a moonless night, as suggested by the tantrik."

At this point Father Timothy's voice dropped down to almost a whisper, "However, something went very wrong with the spell, and soon after, Aamani began to fall ill. It was as if something evil had come into the house and was squeezing the life out of her. She became better when she went away for a few days to the hospital but soon as she came back, she fell ill again and never recovered," said Father Timothy. "She confessed all of this to Luke, Jolly, and myself at her deathbed and begged Jolly for her forgiveness. After she died and Cyril started to feel the same symptoms, we knew that the evil that Aamani invited into her house was not done with the Kurian family and was seeking its next victim. It was then that I told Jolly about this shrine in the forest which belongs to Our Lady of Good Health and is known to bestow favors on those who worship here," he said.

"Why did she come here at night to worship?" asked Raghu.

"It was at my suggestion so she could avoid the curiosity of the village folk," replied Father Thomas.

At this point Josh, who had been listening silently to this exchange sputtered, "What about her roaming around the house at night and muttering words in a strange language?" he asked in an agitated voice.

"She was simply reciting a prayer in Kanarese, her native language, to the Madonna. It's called The Prayer of the Night and is supposed to drive Evil away," replied Father Thomas. "Tonight she came here to pray to the Madonna to spare your life, for she feared that you would be the next victim," finished Father Thomas with a sigh.

Raghu, who had brought a pair of handcuffs with him, proceeded to slap one of them on Josh, who now stood with his head hanging and his body shaking with silent grief and remorse. As Raghu led his prisoner away, I wondered if he shouldn't slap the other pair of handcuffs on me for my complicity in the crime? After all, it was me who had further poisoned Josh's young mind with my half-baked theory about how Jolly had killed off his family.

The aftermath of this affair was as sad as it was swift. Josh pleaded guilty to Jolly's murder and was sentenced to five years in prison. He described in detail how he had resolved to kill Jolly even as he had presented the idea of following her to Raghu and myself, and also how he had easily given the slip to Fat Joseph by feeding him enough leftover rum cake to put Joseph to sleep. Cyril and Aamani's bodies were exhumed and along with Luke's corpse, a comprehensive forensic analysis was performed on all three. The tests yielded no traces of any poison known to man, including the sap of the Arali flower. Raghu even had samples of Jolly's rum cakes tested and they yielded no traces of opiates. Incidentally, the tantrik that Aamani had consulted seemed to have decamped right after her death and vanished in the vastness of India. The police closed the case file after Josh's conviction but some questions still remain unanswered to this day. What really killed the three Kurians? Was there indeed an evil presence in the house that was responsible for these deaths? The village people had accused Jolly of witchcraft but if there was indeed a witch in that house, it certainly was not Jolly, though she paid for another's sins with her life.

I left Koodathayi shortly after Jolly's death and have never returned over the many years that have passed since. However, I am aware that the pastel pink-colored villa that was the Kurian home, still stands empty. It is shunned by the villagers who consider it haunted. The paint is peeling off its walls, the iron gate and fence are covered with rust and the once luxurious garden is overgrown with weeds as most of the trees and plants have died from neglect.

I am told that the Arali flower, however, still blooms there every spring.

IMMORTAL

I remember that it was in October of 1989 that the man came to see me. I also remember that it was on a Sunday, for I had gone to my office at the Royal Institute of Technology in Stockholm, expecting

solitude and to catch up with my work, which is why I had found the man's untimely intrusion particularly irksome. I am certain that there had been a cold bite in the air, for the man had worn a heavy overcoat. The sun had shone through clouds that day, lighting up a pale blue sky while defying constantly falling snow that threatened to obscure the sun's very existence. It's funny, the things you remember while forgetting others. For instance, I cannot for the life of me recall the precise date of this meeting, for I never wrote it down and now too many other events have transpired in the intervening years, thereby clouding my memory.

I was a lowly licentiate researcher in those days, barely out of graduate school and working towards my doctorate. The focus of my research was quantum physics, a subject that has fascinated me for as long as I can remember. Even in my teens, as my friends argued endlessly about whether Elton John's music had more merit than Led Zeppelin or if jeans looked better than bell-bottoms, I was far more comfortable reading up on the works of great physicists like Planck, Bohr, Schrödinger, Heisenberg and of course Albert Einstein. My interest in this field had always been broad-based until the time there occurred two events that caused me to focus on a particularly obscure branch of quantum theory, that has since become my life's work.

The first event was the untimely death of my sister Agneta, who committed suicide at the age of fifteen. Agneta and I had been born ten years apart and we had been close as children, but had slowly drifted apart as I navigated out of my teenage years and got busier and busier with my studies. Agneta had always suffered from low self-esteem and a host of other psychological issues. She had often felt isolated and unable to form meaningful relationships with other people, but she looked up to me and I was perhaps the only person that she ever trusted and confided in. Weeks before her death, she sent me three letters, each filled with increasingly bizarre thoughts and desperate pleas for me to come home. Sympathetic though I was to her obvious distress, I was far more focussed on progressing my career, so I conveniently dismissed the apparent paranoia in her letters as "her usual behavior" and kept putting off the visit to our home in Uppsala for another time.

Then came the dreadful news that Agneta had hung herself in her room. She had tried killing herself once before and this time she had succeeded. Agneta did not leave a suicide note, my parents said, so they were not sure why she decided to take her own life, but I knew! Agneta's letters, that I now wept over, were proof enough of how I had let my sister down. She had hero-worshipped me and I had failed her just when she had needed me the most.

It was a dark place that I went to for a period of time. Egged on by guilt and shame, my capacity for despair and self-destruction knew no bounds. Friends, family, and faculty were all supportive. "He is grieving, give him time," they all said. Perhaps they'd have felt differently had they known my dark secret, the fact that their blue-eyed boy was, in reality, a selfish monster who had cared more about furthering his own interests rather than coming to the aid of his ailing sister. During those dark days, I often contemplated ending my life and all the misery that had descended upon it, but here too I failed due to sheer cowardice. I settled instead on gradually ruining my health with copious amounts of alcohol, smoking, and experimenting with drugs. I was in a dangerous slide towards a point of no return and I desperately needed help, in order to save me from myself.

Consistent with the strange ways in which the universe operates, help arrived in form of a research paper written by Hans Moravec, a copy of which a friend at the institute mailed to me. Moravec was an Austrian physicist noted for his work in transhumanism and his paper spoke of a thought experiment that was built upon the many-worlds interpretation of quantum physics that had been first proposed by Hugh Everett in 1957. In his paper, Moravec claimed that every time someone tried to take their life, the universe split itself into two possibilities, where in one iteration of the universe, the person was successful in killing him or herself while in the second iteration, the attempt was unsuccessful. Moravec even gave his paper the sophisticated title of "Quantum Suicide." The friend who had sent me a copy of this paper had perhaps done so thinking that it may serve as a momentary distraction from my current mood and he had no way of knowing then, of the life-changing effects that this seemingly innocuous paper would have on me.

My depressed imagination was rekindled as I got hooked on the idea. Had she survived her initial attempt at suicide in this world, could another version of Agneta have died in another universe? If so, could the converse also be true and my sister (or another version of her) now be alive in a parallel reality? As a physicist, I was trained to reject anything that could not be explained by science, and here was an opportunity not only to bring my derailed life back on track but also to somehow atone for my having failed Agneta. Just as a drowning man would clutch at a straw, I latched on to this idea and resumed my studies in earnest, and began to research more and more about the theories presented in Moravec's paper. I began to correspond with other intellectuals around the world who shared a common interest in the matter and also began to attend seminars that dealt with the subject. I even wrote a few articles during my research, a couple of which were also published in scientific journals.

Time can heal anything, it is said, and I couldn't agree more. While the scars never really go away, the pain from wounds inflicted by life is eventually reduced to a dull ache, that reminds one of its existence with an ever-decreasing frequency. That was precisely what happened to me as I gradually got back in tune with the rhythm of academic life. My guilt and despair slowly diminished to the point where my thoughts once again became focused on the future, and I no longer dwelt on my sister's death for more than a few fleeting moments. My research into the topic of "Quantum Suicide" also did not reveal any groundbreaking evidence and I became reconciled to the fact that Agneta was gone forever. Therefore I all but gave up my research into the subject and directed my efforts into other areas. Then came the second event that I spoke of earlier, on that wintery October afternoon of long ago, which forced me to once again consider the possibility of parallel realities that may exist around us.

The institute was mostly deserted that day, except for some students in the library and a handful of diehards like me locked away in their tiny offices. I was so engrossed in some material that I was reviewing that at first, I thought I had imagined the soft knock on my door. When the knock was repeated again after a few moments, I wondered who it could be as I was not expecting anyone. "Come in," I said.

The door opened and in stepped a man in his early twenties, wearing a heavy overcoat and carrying an old and weathered leather satchel. "I'm sorry to disturb you, Mr. Tågmark, but I was hoping to get a few moments of your time," he said.

I was a bit peeved at being disturbed when I had come to work on a Sunday especially to have some peace and quiet, so I said rudely "Well I'm afraid we don't have an appointment so you will have to come back tomorrow during regular hours, like every other student." With that I turned towards the pile of papers in front of me, expecting the young man to go away; however, he persisted.

"The thing is Mr. Tågmark, I am only in Stockholm for a few more hours and I was really hoping to speak with you regarding a matter of great importance to me."

I realized that I had mistaken him for a student due to his youth and having been rude the first time, I decided to be more hospitable and see what the man wanted. "In that case, please sit down," I said and the man promptly did as he took his greatcoat off. "Would you like some *kaffe?*" I asked.

"No Thank you Mr. Tågmark," the man replied, to which I responded, "Please call me Eric, and you are?" "My name is Liam, Liam Murphy," the man replied, "Thank you for seeing me, Mr. Tag...Eric, as I said, I have an important matter to discuss."

I looked at Liam with some interest. He was of medium height with a lean, muscular build and a shock of black hair. He had the way of a soldier about him and his old and worn overcoat looked military although it bore no insignia. His non-Scandinavian sounding name and strange accent caused me to surmise that he was a foreigner. "You don't seem to be from around here Liam, are you English?" I asked.

"Irish actually," Liam replied. He spoke Swedish in a halting manner common to those who do not converse in the language habitually so I said "If you prefer, we can also converse in English." Liam looked quite relieved and replied in English "Thank you, Eric. that would be wonderful, for as you can tell, I am not fluent in your language."

"No problem," I replied in the same tongue, "Please tell me how I can help you."

"I have come across your research articles about Quantum Suicide and since I have a personal interest in the matter, I wanted to hear your thoughts on the subject," said Liam.

"Personal Interest?" I asked, "Are you a physicist?"

"Not really but I have my reasons to learn more about this line of thought, reasons that I will disclose to you in due course," Liam replied.

"Well, since you have already read my papers, perhaps it will be better if you ask me specific questions," I said.

"Sure, that is a good idea," replied Liam. "What I am really interested in is if this theory explains how someone can live forever."

"Good God!" I thought to myself. "Is this another one of those lunatics chasing everlasting life?" Such people, crazed with mad hopes often descended upon scientific summits, stalking physicists who attended them. "I'm afraid there is nothing to it Liam," I replied. "Quantum Suicide simply does not support the concept of immortality. Such a thing just does not exist."

Liam had obviously been hoping for some revelation from me, for he looked disappointed, yet he insisted "But Eric, in your articles you wrote about how it is at least theoretically possible for different versions of a person to live on, in alternate universes?"

"Quite true," I replied, "The operative word here is theoretically." With that I got up from my chair and walked over to a small chalkboard that hung in my office, and slipping easily into the role of a lecturer, I began drawing a diagram on the board while explaining to Liam what I meant.

"See here Liam, Quantum Suicide is a thought experiment. What that means is that we can perform intellectual deliberation in order to speculate, within a specifiable problem domain, about potential consequences and outcomes, but without actually performing the experiment in the physical world." Liam nodded and said "Yes I understand that," so I continued "Now because we are prevented from measuring the outcome of such an experiment, for it does not really exist, we can say that in theory, a person can live on, practically forever, through constantly splitting alternate realities, but there is no factual proof to this."

"Ok, I get that," said Liam, interrupting me. "Now let's assume for a moment that the theory is indeed correct. How does it explain a scenario where a person trying to commit suicide fails the first time and then continues to fail in taking his or her own life in each subsequent attempt?"

"Well, let me see," I replied, "Quantum Physics is really all about measuring the quantum particle, also known as a quark. Let's assume that you point a gun to your head, a gun that is controlled by the movement of the quark. If the quark moves clockwise, the gun will fire and if it moves counterclockwise, the gun will not fire. If we are somehow able to control the movement of the quark and keep it rotating in a counterclockwise direction, the man would keep pulling the trigger but the gun will not fire."

"Aha!" exclaimed Liam, "Now we are getting somewhere. What if some supernatural agency were to somehow force this quark that you speak of to always turn counterclockwise, not just for a gun but for any other means of suicide. This would include keeping the cells in the body from dying, for the act of aging is really another form of suicide, albeit at a much slower pace. Wouldn't such supernatural interference make a person immortal?"

I was starting to get a little annoyed at Liam's persistence and said sarcastically "That's quite a stretch, my friend. I'm afraid you misunderstand me!" Then checking myself, I said in a more gentle tone "Look Liam, I know you came looking for an answer to an age-old question, but I'm afraid you will not find it here. If I or anyone else had discovered the secret to immortality, we would not be burning the midnight oil and instead would be fishing off a yacht in some exotic paradise, for all eternity."

Liam gave a wistful smile and said "You say that because you do not know what a burden eternity can be."

I was quite puzzled at this statement but decided to let it go, for I was getting tired of this interaction and anyway, it was time for me to get back to work again. "Look, I will explain this again in another way that will hopefully make sense, but after that, I'm afraid you must leave me to my work as I am quite busy." Liam nodded his agreement so I started again "The fundamental flaw with the reasoning behind quantum suicide is that dying is not a binary event, where you're either alive or dead as the thought experiment assumes. Under normal circumstances, dying is in fact a progressive process, with varying states of decreasing consciousness. You see, in most real causes of death, even those that are most sudden, one experiences such a gradual loss of self-awareness that it does not satisfy the criteria of quantum physics which, if one were to oversimplify the concept, focuses mainly on the binary aspects. Unlike quantum suicide, there is no abrupt transition from alive to dead, when one dies in the real world."

Liam, who had sat silently through my monologue, finally shook his head and said "I appreciate your trying to convince me that immortality is impossible, for that's what you believe in. However, I have reasons to believe otherwise, and I think it is time for me to prove that to you," as he opened his leather satchel and proceeded to take out a revolver, the sight of which sent a cold shiver down my spine, for I was certain that this man was indeed a lunatic who would now proceed to murder me, just to prove some bizarre delusion of his. Noticing my distress, Liam smiled and said "Relax Eric, this revolver is not meant for you, but for me," as he put the firearm in his mouth and calmly pulled the trigger.

I remember a scream escaping my lips, as the sound of the hammer falling seemed to reverberate around the tiny room we were in. Liam had been sitting with his back to the door of my office, which lay a mere three feet away, and what should have happened when he pulled the trigger, was a splash of brain matter plastered all over the office door. Instead, there was nothing. Liam sat there looking at me, very much alive with the revolver still stuck into his mouth. Then he pressed the trigger again and then again a third time, but the revolver failed to fire and I started to relax. This is just a sick prank; there are no bullets in the revolver, I thought to myself.

Liam removed the revolver from his mouth, broke open the chamber and I was stunned to see the chamber full of bullets. Liam laid the weapon on the table and looked at me. "Please examine it," he said in a quiet voice. My father always had a great love for hunting and I had grown up around firearms all my life so I knew a thing or two about them. I extracted the bullets from the chamber and kept them aside. I then examined the revolver carefully but could not see any defects or modifications that would prevent the revolver from firing. He must be using dummy bullets, I again thought to myself.

As if reading my mind, Liam produced a Swiss army knife and extended it to me. "Check the bullets too," he said. Using the knife to pry the cap off one of the bullets, I extracted the fine powder within. It certainly looked and smelled like gunpowder but just to be sure, I carefully separated a tiny amount of it onto a piece of paper and then walking over to the window in my office, I set the paper on the windowsill, struck a match, and held it close to the powder. In a flash, the powder burnt exactly as gunpowder would, and I quickly crumpled the paper to avoid it catching fire too.

Stunned, I returned to my seat, unsure of what I was witnessing. Looking at Liam, who sat in his chair with a patient smile on his face, I said "I think you should explain what's going on here." Liam nodded and began to narrate his story.

"I was born in the year 1626, in Maryborough that lies within County Leix in Ireland. My parents were farmers from a long line of farmers, who had been displaced by English overlords and forced to work as tenants on their own land. We were dirt poor and life was hard. Still, I had a happy childhood and as soon as I was old enough, I started helping my parents with work around the farm. Life went on in our little world but by the time I was a grown man of fifteen, the whispers of discontent that had started a few years ago against the unjust policies of the English started to increase manifold until the time came when after a particularly bad harvest in 1641, the whispers became a roar that shook the very earth and plunged Ireland into a long and bloody war."

Liam paused for a moment and I, who apart from listening to his tale with growing incredulity, had also been furiously performing mental mathematics, blurted out "but...but...that would mean you are 370 years old! How can that be? You don't look a day over twenty!"

Liam smiled and said, "I have been twenty-two years of age for the last 370 years, Eric. As to the question of how I do not know. All I can tell you is when I stopped aging, and the circumstances around it."

"I'm sorry, please go on," I replied so Liam continued.

"Rory O' Moore was one of the few Irish landowners in County Leix and he declared a revolt against the English in October of 1641. He was a bit of a legend in the area and against the wishes of my parents, I joined up the rebel army. I imagined that we would simply go charging into battle and throw the English scum off our land. Little did I know of the horrors and misery that the future had in store for me. My father, who had fought in previous wars, knew what lay ahead, and tried to warn me, but I was filled with nationalist fervor and did not listen. Such is the innocence of the ideals of youth," he finished with a sigh.

The morning had slowly turned into afternoon as I sat listening to Liam narrate his tale. The sunlight outside my window had dimmed but still fought on bravely against the snow that continued to fall in a steadfast fashion. Liam continued "I will not go into the details of the war except that it was long and bloody. I saw death and destruction during that time that I could have never imagined. To this day I do not know why or how I survived, though death came within kissing distance on more than one occasion. While many others weren't so lucky, I think what helped us was the alliance that was formed in 1642 between the Old English and the Gaelic Lords at the Assembly of Killkenny that helped bolster our numbers against the English. While we lost as many battles as we won, by 1649 we seemed to be prevailing as the English fell back further and further. Then came Cromwell with his new model army."

Liam paused and shuddered at the memory. "The man was a monster," he said, "The carnage I had witnessed in the preceding seven years was nothing compared to the brutality that he rained upon us in the following two years, as he systematically decimated the rebel army. Soldiers often told stories of men killing themselves rather than being captured by Cromwell, for that would be a fate far worse than death. I wouldn't have believed it had I not seen it with my own eyes."

Liam closed his eyes for a moment as if recalling a memory from far back in time. Then he said "Even then, I could not fully fathom the desperation that would drive a man to take his own life, until the day it was my turn to experience this particular dilemma. My unit was ambushed by Cromwell's men and it was a massacre. I was hit by a bullet in the shoulder and passed out. I'm not sure for how long I was unconscious but when I slowly regained my senses, I could see the battlefield littered with my dead and dying comrades. Cromwell's men were methodically going across the field, hauling off survivors who were not too badly injured and executing any who were unable to walk. I knew then that my options were limited. I was in no condition to escape, and capture would mean a death far more terrible than if I were to just shoot myself. I really had no choice, so taking my revolver, I put it into my mouth and closed my eyes for a moment to think of my parents, the memory of whom gave me strength. When I opened my eyes again, I was startled to see a robed and hooded figure of a man standing and looking down at me, with shadows of the gathering dusk dancing around him. The man, if you could call that thing a man, had a smooth, ageless face and his robes reminded me of the legends of Celtic druids that my mother used to narrate to me when I was little.

"The figure stared at me for a few moments and then with a cackling laugh and a voice that sounded both ancient and evil, he said the words *'Gun bhàs do thràill,'* which in the Gaelic language literally means 'No Death For You, Slave.' He then started waving his arms together to form a circle in the air and I saw sparks of blue energy emanating from his fingertips which swirled round and round, growing in intensity until a portal appeared out of thin air. The hooded figure then grabbed me by the hair and started to drag me into the portal as I screamed and kicked to break free, but to no avail. My revolver had slipped from my hands in the struggle so I could not even shoot in my defense."

Pausing for a moment, Liam continued "Suddenly there was a lot of yelling as shots rang out. It seemed that the commotion caused by my struggles had caught the attention of Cromwell's men and they were now shooting at the apparition before them. The figure had by this time managed to drag me almost to the edge of the portal. He took one step into the portal and pulled my head inside with him and through that swirling oval, I saw visions of another world that could only have been hell. The landscape was barren and charred as if a great war had been fought there, and had scorched the very land. Distant mountains with jagged peaks rose up to impossible heights, slicing into a sky that was choked with thick smog.

"The hooded figure now stood half in and half outside the portal as he attempted to drag the rest of my body inside, when suddenly one of the bullets fired by Cromwell's men found its mark. It crashed into the hooded figure's arm causing him to emit a piercing scream and let go of my head. There was a sudden, blinding flash of light and then, nothing.

"When I came back to my senses, I felt like my entire body was on fire. The agony that I felt can not be described in words, but it seemed like every fiber of my being was being twisted and turned inside of me. Mercifully, the feeling only lasted for a few moments and then vanished. This was to be the last time that I ever experienced lasting pain again. I sat up and checked my shoulder and was startled to see that the wound created by the bullet had already healed, barely leaving a scar. I looked around me and could only see the bodies of my dead comrades, while of the hooded figure and of Cromwell's men, there was no sign. Getting up from the ground, I walked around the battlefield and upon examining a few bodies that lay strewn around, I was shocked to see the advanced stage of decomposition that they were in as if they had been dead for days and not mere hours. Slowly, I pieced together what must have happened. When the hooded figure let go of me, I must have passed out and Cromwell's men, thinking me to be dead, left me there with the other bodies instead of taking me prisoner. I must have been unconscious for days, but it was a fortunate escape, or so I thought at the time. Unable to fully comprehend the implications of my encounter with the supernatural, my immediate thoughts were to get back to my parents, and so retrieving my revolver from where it had fallen, and using the cover of darkness as a shield, I embarked on a journey back to Maryborough that took me three days, for out of necessity I hid in the forest during the day and could only travel at night, due to my fear of running into Cromwell's men again."

Liam paused here for a few moments with a drawn expression on his face, as if reliving a memory from long ago that, despite its antiquity, remained painful to him even now. Then he said "When I arrived in Maryborough, I found that all was lost. Cromwell and his men had burnt the fields, destroyed my village, and executed all men, women, and children within it, including my parents. I went almost insane with grief as I sat within the ruins of my erstwhile home, with the bodies of my parents before me, grotesque in the aftermath of death, as nature took its course. I sat there in the gathering darkness for a long time, taking stock of my life, and realized that I had truly lost everything. My family, home, land, and friends were all gone. I had nowhere to go and no one to turn to. It would be quite hard for someone to imagine the depth of despair I felt unless one has lost everything they once cherished," said Liam with a sigh, "That was when I decided to end my life. I figured that I really had no reason to live on, and perhaps the brief respite I had been granted at the battlefield was so I could give my parents a proper burial, before joining them in death. Once the idea was let loose in my mind, it steadily gained strength until I was convinced that suicide was my one and only option. So after digging two graves for my parents, I dug the third one, for myself. That night, I buried both my parents, said a prayer over their graves, and then getting down into the grave I had dug for myself, I asked God for forgiveness, held the revolver against my temple, closed my eyes, and pressed the trigger."

I had been making kaffe while Liam narrated his tale and extending him a full cup, I asked "What happened then?"

Liam smiled and said "Nothing happened, same as what you witnessed today. The revolver's hammer just fell and fell again as I kept pressing the trigger, but to no avail. I checked the firearm much as you did today and could find no reason why it would not fire. Puzzled, I decided to try another way and walked a few miles in the dark to where I knew the enemy lay encamped. As I neared the encampment, I ran into two sentries who challenged me and I raised my revolver and stood waiting for the fusillade that I knew would come in short order and end my miserable life but alas, that was not to be. The sentries aimed their rifles at me and tried to fire but all that came was the now-familiar and futile falling of the hammer. The sentries' rifles simply wouldn't fire when pointed towards me. I can still recall the confused looks on their faces as I shot them both through the heart, with the same revolver that had hitherto refused to help me end my life. As one of the sentries fell dying to the ground, he reflexively pressed the trigger to his rifle again as it pointed towards the sky, and it went off with a great boom. A commotion started in the enemy encampment as other soldiers grabbed their rifles and came rushing out. Try as they might, their rifles refused to fire at me and I shot four more with the bullets I had left. A brave soul then tried to run me through with his sword, but the metal seemed to just bounce off my body and I grabbed the sword from him and stabbed the poor sod through the heart as he stood looking at me in disbelief. After this, the rest of the enemy soldiers dropped their arms and fled into the forest, rather than face what their poor minds must have perceived to be a demon arrived straight from hell."

Liam took a sip of his kaffe as I stood near the window watching the winter wonderland that lay outside. The land lay blanketed in white, powdery snow and icicles were beginning to form on the ledge outside the window. Pale sunlight cast an eerie glow on the atmosphere and a hush seemed to have fallen over the world. I inadvertently shivered, whether from cold or something else, I could not tell, as Liam continued. "I knew then that my encounter with the hooded figure in the battlefield had somehow changed me. My entry into that portal to hell, however brief, had somehow equipped me to cheat death at will. That, however, did not stop me from trying to kill myself in a variety of ways, but at the end of it all I was left only with the knowledge that I just will not die, cannot die. Fire will not burn me, water will not drown me, poison has no effect, just as the metal will not pierce my skin, and guns refuse to fire when pointed at me. It was as if somehow when it came to a manner of dying, it would always have the opposite effect, no matter what instrument I tried to use. For over three centuries I have wandered this earth in search of an answer, an answer that has eluded me, until today."

I looked back from the window towards Liam and said "What do you mean?" and Liam replied "Don't you see Eric, your explanation of this quark particle makes perfect sense. Somehow my exposure to this portal has changed how the universe responds to my actions. I can go about and live a normal life for everything except when it comes to dying, there the universe will do exactly the opposite of what should happen as if some unknown power is controlling it."

"But Liam, nothing can control the quark," I replied.

"Maybe not now, not in this reality, but what if there were other worlds that have discovered the secret already? In fact, I know there are other worlds, for I have seen glimpses of at least one of them. Think about it Eric, the technological advancements you take for granted today would have been seen as nothing short of magic and witchcraft in my time. Why is it inconceivable that the world where that monster was trying to drag me off to is far more advanced in terms of technology than our world, and that they have somehow figured out a way to control the most fundamental elements of the universe, and thereby cheat death?"

I was at a loss for words against this line of reasoning. There was no doubt that what I was witnessing was outside the realm of science as we knew it and the phenomenon that Eric had demonstrated was no mere parlor trick. However, my years of scientific training and conditioning demanded further proof of this unbelievable tale, so I asked "So what happened after you discovered that you could not die?"

Liam replied "For a while I wandered all over Europe, trying to find new ways to kill myself, but eventually I began to realize that it was a futile effort, and I also began to enjoy my travels and seeing new places. A few years passed thus when I began to notice my unchanged appearance. In addition to being impervious to any method of execution, it seemed that I was also to remain unaffected by age. This posed a particular problem for me, especially if I stayed in a place for too long. Time and again, I would find a town that I liked and would try to settle down, and invariably after a few years, my seeming agelessness would be noticed and tongues would begin to wag, and I would have to move on. Admittedly, as the world has become more populated and travel easier, it has made it possible for me to hide among the crowds, but I still have to be on my guard at all times." With that statement, Eric once again dug into his satchel and produced what looked like pages from old newspapers and laid them on my table. "Here is further proof to everything that I have just told you," he said.

Sitting back on my desk, I took a closer look at the pages Eric had laid down. The first was a copy of a French newspaper called *Le Temps* with a date of 2nd April 1889. It was an article about the then newly constructed Eiffel Tower with a daguerreotype depicting a crowd at the base of the tower. I peered closely at the image and there was Liam, standing in the crowd in a black frock coat in the style of that period.

The second was an English newspaper called *The Atlantic* with the date of 25th March 1916, which had a picture of some French soldiers with plumed helmets being awarded the Military Medal for their bravery in the Battle of Somme during the Great War. I scanned the faces within the photograph and again spotted Liam, standing ramrod straight at attention as a general pinned a medal to his chest.

The third and last newspaper was a copy of the *Nottingham Evening Post* with a date of June 12th, 1944. It showed a group of soldiers milling about in the aftermath of D-Day, the invasion of Normandy during the second world war, which had taken place just six days prior before the publication date. There was Liam again, in the picture, wearing the same greatcoat that he had worn to my office.

I looked over the newspapers that were yellowing with age. Though I was no expert on historic documents, I was convinced beyond doubt that these were genuine. To say that I was thrilled looking at this irrefutable proof would be an understatement. Turning towards Liam, I asked, "What would you like me to do?"

"I'd like you to help me better understand what has happened to me and if there is a way to reverse it. I have had a long life. I have traveled the entire world, seen everything there is to see, and I am tired. If there is a way to end this lonely existence, I want to do it," he replied.

I considered what Liam was asking me to do and to say that I was not tempted to take him up on the offer would be tantamount to lying. Visions of grandeur filled my mind as I imagined the fame and publicity that I would garner, not just in the scientific community but the entire world, with this discovery. My name and place in history would be assured as the man who proved that immortality is indeed possible, even if it may fall upon others to divine its true secrets. All in all, it was as if the gods had finally smiled and given me this present, and it was now up to me to use it as I saw fit. It was then, as I stood daydreaming in my little office, that I heard her voice.

Agneta! It was as if she spoke to me! "Don't do it, Eric," her voice said, "Think of what would become of Liam, if you expose his secret." I realized in a flash what the voice in my head meant. If the world came to know about Liam, the anonymity he craved would be lost forever, and with that, his freedom. I could almost see hordes of government agents descending upon him and hauling him away to some secret lab where he would be experimented upon mercilessly, like a guinea pig, and would never see the light of day again.

A struggle of epic proportions now began to rage inside my head. A part of me said that this was an opportunity that was a godsend and that I'd be a fool to let it go. Here was a chance for me to go down in history and to amass the kind of wealth and fame that I could otherwise only dream of. The other part of me appealed to my humanity and decency and said that no matter what, I should not subject Liam to the horrors that would be visited upon him if I were to expose his secret. On one side lay a golden future, albeit with blood on my hands, while on the other side lay an ordinary but unblemished life. For a long moment, I stood there, torn with indecision. Finally, it was the thought of Agneta that helped me decide. I had failed her once and I decided that I would not fail her again.

So I chose decency over glory and turning to Liam, I said "I'm afraid I can not help you Liam, and if I were you, I'd never repeat what you have said and shown to me, to anybody else, or they will likely have you committed to a mental asylum, for life."

The look of hurt on Liam's face almost broke my heart. He had dared to open up to someone for the first time in over three hundred years and this was not the response he had been expecting. He started to protest but I said firmly "No, Liam! Remember what I said—they will imprison you!" as I added special emphasis to the word "imprison."

Understanding finally dawned in Liam's eyes, and gathering his revolver and papers quickly, he stuffed them into his satchel, looked at me with a sad smile, and said "Thank you." Then he was gone. I sat in my office for a long time, as the fading twilight made the shadows dance on my windowsill, thinking about Liam. Finally, with a sigh, I got up and left my office and went home.

I moved to California the year after this meeting took place, in order to complete my doctorate at the University of California, Berkeley. After that, I decided to remain in America and took up a teaching position at the University of Pennsylvania. I found life at the university to be quite satisfying, even if somewhat boring, and I took great pleasure in helping young minds expand their view of the physical world, while all along being intensely aware of how much my own view of the universe had been changed, in a single meeting with Liam.

I saw Liam only one more time after our first meeting. I was in New York, in the spring of 2017, delivering a lecture. Once the event had finished, I had a few hours before my flight out of LaGuardia so I decided to spend some time in Manhattan. I was standing in Times Square, admiring the splendor of the large screens that adorned the buildings, when I saw Liam, walking across the street. He had a beautiful woman with black hair hanging on to his arm as they laughed and talked. Suddenly Liam looked in my direction and our eyes met. He stopped, as did his companion, and Liam stared at me from across the street. At first, I thought something was wrong but then I realized that he was trying hard to recognize me. Of course! It had been twenty-eight years since our last meeting, and while Liam had not aged a day since, I now bore the ravages of middle age, so I waved at him to confirm that it was indeed me, Eric Tågmark, that he saw. Upon my confirmation, Liam's face broke into a smile and he waved back. He said something to his companion, who looked across the street at me, smiled, and nodded her head, as if in silent acknowledgment. Then they were lost in the crowd and I never saw Liam again.

On some nights, when the weight of the world is upon my shoulders, I like to sit in my backyard with a tumbler of scotch in my hands as I gaze towards the stars. The universe is vast and full of mysteries, while our understanding of them is quite minuscule. Those of us fortunate enough to have been given a peek beyond the veil hold immense hope that one day, mankind too will uncover these secrets. Whether man will use this knowledge for his betterment or for his destruction, I cannot say.

It is at such times that I also think of Liam, with both affection and sadness. While I have never once doubted my decision of keeping his secret, I cannot help but feel occasional pangs of regret, for I came face to face with a being that was truly godlike, and yet I had to let him go, so as to prevent his godliness from being defiled by the cruel curiosity of science. It's a small consolation to me that even though I had not been able to help my sister, I have honored her memory by doing the right thing for Liam and I also like to think that he finally found happiness.

Since my first meeting with Liam, I have tirelessly searched for ways to prove the existence of parallel universes, in the hope that one day, I will be reunited with Agneta.

THE WOMAN IN THE LAKE

"To summarize what we have learnt today, a vowel is a speech sound made with your mouth fairly open, while a consonant is a sound made with your mouth fairly closed," said James Polley, to the Japanese students attending his English language lecture. "Read up on this guys, as there will be a test next week," he finished just in time before the bell rang, marking the end of the period and also the school day. As the students filed out of the classroom in an orderly fashion, James smiled and marveled yet again at the contrast in discipline between Japan and his native country of Canada, where the last bell would have signalled a mad dash for the door amongst his erstwhile pupils.

James ("Jim") Polley, "Jimu-San" to his friends and "Polley-Sensei" to his students and colleagues, was a twenty-nine-year-old expat who had been teaching English for the last four years at the Shane English school, located in the coastal city of Kamakura, Japan. Since childhood, Jim had held a love for travel and Japan had captured his fancy since an early age.

After graduating from university, Jim had spent a few years helping new immigrants to Canada learn English as their second language, and when an opportunity to teach in Japan came his way, Jim took it up immediately. He had long dreamt of going to Japan, and now that he was here, Jim had no intention of ever leaving. He loved everything about the land and its people, and had painstakingly learnt the Japanese language and customs, until he was almost fluent in the former and able to rigidly practice the latter.

Jim was broken out of his reverie by a soft voice that reminded him of tiny bells tinkling in unison. "Polley-Sensei? Polley-Sensei?" said the voice and Jim turned around to find Fuyuko Sasaki, the school's administrative secretary, smiling at him from the classroom door.

"*Gomen-ne,* Fuyuko-San," said Jim, "I did not notice you standing there."

"It's all ok Polley-Sensei," replied Fuyuko, in English.

"It's all right, not all ok" said Jim, correcting her. "I see that you have not been practicing," he said with mock severity.

Fuyuko blushed and said "*Gomen nasai,* Polley-Sensei, I will do better, I really will."

Jim, who had been coaching Fuyuko on her English skills, in exchange for her help in learning Japanese, smiled and said "Now then, what's with the Polley-Sensei bit eh? I thought we agreed that since we are friends, you may call me Jim."

Fuyuko, who quite obviously carried a torch for Jim, was now positively turning red, both from shame that was culturally requisite in such situations, and not a small amount of guilty pleasure. Quickly changing the subject, she asked "Polley...errr...Jimu-San, some of the faculty and staff are planning to go out for drinks this evening, would you like to join us?" Jim, ever ready for a round of pint agreed enthusiastically and after giving him directions to the meeting point, Fuyuko left. Jim collected some papers that he meant to grade over the weekend, and headed home as well.

Jim lived in a small garden flat located in the 2nd chome (city district) of Komachi, a neighborhood in the Kanagawa prefecture of Kamakura. The flat was within walking distance of the Yokosuka line station and therefore quite convenient. When Jim entered the flat, Okami, his three year old Hokkaido, came running to greet him and danced around his legs as Jim made his way inside. Jim put his bag down and headed to the kitchen to make tea in Japanese style, a daily ritual that he enjoyed immensely. Once his cup was empty, Jim puttered around the flat, with Okami following him everywhere, until finally giving in to the dog's silent demands, Jim picked up the leash and took Okami for a walk around the neighbourhood. When they got back to the flat, Jim changed clothes, combed his hair and after throwing on some aftershave, he bid goodbye to

Okami and walked towards the station in order to take the train to his rendezvous with Fuyuko and the others.

The directions given by Fuyuko led Jim to the neighbourhood of Hase, an hour's train ride away from his flat. The meeting point was an Izakaya, a traditional Japanese tavern, by the name of Tempo. It was a delightful little place with a great selection of drinks and a small tasting menu of snacks. Upon arriving, Jim found his colleagues already seated so he joined them at the table. Fuyuko had saved him a spot right next to her, which put Jim squarely across from a British expat called Oliver Hanson, much to Jim's dismay. Oliver also taught English at the college and both men detested each other immensely for multiple reasons, chief among which was soccer. Oliver was from Liverpool and therefore naturally supported the Liverpool football club while Jim's family was originally from Manchester and he was therefore a diehard fan of United. It was no secret that the bitter rivalry between the two soccer teams was also shared by their respective fans around the world, and Oliver and Jim were certainly no exception.

Jim ignored Oliver as he chatted with Fuyuko and his other colleagues, and at first Oliver seemed only too happy to do the same. However, as the evening wore on and Oliver got more and more drunk, he started directing snide remarks towards Jim, who continued to ignore them, until finally Oliver rudely interrupted something Jim was saying, by blurting out "Oh shut up, you are talking out of your arse, mate. You colonials think you are so smart, well let me tell you lad, you are just full of shit!"

The group around the table went silent as everyone looked at the two men, now engaged in a staring contest. Jim felt Fuyuko squeezing his hand from under the table, in a silent plea to ignore Oliver and so Jim took a deep breath to get a grip on his mounting anger. In an effort to ease the tense mood around the table, he raised his beer glass in the air and said "If you say so mate, cheers!" However, Oliver seemed bent on escalating the confrontation, and with a smirk he drawled "What a pussy! Well what can one expect from a United fan?" Turning to the rest of the group he added "Do you guys know what the similarity is between Manchester United and a three-pin plug? They're both useless in Europe," he finished, roaring with laughter, oblivious to the fact that nobody else in the group seemed to share his mirth.

Jim felt his ears starting to burn with rage. While he could possibly let Oliver's other insults go, the transgression against his beloved soccer team was a bridge too far and retaliation was therefore necessary. Raising his beer glass in the air once again, Jim chanted:

> *"Build a bonfire build a bonfire*
> *put the Scousers on the top*
> *put Man City in the middle and*
> *then burn the feckin' lot."*

Hearing the familiar chant known to United fans and foes alike, Oliver's face went red with anger. "Why you rotten son of a bitch!" he screamed as he suddenly lunged across the table towards Jim, who promptly threw his beer in Oliver's face.

"Take that, you Scouse bastard!" snarled Jim, while leaping away from his seat so he was out of Oliver's reach. Things were starting to look ugly, but thankfully others in the group intervened. The party broke up as some of the colleagues hauled a drunk and stumbling Oscar away, while Fuyuko led Jim out of the Izakaya into the warm summer evening. Jim was a pacifist by nature and the confrontation with Oscar had left him shaken. "*Gomen nasai,* Fuyuko-San," he said, "I am sorry for ruining your evening. God knows I tried to avoid Oscar, but I don't know what got into him today."

"No Jimu-San, it is I who should apologize," said an embarrassed Fuyuko, "Oscar had asked me for a date earlier today and I refused. I knew that made him angry and I know that you both do not get along, and still I made you sit near him. It was my mistake," she said in a miserable voice.

Ah, thought Jim, that explains Oscar's fouler than usual mood and why he was trying to pick on me. Fuyuko's romantic intentions for Jim were no secret and though Jim liked her immensely as a friend, he did not reciprocate her feelings, nor was he looking for a committed relationship, which he knew was something that Fuyuko wanted. I'm going to have to find a way to gently let her down and also set things straight with Oscar, so he knows that I am not a hurdle to his amorous pursuits, thought Jim, smiling to himself as he and Fuyuko walked down the street.

Jim knew that Fuyuko lived somewhere nearby, so he had naturally assumed he was just escorting her home and was therefore quite surprised when Fuyuko stopped at the gates of a park and proceeded to step inside. "This park has a Buddhist temple within it. I come here often to pray. It's beautiful and very peaceful," she explained. Jim saw a plaque at the entrance to the park with characters in Japanese script which he mentally translated to mean "*K tokuin,*" as he followed Fuyuko into the park. Once inside, Jim found himself on a wide stone path, flanked by marching rows of beautiful Japanese Maple trees on both sides. The path led up to the gates of the temple, where a pair of marble lion-dog statues were situated, one on each side of the door. Fyoko pointed towards them and said, "These are called *koma-inu;* they are symbolic guardians of shrines and temples. They drive evil spirits away from sacred grounds." The temple gates were closed; however, visitors were streaming in and out from a temporary entrance set up towards the left of the gates. Unlike Shinto shrines that were free to visit, Buddhist temples in Japan charged a modest entry fee, so Fuyuko dug into her purse to deposit a few coins in a box, as she and Jim entered the temple premises.

The temple was made up of a single-story building with a tin roof that ran around a large stone courtyard in the shape of a horseshoe. In the center of this complex stood one of the largest Buddha statues that Jim had ever seen. He had of course seen the great Daibutsu statue in Nara and also knew of its contemporary here in Kamakura, but this was his first opportunity to visit. The sculpture was made of bronze, and in Jim's estimation was at least forty feet tall. Fuyuko mentioned that the structure was hollow inside and one could enter it after paying an additional fee. She asked Jim if he wanted to enter the temple to pray, but being an atheist himself, Jim politely declined, so leaving him to explore the courtyard, Fuyuko entered the temple's sanctum.

Jim wandered about the temple complex, reading the various plaques that spoke of the history and interesting facts about the temple. He was pleased with himself when one of the plaques confirmed that the Buddha statue, built in or around the year 1252, was over forty-three feet tall, close to his own estimation. Jim also noticed plaques under some of the pine trees and after reading one of them, he discovered that several kings and princes of Thailand, another majority-Buddhist country, had also made pilgrimages here, and planted commemorative pine trees to mark their visits. Jim also noted that a lot of the people milling about in the courtyard had their dogs with them, though none seemed to be taking the dogs into the temple building.

Eventually, Jim came upon a small dirt path that led away from the temple premises and down a gentle slope. The path bent at the end of the slope and disappeared into the undergrowth so Jim could not see what lay beyond. He noticed a small sign placed at the entrance of the path with a single word printed on it, *Go-Ch i,* which is Japanese for "Beware." Even though a lot of people seemed to be visiting the temple, the path itself lay deserted. Intrigued, Jim walked along the path and down the slope until he came to the bend where the undergrowth started. Peering through the vegetation, Jim got a glimpse of water beyond, made his way through the foliage and emerged on the other side, where he found himself looking at perhaps the most idyllic scene he had ever witnessed. There lay before him a small, oval-shaped lake, ringed by a dirt path that ran around its perimeter and which had *tamukeyama* trees, a dwarf cousin of Japanese maple, growing along the lake's edge. A boardwalk stretched to almost the middle of the lake, ending into a small viewing deck made of wood. The surface of the lake lay deathly still, unbroken save for small ripples caused by a frog diving inside, startled by Jim's unexpected appearance.

Deciding to explore the opposite shore of the lake, Jim started walking in a clockwise direction. As he strolled along the dirt path, Jim noticed small benches made of wood that had been placed in strategic spots, providing views of the picturesque lake from different angles. Pity, thought Jim to himself as he considered the throng of visitors at the temple. I wish more people would come here and enjoy what's truly divine, instead of chasing false gods and deities of our own making. In a short while, Jim reached the opposite side of the lake where his progress was arrested by the sudden change in lighting conditions. Jim found the path covered with dark gloom, in stark contrast to the sunlit boardwalk and viewing deck that he could see across the water. The side of the lake where Jim now stood had a small hill adjacent to it, covered with large trees and thick foliage that somehow seemed to blot out the sun. It was an easy enough explanation for the murky light, yet somehow it gave Jim pause, as he stood there looking at the path ahead of him, unsure whether to proceed or return the way he came. Something stirred in the water and slithered away, leaving small telltale signs on the surface, though Jim could not make out what it was. The air too became decidedly cooler, causing Jim to shiver involuntarily. Silence reigned for a few more seconds and was then suddenly broken, as the haunting melody of a flute filled the air.

For those who have never heard a Japanese flute play, it is virtually impossible to describe the raw emotions that are embedded in its music. No other instrument in the world can convey the longing and loneliness with such precision as the Japanese flute, its melody the very embodiment of eternal loneliness. Such was the music that now took over Jim's senses as he made his way towards its source as if pulled by an invisible string. His feet, as if having developed a mind of their own, led him onwards on the path until he reached the point where the lakeshore started to curve again towards the opposite end. There, on a stone bench, sat a petite woman, dressed in a white kimono and sitting still as a stone, the only movement coming from her fingers that danced in rhythm over a flute that she played with considerable skill. For a long time, Jim stood listening, as if in a trance, while the woman kept playing one heart-rending melody after another, and if she was aware of Jim's presence, she did not show it.

At last, the woman in the white kimono put down her flute and turned her head towards Jim, revealing the most beautiful face that he had ever set his eyes upon, and which sent his heart aflutter. She had a perfectly oval face that was set between long, raven black hair. Her large eyes were exquisite in their beauty, complemented by a small delicate nose. Her lips, thin and graceful, quivered with the ghost of a smile as she looked up at Jim with a child-like curiosity.

"*Na...Na...Nanto osshaimashita ka,*" an embarrassed, Jim managed to stutter, "I beg your pardon, I didn't mean to intrude."

The woman's face lit up with delight. "I see you speak our language well, *gaijin-sama,*" she replied, using the Japanese word for foreigner (*gaijin*) and the honorific *sama* (Mister) to address Jim. "It's no intrusion at all. You are welcome to stay and listen."

"*Arigatou gozaimasu, Ojou-san* (Thank you, Miss)," said Jim, as he felt grateful to Fuyuko for having insisted that he learn the myriad ways in which one must address strangers in Japanese, "My name is James Polley but my friends call me Jim."

A puzzled look crept over the woman's face and she asked "Why do your friends not call you by your name?"

Jim was taken aback for a moment, confused, then understanding dawned and he burst out laughing, as the woman stared at him with a quizzical expression on her face. "*Gomen nasai, Ojou-San,*" he said, "I am not laughing at you, it's just that no one has ever asked me that before. You see, in my country, it is a custom for friends to call each other by shorter versions of our given names. It signifies affection and familiarity," he explained.

"It's a strange custom indeed," replied the woman, "Tell me more about your country."

"I am from Canada," said Jim and he proceeded to tell her about the great northern cities and the vast and beautiful landscapes that surrounded them. "It snows a lot in the country I am from, and it gets really cold up there," he finished with a smile.

"Ka...na...da," said the woman, rolling the name slowly off her tongue, as if hearing it for the first time, "You say your country is very cold. I too am cold, always cold, and always lonely," she said with a sigh.

Jim didn't know quite what to make of that statement. He knew that Japanese women weren't quite as direct as their western counterparts, but just the same, he couldn't decide if this was a mere statement of fact or a veiled invitation. Embarrassed, he changed the subject by asking "Do you come here often?"

"I am always here; where else would I go?" replied the woman with a tinkling laugh that filled Jim's ears like sweet music and set his heart thudding so loud, he was afraid the woman might hear it. Jim was about to say something when he heard Fuyuko calling for him in the distance.

"Jimu-San? Jimu-San?," she called and Jim slapped his forehead. Oh crap, he thought, I forgot all about Fuyuko! Turning to the woman in white he said, "My friend is calling for me. Let me go fetch her. I am sure she will be delighted to hear you play the flute." The woman in white didn't respond so Jim turned around and sauntered over to the other side of the lake, and up the slope where he found a very worried-looking Fuyuko waiting for him.

At the sight of Jim, Fuyuko cried out "Jimu-San! Where did you go? I looked for you everywhere! Even inside the Buddha statue. Then somebody mentioned that they saw you going down this path. I saw this sign that says beware, and I was so worried!"

Jeez, thought Jim, a bit annoyed, does she think she is my mother? Then realizing that Fuyuko's concern for him was quite genuine, he said "Sorry Fuyuko-San, I just decided to take a look around. There is a lake down there and I met this most wonderful lady who plays the flute like you wouldn't believe!"

"A lady?" inquired Fuyuko, her ears and hair both prickling at the mention of a potential competitor for Jim's attention.

"Yes indeed. Come with me and I'll introduce you to her," said Jim excitedly as he half dragged Fuyuko down the path, towards the lake.

Upon reaching the spot where Jim had encountered the flute player, they found the stone bench empty and no sign of the woman in white. Jim looked all around but didn't see her. Strange, thought Jim, feeling a bit dejected, there doesn't seem to be another way out of here and she certainly didn't pass us on the path. Where could she have gone? Turning to Fuyuko, he said, "I don't know where she went. I told her that I would go fetch you and that you would have loved to hear her play. I guess she had to leave anyway." He decided that there must be another route leading away from the lake and the woman must have left that way. He felt a curious sense of loss which he could not explain, so he shook it off as the duo headed back towards the temple.

Along the way, Fuyuko asked Jim "What was this woman's name?"

Jim was startled with the realization that he hadn't even bothered to find out. "Er...I never asked," he responded, with a sheepish look on his face. Fuyuko smiled and shook her head for she was convinced that Jim had made up this imaginary flute player just to make her feel jealous. Neither of them saw the bubbles forming in the water as if something waited and watched from below the surface of the otherwise placid lake.

Jim didn't sleep well that night. He kept tossing and turning in his bed as visions of the woman in white kept flashing in his mind, and the haunting melodies of her flute filled his ears. As a result, he arose in the morning, feeling tired and disoriented. Fortunately, the school was closed on weekends, so he sat in his living room drinking gallons of tea until he started to feel a little better. You are infatuated, son, said Jim to himself, like a sick teenage puppy. You call yourself an adult? Shame on you!

During the day, he tried to keep himself busy by puttering around his flat and running errands, but try as he would, he just couldn't get the woman in white out of his mind. The ache in his heart only intensified as hours marched on towards the afternoon. Finally, as evening approached, Jim had had enough and decided that he needed to visit the lake again. I'm sure she will not be there, and I can finally put this adolescent nonsense to rest, thought Jim. At the last minute, he decided to take his dog, Okami with him. What if I run into Fuyuko near the temple? I can always claim that I came there to let Okami run free as there aren't many other spots where I can do so, he reasoned. So the dog and master walked briskly to the Yokosuka line station, to board a train that deposited them near K tokuin an hour later.

Jim deposited a few coins at the entrance of the temple and then made a beeline for the spot where the path to the lake started. He noticed that compared to the day before, the crowd of visitors to the temple that day was visibly thinner. He also saw a lot of monks tending to the pine trees within the temple premises. A couple of them looked at Jim curiously as he and Okami walked by, but did not say anything. Jim went down the path towards the lake and soon reached the spot of his encounter the day before. The stone bench was unoccupied and again there was no sign of the woman in white, and even though Jim had expected as much, he felt sharp pangs of grief pierce his heart, an emotion that he could neither explain nor justify. With a heavy heart, he turned around to head back when once again, the sounds of a flute playing filled the air, and Jim's heart filled with joy, the likes of which he had never experienced before. Jim started following the music to its source, which led him on the dark, gloom-enshrouded path he had traversed the day before. Soon enough, he came upon the woman in white, leaning casually against a tree, playing her flute.

At the sight of her, Jim's face broke into a smile and he said loudly, "Well hello! Nice to see you again!" The woman did not return his greeting and instead stared at Okami, the dog, with a wary expression on her face, upon seeing which Jim said "Are you scared of dogs? Don't worry, Okami is quite friendly and loves people."

Scarcely had the words left Jim's mouth when Okami gave a blood-curdling growl and lunged into the air, his snapping jaws aimed squarely at the woman's throat. Jim instinctively yanked Okami's leash, which caused the dog to fall back before he could reach the woman. Landing on the ground, Okami started barking furiously at the woman as Jim struggled to control the animal. "I'm terribly sorry," he said to the woman, "I don't know what's gotten into him. He has never behaved this way before."

"He is only trying to protect you," replied the woman while keeping her distance. Protect me? From what, wondered Jim, but he gave the woman's mysterious words no further thought, for he was fully engaged in calming down Okami, who was struggling to break free of his leash and attack the woman. Finally, he dragged Okami a few feet away and after tying the dog to a tree, he walked back to rejoin the woman, ignoring Okami's howls of protest.

"Gomen nasai, Ojou-San," he said, "I'm sorry if my dog frightened you." The woman just smiled mysteriously and didn't say anything and an embarrassing silence ensued. Finally, clearing his throat, Jim spoke again, "Where did you go yesterday? I came back with my friend but you were gone."

"I was here, just hiding so your friend couldn't see me," said the woman in a playful tone, "I don't reveal myself to most people, only to whom I choose," she said with yet another mysterious smile.

Jim was now certain that the woman's words hid a double meaning so he decided to play along. "Well, it's just the two of us here now, not counting the dog, so reveal away," he said with a naughty smile.

"All in good time, Jimu-San, be patient," replied the woman in an equally naughty tone.

"Ah! You remembered my name!" said Jim, thrilled beyond words.

"I heard your friend call you that yesterday. What an exotic name, just as exotic as your blue eyes and golden hair," replied the woman as she moved towards

Jim with her hand extended, as if wanting to stroke his face, but stopped when Okami, who by now had settled into a watchful silence, erupted into another bout of furious barking.

Jim, oblivious to the din caused by the dog, and by now quite enamored with this mysterious woman, blurted out "Thanks for remembering my name, but you never told me yours."

The woman giggled and said "That's because you never asked me, Jimu-San," as she batted her eyelids and purposefully put emphasis on Jimu-San, in a manner that could only be termed as flirtatious.

Jim, now positively in seventh heaven, said "Well, what is your name, do tell?"

The woman bowed formally towards Jim and said "I am the Lady Aiko, of the house of Yoshikane."

Hmmm, thought Jim, that sounds like a made-up title. She must be joking. Assuming that Aiko was play-acting, he decided to play along too. "A royal lady? You don't say! Did you know that I am the great-great-grandson of the 7th queen of England and therefore 450th in line to the throne?" quipped Jim.

For a moment, Aiko looked at Jim with a strange expression on her face, then nodding her head, she said softly to herself, "A prince. A foreign prince. Of course, it must be so." A tear escaped her exquisite eyes and traveled down the side of her small, regal nose.

"Aiko-San! Why are you crying?" exclaimed Jim, "I'm sorry if I said something that hurt you."

Aiko smiled sadly and said, "No Jimu-San, it's nothing that you said. You just remind me of someone I knew, a very long time ago."

Jim and Aiko stood talking for a long time as sunshine slowly faded to twilight, heralding the arrival of approaching night. Their conversation was long and uninterrupted, except for the occasional whimpering from Okami who sat tied to the tree a few feet away. Jim was both fascinated and yet puzzled with Aiko. She was extremely beautiful, talented, and obviously quite intelligent, and yet she seemed stunningly uninformed of things that were commonplace in modern life. She avoided giving straight answers to questions about her life or family. If she did choose to speak, her references to people or events seemed to point at a time that lay buried in the annals of ancient history. She spoke like someone who had lived a very long life, even though to Jim she didn't look a day over twenty years in age. Her hairstyle and her kimono, even to Jim's uninitiated eyes, looked dated, unlike the modern styles he had seen other women wear in Japan. All in all, Aiko was an enigma, a strange woman about whom Jim knew very little, and yet, he felt himself falling hard for her. It wasn't lust that Jim felt, though God knows Aiko was gorgeous, but a far deeper connection that he could not explain. If there is such a thing as love at first sight, this is it, Jim thought to himself, for in her company, he felt more at peace than ever before in his entire life.

Time marched on, yet Jim and Aiko did not tire of their ceaseless conversation. The shadows that had previously been confined to the side of the lake where they stood, now slowly began to encroach upon the other shore, on account of the late hour. "So what else do you like, apart from music?" asked Jim.

Aiko thought for a moment and replied "Poetry. I remember that I used to love hearing recitations from poets visiting my father's house. It brought me great joy to hear words cleverly arranged together to convey hidden meanings," she said with a faraway look in her eyes. "It's been a long time since I heard a poem," she added with a wistful look on her face.

"Well, we need to rectify that," said Jim with a smile, "I shall write a poem for you."

Aiko looked at him with a dreamy expression and said "You will do that for me?"

Jim looked into her eyes and said softly "I will do anything for you, Aiko-San."

"My sweet foreign prince," replied Aiko in a thick voice, tilting her head closer to Jim, who took it as an invitation for a kiss. As he was bending to do just that, Aiko suddenly whipped her head around to look towards the other side of the lake. Jim followed her gaze and saw the silhouette of a monk standing on the other shore, waving and gesturing for them to come over. "He has come to take you away," said Aiko in a sad voice.

"The temple must be closing for the day," observed Jim, "Why don't you come with me, Aiko-San? We can get dinner somewhere."

"If only I could, Jimu-San," said a visibly miserable Aiko, "but alas, I can not go with you, for I must return to my home. Will you come back tomorrow? Same time?"

"Nothing will stop me from meeting you tomorrow Aiko-San, I promise you that," said Jim, putting on a brave face, even though his heart filled with dread at the thought of the empty hours that lay between this parting and the next time they would meet.

"Will you do something for me?" asked Aiko in a soft voice.

"Anything for you, Aiko-San, just say the words," replied an eager Jim.

"When you return tomorrow, could you not bring the *koma-inu* with you?" said Aiko while pointing towards Okami, who bared his teeth and glared at her with obvious hatred.

Jim laughed at this and said, "Ha! That's a clever nickname for Okami! A dog who thinks he is a lion. Sure Aiko-San, I won't bring him with me when I come tomorrow."

Aiko smiled at this and said, "*Domo arigato* (thank you), Jimu-San. I cannot wait to see you again."

"*Sayonara,* Aiko-San," said Jim, "Believe me, I will be counting every minute that passes by."

Leaving Aiko where she stood, Jim collected Okami from the tree he was tied to and walked across to the other side of the shore, where the monk stood waiting for him. He turned out to be a novice, barely out of his teens.

"Jimu-San," said the monk as he smiled at Jim, "I saw you enter the temple compound today but didn't see you leave, so I thought I'd check here before we lock the gates."

"How do you know my name?" growled Jim with uncharacteristic rudeness, annoyed at the monk having interrupted what would have been his and Aiko's first kiss.

"My name is Hakkun," said the monk. "My cousin Fuyuko works with you at the school," as he patted Okami on the head while the dog wagged his tail.

Jim instantly regretted his rude behavior and said "Gomen nasai, Hakkun-San, and thanks for checking on me. Domo arigato."

The monk waved away Jim's apology and instead asked "What were you doing for so long at the lake, Jimu-San?"

"I was just talking to my friend over there," said Jim as he turned to point towards the other side of the lake, expecting to see Aiko standing there for a final wave of goodbye, but there was no sign of her. How does she do that, vanish into thin air, wondered Jim.

"Is there another way out of here?" he asked the monk.

"No, Jimu-San," said the monk, looking at Jim with a strange expression, "This path is the only way out." Then in a quiet voice, he added, "Jimu-San, this place is not safe, especially after dark." Jim didn't respond to that comment and both men walked in silence up the path until they reached the temple gates, where another monk stood waiting to lock up. Hakkun lived in a monastery building next door so bidding him goodbye, Jim walked towards the train station with Okami in tow. Aiko's mysterious ability to vanish at will and the monk's ominous-sounding warning seemed to only have deepened Jim's longing for his newfound love.

Jim again had difficulty sleeping that night, for his dreams were once again invaded by strange visions, with increased intensity. He somehow managed to pass the night while staying awake, and as a result, ended up sleeping through most of the following day. He arose shortly before four p.m., feeling refreshed and full of enthusiasm at the prospect of meeting Aiko. After taking a quick shower and putting on fresh clothes, Jim started to head out of his flat but found his way barred by Okami, who let loose a volley of barks as he tried to prevent Jim from leaving. It was as if the dog knew where Jim was headed and didn't like the idea one bit. Jim somehow managed to bypass the dog and left his flat but he could still hear the dog's frantic yelps when he reached the end of the street. If he keeps this up while I'm gone, the neighbors are going to throw a fit, thought Jim to himself. With a sigh, Jim headed back to his apartment as he racked his brains to come up with a solution to this new annoyance. Seeing Jim return, Okami immediately calmed down and retreated to a corner where he sat wagging his tail. "You are a killjoy and a royal pain in the ass," said Jim scolding the dog.

He made a telephone call to Fuyuko praying that she was home. Fortunately, Fuyuko answered after a couple of rings and was happy to hear Jim at the other end. "Jimu-San! What a nice surprise! How are you?"

"I'm doing ok, Fuyuko-San," replied Jim, "Listen, I'm sorry to bother you but I was wondering if you can do me a favor? I have some business to attend to near where you live and for some reason Okami is creating a racket, so I can't leave him here. Can I drop him off with you for a little while?"

"Of course Jimu-San, I am very fond of Okami and will be happy to watch him for you," replied Fuyuko as she gave Jim her address.

"You are an angel Fuyuko-San! We will see you in an hour or so," said Jim as he hung up. Putting Okami on a leash, he left his flat and hurried towards the tube station.

"Hello, Jimu-San! Hello Okami! Please, please do come in," exclaimed a beaming Fuyuko, as she opened the door. Okami bounded inside and landed straight into Fuyuko's arms, as Jim followed after taking his shoes off outside. He had never been to Fuyuko's home before and was quite impressed with the tasteful decorations and how neat she kept the place. "Would you like some tea Jimu-San?" asked Fuyuko as she ruffled the fur on Okami's head.

"Oh no, Fuyuko-San," said Jim, "I am getting late for my appointment and need to get going." Upon hearing this, Fuyoko's face fell which made him feel immensely guilty and so he hurriedly added "Perhaps when I come back to collect Okami?"

Fuyuko simply nodded and Jim took his leave. As he briskly walked away towards the temple, he couldn't shake off the feeling that he was taking advantage of Fuyoko's affections. All is fair in love and war, me old son, he said to himself as he entered the temple gates and made his way towards the lake, where Jim knew he would find Aiko waiting for him.

As usual, Jim heard the haunting melody of her flute before he saw Aiko appear. Familiarity had, however, given him confidence, where he did not get agitated at failing to spot her immediately, upon his arrival at the lake. "*Konnichiwa* Aiko-San," said Jim by way of greeting Aiko.

"Konnichiwa Jimu-San," she replied with a smile that lit up Jim's world, "I have been waiting for you." Aiko walked towards Jim but then stopped, looking around as if to determine if he had arrived alone, or with company.

"It's just us today, Aiko-San," said Jim, and hearing this, Aiko smiled again and drew nearer until she was within touching distance.

"My sweet prince," she crooned as she moved as if to kiss Jim, but he caught her hand, which felt clammy and cold to the touch.

Looking into her eyes, Jim said "Aiko-San, you and I have only known each other for a very short time, yet I feel I have known you my entire life. I think I am falling in love with you."

"I feel the same, my sweet prince," said Aiko with a dreamy look in her eyes.

"Aiko-San," continued Jim, "I have never felt this way ever before, and I am ready to spend the rest of my life with you, but..."

Aiko looked sharply at Jim, her dreamy expression evaporating, and asked "But? But what Jimu-San?"

Jim cleared his throat and replied, "If we are to be together, you must be completely honest with me."

"What do you mean? You are talking in riddles. Is this what they call romance in your country?" giggled Aiko.

"I'm serious, Aiko-San," said Jim with some feeling.

Aiko too became serious and replied, "Gomen nasai, Jimu-San, please ask me what you want. I will be honest."

Despite being head over heels in love with Aiko, Jim was no fool, so he asked "Who are you, Aiko-San? Where do you live? Where is your family?"

Aiko just stared at Jim with an inscrutable expression on her face so he continued, "Where do you go when you seemingly vanish into thin air? You do not leave here using the path to the temple and you certainly did not do so last night, for I saw the gates being locked behind me. I also know there is no other way out of here. Where did you go?" Aiko had a calculating look in her eyes that Jim did not like one bit, but he patiently waited for an answer.

Finally, with a sigh, Aiko said to Jim, "My sweet prince, you have so many questions, and I so little time. It will be easier if I just show you." With those words, Aiko caught Jim's head in her hands and kissed him full on the lips, and there was a flash of lightning that obscured the world around Jim with blinding light.

The light receded just as quickly as it had appeared, and Jim found that Aiko had vanished and he had been transported to inside a scene that could only be feudal Japan. He found that he could neither move nor speak and was, therefore, a mute and motionless spectator to the events unfolding around him. He saw men in traditional Japanese clothes with *katanas* (curved, single-edged swords) attached to their belts walking down a street that led to a large castle, five stories tall with a curved roof at each level. The scene changed and he now stood inside a giant hall, where the same men he had seen previously knelt in front of a throne on which sat an imposing-looking man with a hard face. Jim suddenly spotted Aiko standing next to the throne, but try as he might, he could not catch her attention. The scene changed again and Jim found himself in a beautiful garden adjacent to the castle, where he saw Aiko sitting with her lady attendants, while an effeminate-looking man stood and recited haikus, much to Aiko's apparent delight. It was then Jim realized that what he was witnessing were scenes from Aiko's life. He also figured that he was invisible to the people around him, for they carried on without once glancing in his direction.

Suddenly there was the sound of a horn blowing and Aiko looked up, curious about the source of the disturbance. A grand procession could be seen entering the castle gates, with men on horses carrying standards that had the emblem of an elephant on them. The scene shifted once more and Jim was back in the great hall where he saw the man on the throne, whom he guessed to be Aiko's father, welcoming a prince from Thailand. Aiko stood next to her father, smiling shyly at the prince who, despite keeping a straight face, kept stealing glances at her.

The scenes now began to change rapidly as Jim saw Aiko and the prince running into each other on multiple occasions around the castle, Aiko and the prince walking together in the garden, under the watchful eyes of their respective attendants. The star-crossed lovers stealing away from their minders to sit in the dark and talk for hours. Their first kiss under the stars. Their passionate lovemaking next to a lake, that Jim recognized as the one where he met Aiko for the first time, after which Aiko and the prince lay spent on the grass, she wearing the white kimono that Jim knew only too well. Then came the sound of running feet and they were suddenly surrounded by armed men. The prince was hauled away by his minders, while her father's soldiers caught hold of Aiko and dragged her to the edge of the lake where her father stood waiting, with a katana in his hand. "You have brought shame to our family's name," he said sadly to Aiko, before running the sword through her abdomen. For a second, Aiko stood still, as if in shock, then she turned to look directly at Jim, as she started to fall back into the lake, her arms stretched out into the air.

That was when the spell that bound Jim broke and a scream escaped his lips. "Nooooooooo!," screamed Jim, as he ran towards the spot from which he had seen her fall. Aiko's father and his men seemed to vanish into thin air and looking into the lake, Jim saw Aiko, floating just under the surface, her eyes wide open, as if in shock. "Save me, my sweet prince," came her voice inside Jim's head, and without a moment's hesitation, he dived into the lake after her.

As Jim reached Aiko's floating body, he got a firm hold of her and turned around to swim back towards the surface, but he was startled when Aiko's arms suddenly encircled him in a vice-like grip. He turned towards her and got the fright of his life, for instead of Aiko's beautiful face, the grotesque visage of a rotting corpse now stared back at him, its eyes bulging out of the sockets. Jim struggled to get free but Aiko, or whatever she had now become, proved too strong and they slowly sank together into the inky depths of the lake. "Hush, my prince," came Aiko's voice from inside Jim's head, "Do not fight this and soon we shall be together, forever." Jim's lungs were on fire and his attempts to free himself were getting more and more feeble.

Then a miracle happened, and like an avenging angel, the small shape of Okami streaked through the water and descended upon them. Through his fading vision, Jim saw the dog bite down hard on the corpse's arm. A terrible scream of rage and frustration reverberated inside Jim's head, but suddenly he was free of Aiko's deadly embrace. With the little strength that he had left within him, Jim swam back up the surface, as the corpse, with Okami still attached to its arm, continued to sink into the murky depths below.

Jim burst through the water's surface, gasping for air. He swam back to the shore and crawled out of the water, falling into the arms of Fuyuko, who stood there waiting for him. "Jimu-San, are you ok?" she cried.

For a few minutes, Jim sat shivering, unable to speak, then looking at Fuyuko he asked "O-O-Okami?" Tears ran down Fuyuko cheeks as she sadly shook her head. Jim turned to look towards the lake, whose surface stood as placid as ever. Then in a shaking voice, he narrated the entire tale to Fuyuko, who listened in silence.

When he finished, Fuyuko replied "My cousin Hakkun, whom you met yesterday, called and told me that he observed you from across the lake, talking to yourself.

He said that you told him you had been speaking with a friend, but he swears that he saw no one else with you." Jim looked up at her, but said nothing, so she continued. "Today when you left Okami with me, I had a feeling that you were headed here again and I was worried about you, so decided to follow you. I brought Okami along as he was getting very restless, and we stood watching you from a distance for a while. You were talking to yourself, then you suddenly screamed and ran towards the lake and dived in. That is when Okami suddenly pulled hard against his leash, breaking it, and ran and jumped into the lake after you."

Jim sat up and said "You don't believe a word I have said, do you? You must think I am going crazy."

"No, Jimu-San!" exclaimed Fuyuko, "I do believe you. I know you experienced something terrible today. I think you encountered what legends call an *ayakashi,* a kind of a *yokai* (spirit) that is found near rivers and lakes." With a shudder she continued "People around here avoid this lake, for there are whispers of ghostly sightings. Some have reported seeing a white-clad figure of a woman walking among the trees and some have also reported hearing flute music coming out of nowhere." With fresh tears streaming down her face, she sobbed "I'm sorry Jimu-San, I should have warned you, but I didn't. You ended up getting ensnared in the ayakashi's trap, nearly drowning, and poor Okami gave up his life to save yours."

Finally, Jim too could no longer hold back the flood of emotions inside him, falling once again into Fuyuko's arms. For a long time he sobbed, overwhelmed by grief from the loss of Okami, and despite its evil designs, pity for the lonely and wretched being called Aiko, as Fuyuko gently rocked him back and forth.

A few months after this incident, Jim and Fuyuko were married in a simple ceremony, and shortly thereafter, they left Japan for Canada, never to return. Settling in Toronto, Jim tried his hand at a variety of things for a while, before landing an executive role with a prestigious university. They recently bought a nice house in a trendy neighborhood that is a stone's throw away from Lake Ontario. Fuyuko is a model wife and tries to keep Jim happy, but she is aware that the encounter with the ayakashi has somehow changed him, and there is now a melancholy that lies deep within him and which takes hold on days when the moon is full and the tides run high. Fuyuko believes that during such times, it is best to leave Jim alone, as he takes long walks on the lakeshore near their home.

If only she knew the truth—that whenever Jim sits on the lakeshore staring at the horizon, the waves carry over them the faint sounds of a Japanese flute, the siren song of the woman in the lake.

FAMILY TIES

"Ladies and gentlemen, we have now begun our descent into Berlin," announced the captain to the passengers of the Lufthansa flight, as I woke from my deep slumber and looked out the window at the German countryside visible below. The pilot continued the rest of the announcement, as flight attendants went up and down the aisle to collect the last of the trash, and to ensure that passengers had their seat belts on. I yawned and handed over the remains of my breakfast

to the smiling attendant and then settled back to pass the remaining ten or fifteen minutes of flight time left, usually a difficult wait, and today even more so due to my mounting excitement.

My name is Laura Griffith. I am twenty-eight years old, unmarried, and definitely unattached. I was born in Austin, Texas to Albert and Rebecca Griffith, both of whom died in an accident when I was just three years old. My memory of them is faint but treasured nevertheless, kept alive in my heart all these years by my grandmother Katherine, who brought me up after my parent's death. She too passed away shortly after my twenty-seventh birthday last year, leaving me all alone in this world as I had no other living relatives that I knew of.

Fate, as we all know, never misses a chance to add insult to an injury. A mere six months after my grandmother's death, I was diagnosed with terminal cancer. "It has spread through your pancreas. You have maybe six months left, twelve at most, if we are lucky. I'm really sorry," said the doctor. Then as an afterthought, he added "You know, this form of cancer is extremely rare. Less than 200,000 cases are reported in the United States each year." Gee, Thanks Doc! I remember thinking to myself, lucky old me! Winning the cancer lottery. So what if I am also losing the race for life? Hey! You gotta take the good with the bad right? Sure Doc, thanks for that gem of trivia, very helpful indeed! I of course did not say any of that to the doctor, for that would have been contrary to my nature. Instead, I did what I had always done whenever fate dealt me a rotten hand. I crawled into my bed and cried my heart out.

Weeks went by while I drank myself to delirium. Alcohol will be the death of you, said a voice within my head. Nah! Cancer got first dibs on you girl, said another voice inside my inebriated mind. You guys wanna take bets? I asked with a giggle, that soon escalated into hysterical laughter, before devolving once more into the inevitable bout of bawling. In retrospect, I went through the classic phases of grief, though not in the usual way. You see, the first stage of grief is denial, where most people take the position that this can't be happening to them. In my case, I firmly believed that fate had plotted against me since the day I was born, so asking that particular question would have been rhetorical. The second phase is anger, and there too I scored a whopping goose egg since I am not, and never have been angry about anything. I therefore skipped the first two stages and proceeded straight to stage three, which is depression, and I stayed there for a while—months in fact—before proceeding to the next stage, which was bargaining, as I took stock of my life thus far.

After much retrospection and soul searching, I came to the realization that as it stood, I had accomplished very little in life. Since childhood, the protective shadow of my grandmother had been there to help me navigate through the world and its tedious ways, and I had simply followed her commands well into adulthood. I had always been a loner, more interested in books (I was a voracious reader) than people, which is why I had never made any lasting friendships through the school years. Now, all alone and with my time literally running out, I wanted to accomplish something all by myself. I wanted to achieve at least one thing that I could say was all my idea, and my effort, before the curtains dropped and I exited the stage of life, never to return. Knowing that the future had zero prospects, I therefore turned my gaze towards the past.

I decided to find out more about my roots, facts about where my family came from. The more I thought about it, the more the idea appealed to me, even though I knew that the task was far more difficult than it sounded, for my grandmother had always been very tight-lipped about her past and my father, who may have been able to shed some light on our family's history, was dead as well. The few facts that I did have were simply that my grandmother had fled war-torn Germany during the second world war with my father, who at that time was only five years old. They had arrived in America as refugees and had rebuilt their lives here. I also knew that my grandfather had perished in the war, for even though my grandmother seldom spoke of him, she had shown me a grainy picture of him, that showed a handsome man in his thirties, wearing a smart military uniform, with a hint of a smile on his face. It was this picture that I decided to start my research with.

I looked through the photo albums that my grandmother had kept meticulously over the years, and some of the pictures brought back bittersweet memories of happier times and I couldn't help but shed some more tears. However, the photo of my grandfather was nowhere to be found, and after having exhausted all the options at hand where she could have kept the photo, I looked towards the small metal safe in her room which had always been off-limits to me since childhood. In fact, so strictly was this rule ingrained in my mind that I had not thought of opening the safe even after my grandmother's death, though she had left me its keys (along with the house and a substantial inheritance) in her will. Even now, the thought of rifling through her personal belongings filled me with a sense of guilt, but I told myself that since she was dead and I was an adult, I had all the right to do so. Our family attorney had handed over the safe's keys to me after my grandmother's funeral, so I picked up one from the bunch, inserted it into the keyhole, and turned the handle down. There was a loud click and the safe door swung open, at last revealing the secrets my grandmother had kept hidden from me all these years.

I found my grandfather's photograph in the safe, amongst other things contained in an oilskin packet that my grandmother must have placed there for safekeeping. The picture had the name Albert Greifswald written on its back with the date June 2nd, 1942. So my grandfather's name was also Albert, the same as Dad, I thought, thrilled at this first clue. Inside the packet, I found old letters written in German and dated from before the war. There was also a silver pendant, tarnished with age, and some other black and white photographs. I also found my grandmother's old German identity card which had the name Katherina von Greifswald on it. I couldn't understand any of the other information on the card, so put it aside for further research. Next, I looked at the photographs which were mostly of my grandparents and seemed to have been taken before the war. My father featured as a little boy in a few of them. I noticed that most of the photographs had a castle atop a hill in the background, and upon further examination, I confirmed that it was the same building in all the photos. I started to feel a little excited, for here was a clue, albeit small, to where my family lived prior to their flight to America.

Why learn a new language when one has Google? Well, alright, it's an excuse often provided by the linguistically challenged, but still, that's the best one I could come up with. My grandmother had never shown any interest in teaching me German, but I wish I had taken some initiative and pushed her harder. Anyway, it was too late for regrets, so picking up my grandmother's *kennkarte* (identity document), I started typing the words off of it into my computer, hoping that Google would decipher their meaning into English, thereby providing me with additional clues. Sure enough, with the help of the language translator, foreign-sounding words like *Gerburstag* (Birthday), *Geburtsort* (Place of Birth), and *Rennort* (Place) began to reveal their true meaning, and soon I was able to piece together some facts about my grandmother. I now knew that she had been born on August 12, 1920, which means she was only twenty-five years old when she fled to America with my father. Her kennkarte was issued in May, 1943 and the place of issue was listed as Greifswald, which incidentally was also the family name listed in her ID card. The other item of interest in the kennkarte was the section titled *Beruf* (Job), which listed only the word *Gräfin* as her occupation, and for the meaning of which I once again turned to the internet.

"*Graf* (male) or *Gräfin* (female) is a historical title of the German nobility, usually translated as 'count.' Considered to be intermediate among noble ranks, the title is often treated as equivalent to the British title of earl," said Google, the internet god of wisdom, and my new best friend.

German nobility? My grandmother? Really? The more facts I put together, the more questions popped up in my mind. For starters, why would an obviously wealthy aristocrat flee her country to become a refugee in a foreign land? I knew that she had arrived in America with her son, the clothes on their backs, and little else. Secondly, my grandmother had never remarried, so I had always assumed that Griffith was our family name, but I now knew that it really should have been von Greifswald. Why did my grandmother decide to change her first and last name? Was it to assimilate better with the general population in her adopted country, perhaps even to hide her German origin, or was there another hidden, and more sinister reason that I did not know about? My hunt for clues thus far had managed to yield more questions than answers, so I decided to now focus on the town of Greifswald, where my family had lived as nobility prior to the war.

"Tell me more about Greifswald in Germany," I commanded Google.

"The town of Greifswald (from German *Greif,* 'griffin,' and *Wald,* 'forest'), is is a town in northeastern Germany located on the shores of the Baltic Sea, about 200 km (124.3 mi) to the north of Berlin, with a population of roughly 55,000," came the response. The search results also showed the town's coat of arms, which featured a strange lion-like creature, which upon further reading turned out to be the griffin, a mythological creature with the body of a lion and the head of an eagle. Suddenly I remembered my grandmother's silver pendant that I found in the safe and snatching it up, I examined the design on it. Even though the pendant was black with age, I could clearly see the griffin etched into the metal, identical to the town coat of arms I saw online. Curiouser and curiouser, I thought to myself, like Alice in wonderland, so much surprised by this discovery, that for the moment I quite forgot how to speak good English, just as Alice did in the fictional world created by Lewis Carroll.

My head was starting to hurt from all the fact crunching, so I got up to make myself some tea. Then as I sat down with the steaming mug, I considered what I had learned from my snooping thus far. My grandmother (and logically my grandfather) were German nobility who hailed from the town of Greifswald. My grandfather had perished in the war, presumably fighting the allies, shortly after which my grandmother had fled to America with my father. Why she fled her home and why she changed her name was, however, still a mystery. The more we learn, the less we know, I paraphrased Einstein, with a sigh.

There were no other clues to be found in my grandmother's safe or her belongings and my career as an amateur investigator seemed doomed to be short-lived (ha! pun intended). Dejected, I sat lost in my thoughts for awhile, until inspiration finally struck. Of course, I thought to myself, if you want to dig up the past, you need to do it where it all started, which was in Greifswald.

On the spur of the moment, I decided to travel to Germany, and with mounting excitement mixed with not a small amount of trepidation (I'm a meek, sheltered homebody, hello?), I researched airlines, hotels, and rental cars that I would require during the course of my adventure. The Internet is one of the greatest enablers behind making the world smaller, and I proved it by booking my entire trip online in a matter of minutes. The game is afoot! I said to myself, although I had no illusions about my powers of deduction which were decidedly lame when compared to the great detective whose famous quote I had just appropriated.

I almost didn't go. A few days before my scheduled flight to Berlin, I started feeling bouts of intense and debilitating pain that racked through my body for hours on end. Pain, you ask? Yes dear, pain, caused by that tiny but lethal enemy that stormed through my body in its relentless quest to kill me. Does cancer ring a bell? Or did you forget all about my disease, just because I haven't mentioned its terrible symptoms thus far? Perhaps I wanted to spare you the ghastly details of the extreme fatigue, bowel problems, weight loss (not that I was ever big), and the general sick feeling that you get when you know you're dying, albeit slowly. All of those, and the pain. Fortunately, "Dr. Helpful," of whom I spoke earlier, was able to prescribe some medication for pain management, which helped a lot even though it made my mind somewhat foggy. He did, however, warn me that the pain would only get worse over time until even medications would not help. Jeez Doc, would it kill you to not be so brutally honest? I wanted to say. Anyhow, the medications helped, and aboard I went on that gleaming Lufthansa jet that flew me across the Atlantic to Berlin.

The Berlin-Tegel airport was smaller than I had expected, even though this was the first time I had flown anywhere outside the United States. The customs and immigration check was right on the jetway which was interesting (and to be honest, a bit annoying. I mean, let a girl stretch her legs after a long flight). Nevertheless, I breezed through it in short order. My flight had arrived in Terminal A and after collecting my baggage, I followed signs for *mietwagen,* which I now knew meant rental car in German. I had checked online about German traffic rules and had been relieved to find that they drove on the same side of the road as Americans do and their traffic rules were also similar. I had also read about the Autobahns, German highways with no speed limits, which I had found unbelievable and possibly dangerous. The lady at the Hertz counter spoke excellent English and waved away my AAA International Driver's Permit that I had spent twenty dollars on, stating that my Texas driver's license would suffice. (Gee, thanks AAA. Shame on you for the misleading marketing spiel.) She put me in a nice Volvo SUV with a GPS system, and after handing me the paperwork, directed me towards the car lot where I could pick up the vehicle. At the car lot, a handsome young man helped me find my vehicle and switch the

GPS interface from German to English. Then, finally! I was on my way to Greifswald.

The Autobahn really does not have a speed limit. While I drove, keeping a sharp eye on the speedometer and never going past 120 km per hour (equivalent to 75 miles stateside), other cars zipped past me like I was standing still, quickly becoming a speck in the distance. There wasn't much traffic once I left the city and followed the GPS directions that put me on the A11 highway, a simple two-lane road that winded through small towns and countryside. Along the way, I kept seeing the word *ausfahrt* repeated at every exit, and I guessed that's what the word meant in German, but that didn't stop my witty self from remarking My! They sure have a lot of cities called Ausfahrt in Germany. Lame, I know, but hey—anything to pass the time, right? The helpful young man back at the Hertz car lot had also helped me connect my iPod with the Volvo's music system, so humming along to my favorite playlist, I drove for a little over two hours before signs for Greifswald began to appear on the highway.

I had always imagined European towns to be quaint and romantic little places where time flows more slowly than it does in the surrounding world. Knowing that my expectations were largely built upon musings of daydreaming novelists and of course, Hollywood, I won't go as far as to say that Greifswald disappointed me in this regard. It's just that I found the town to be neither quaint nor romantic, though it was charming enough in its own right. Greifswald turned out to be a small town, filled mostly with the customary tall and narrow houses built against each other, with red-tiled roofs and pretty little windows. The only gap among these homes were small storefronts with modern glass windows and a gas station or two that I passed by. The roads were narrow but well maintained and small trees lined them on both sides. The town's skyline was dominated by imposing bell towers of three churches that were visible in the distance. All in all, were it not for the German signs on the road and storefronts, I might as well have been driving through one of the countless little fishing towns in New England.

My hotel was near the harbor, built on the banks of the Ryck River that runs into the Baltic Sea. I parked my SUV near the hotel and walked over to its front entrance. After checking in, I was shown to a lovely little room with a view of the river and the harbor where I could see many sailboats floating about. I took a quick shower, changed my clothes, and out I went again, eager to explore this land of my ancestors. Through my research, I knew that most German towns had a *rathaus,* the town hall that contained historic records. Following the GPS directions to Alstadt (Old Town), I soon found my way to the building that I was looking for. As it was, the structure was hard to miss.

The Greifswald town hall was located in the old quarter, nestled among other historic buildings. It was also the largest establishment in the area, flaming red in color and adorned by striking volute gables that gave the structure a unique shape. A large and heavy bronze door stood open, providing access to the building and upon entering, I found myself in a large hall that was a perfect blend of the old and the new. Baroque style carvings in gold covered the ceiling along with antique chandeliers, while modern-looking counters with glass windows were situated along the periphery of the hall. There were also a few automated kiosks that looked equally out of place as the counters in this throwback to earlier times. I saw a counter with a sign that said Information, one of the few words that German and English have in common, so I made a beeline towards it. A smiling woman behind the glass panel greeted me by saying "*Guten Tag,*" to which I replied "*Guten Tag! Sprichst du Englisch?*" in halting German that I had managed to learn in preparation for this trip. "*Entschuldigung, ich spreche kein Englisch,*" replied the woman, which I understood to mean that she didn't speak any English. The woman gestured for me to wait, as she got off her chair and went off towards offices that lay further behind the counter.

In short order, she returned and again motioned for me to wait. In a few moments, a door that stood next to the row of counters opened, and out stepped a man of medium height, dressed in a dark suit and a shock of blond hair. "Hello," he said to me with a pleasant smile, "My name is Gunther. How can I help you?"

Relieved, I responded, "Hello Gunther, I am Laura and I was hoping to see the town records between 1920 and 1945."

"Ah 1945, the year of Germany's surrender to the allies," said Gunther, "Are there any particular type of records that you are looking for?"

"What type of records would help me learn more about the people that lived here during that time?" I responded with another question.

"Well, let's see, we have voter records, birth certificates, marriage certificates, tax records, and of course certificates of death," replied Gunther, "but you must have a legitimate reason before we can provide access to this information," he added.

"My father and grandparents used to live here," I replied, "They have all passed away and I am trying to learn more about my family's roots."

"Oh, I see. What were the names of your grandparents?" asked Gunther.

"Albert and Katherine von Greifswald," I replied, giving my grandmother's adopted first name.

Gunther's eyes widened in surprise and a strange look came over his face. "You mean 'the' Graf Albert von Greifswald and his wife, the Gräfin Katherina von Greifswald?" he exclaimed.

"Yes," I replied, thrilled that he recognized the names of my grandparents.

"But that's impossible; it's well known that the Graf died in the war and his family perished in a fire at the castle shortly thereafter," said Gunther, looking at me suspiciously.

"No, they did not," I replied, "My grandmother fled to America with my father just after the war."

Gunther still looked skeptical so I showed him my grandmother's kennkarte and some pictures of her in America with my father as a boy that I had found in her safe. "I see," said Gunther, "Please follow me and I will try to find the records." He scanned a card at the door which opened with a click. Gunther held it open for me as I stepped inside and then he led me down a long corridor until we reached a tiny room that contained a round table with four chairs. "Please wait here," said Gunther, "I will collect the records and bring them to you in a short while."

Thirty minutes later I was wondering if Gunther had forgotten all about me, when I heard the squeaking of wheels in the corridor and Gunther appeared with a mail cart full of files. "I must apologize in advance, for there really are not many records available," he said.

"Why is that?" I asked.

"Well, you see, when Germany surrendered to the allies, the Red Army was rumored to be just a day away from Greifswald, and there had been rumors, terrible rumors, of the looting and destruction the Russians had wrought in other towns," replied Gunther. "So the town council decided that all our records would be moved to an undisclosed location for safekeeping. Fortunately, when the Red Army arrived, our town was spared; however, the building where the records were kept was destroyed in a mysterious fire, and only some of the records survived," he finished while pointing at the records in the cart. Indeed I could see the charred edges on some of the documents that had survived the fire. "There is not much in here," said Gunther apologetically. "However, I took the liberty to call my father, who was there when these events occurred. He is on his way and should arrive momentarily. Hopefully, he will be able to answer some of your questions. He is old but still has a sharp memory." "Thank you Gunther," I said with heartfelt gratitude. He smiled, nodded, and left me with the files.

Another twenty minutes passed by and I spent the time browsing through the files that Gunther had left with me. They were all in German and filled with figures and numbers so I figured they were mostly tax records and therefore didn't provide any useful information. Then there was a soft knock on the door and a kindly-looking old gentleman peeked in. "*Fräulein* Griffith?" he asked. I nodded and he came inside and sat down on the chair opposite to the one I was sitting on. "I am Werner Huber, Gunther's Papa," he introduced himself, "I understand that you have some questions about the von Greifswald family?"

"Yes *Herr* Huber," I replied, "I belong to that family. Albert and Katherine were my grandparents."

Werner studied me for a few moments before responding "You must forgive me if I sound skeptical, but it is well established that the Graf and Gräfin, along with their son Albert Junior, perished towards the end of the war," he said. "The Graf died bravely defending the Fatherland, while the Gräfin and Albert Junior died in a fire at the castle."

"The part about my grandfather dying in the war is true, but my grandmother fled to America with my father right around that time," I replied as I showed him my grandmother's kennkarte and her photos from America. "I am here to try and understand why she fled, and why it's such a mystery."

Werner looked thoughtful as he examined the documents and then looked at me in silence for a few moments. Then, he seemed to come to a decision and said "Very well, there is someone that you should meet. He can provide all the information that you seek."

"Really? That's wonderful!" I exclaimed. "Who is this man?"

"I'd rather that he tell you himself," replied Werner. "Let me get in touch with him and I will set up a meeting. Where are you staying?" I gave Werner the name of my hotel and after promising to call me there as soon as the meeting had been set up, Werner escorted me out of the rathaus. Standing near the great bronze door, he gave me a final searching look and said "*Auf Wiedersehen Fräulein,* and I sincerely hope that you have told me the truth about the Gräfin and Albert Junior, for this man we are going to see, he doesn't take kindly to frauds." With those words, Werner turned and walked away. I spent a couple of hours exploring tourist attractions in Greifswald before returning to my hotel.

The shrill ringing of the telephone rudely interrupted my jet lag-induced slumber. Groggily I reached for the instrument and managed to mumble "Hello?"

"Fräulein Griffith?" said the voice of Werner Huber on the other end, "I have contacted the man that we spoke of. Can you meet me in your hotel's lobby in an hour?"

Excitement tore through the fog of drowsiness clouding my mind as I sat upright in my bed and replied "Yes of course! Will this man meet us in the lobby as well?"

"No, he will meet us at the site of where the von Greifswald castle used to be. The place is in ruins but I'm sure you would still want to see it," replied Herr Huber. I readily agreed and after cautioning me to dress up in warm clothes as the evening was promising to be chilly, he hung up. I sprang from my bed, only to collapse onto the floor feeling weak and dizzy. I realized with horror that I had not eaten anything since my meal on the flight that morning and had also forgotten to take my medication on account of having fallen asleep immediately upon my return to the hotel. Predictably, my fall was followed by waves of intense pain that washed over my body as I crawled towards the bedside table where I had kept my medicines. Somehow, amidst the agony that seemed to cut through my very soul, I managed to pop a few pills into my mouth, and then collapsing on my bed once again, I waited for the pain to pass, as I knew it would.

An hour later, I went down to the hotel lobby where I found Werner Huber already waiting for me. We sat in his car and he drove in the direction of my family's erstwhile home. "I have fond memories of the castle," said Werner with a sigh. "Those were the good days before Hitler came to power and the world turned upside down."

"You knew my grandparents?" I asked, surprised that Werner had not mentioned it before.

"My father worked for Graf Albert and I visited the castle many times as a boy," he replied.

"What was my grandfather like?" I asked, eager to know more.

"He was a good man," said Werner looking at me. "Tough, but fair."

"Was he a Nazi?" I asked, finally blurting out the question that had bothered me for a while, and which I had thus far hesitated to voice.

"Not at all!" exclaimed Werner. "Why do you ask?"

"Well, he did go off to fight the allies," I replied.

Werner gave me a look and said gruffly "It's sad that people think all Germans who fought in the war were Nazis. Graf Albert was an honorable man who despised the Nazis. In fact, he helped many jews in our village escape to safety. Still, he was a proud German so he went to fight for his country, not because he agreed with the Nazis but because he believed that it was his patriotic duty to do so."

I was relieved to hear this and replied "I'm sorry if I offended you. I am glad he was not a Nazi." To this Werner just grunted and we drove in silence along a winding road that led up a hill as I stared out of the window. Daylight was fading fast and as we turned along a bend in the road, the ruins of my family's erstwhile home suddenly appeared in the distance. I could almost see the resemblance between the beautiful castle in my grandmother's old pictures and this sad remnant of its former glory.

Soon enough, Werner stopped the car by the roadside. "We are here," he announced in a quiet voice. We left the car parked by the roadside and entered a thick patch of woods that lay between the road and the castle ruins. A thin trail led through the trees and we followed it until we emerged into a clearing where the entrance to the ruins lay. There was no door at the entrance, simply a stone archway that led into a large courtyard with paved stones that was overgrown with weeds sprouting around the edges of the brickwork. To our left and to our right were the ruins of a smaller and a slightly larger structure respectively. Werner introduced them as the servant's quarters (to the left) and horse stables (to the right). Directly in front of us, and at some distance from where we stood, lay the main part of the castle which Werner referred to as *hauptfestung,* and also provided translation of the same to mean "the main keep" for my benefit. The main keep was significantly larger, with battlements running across its crumbling walls from one turret to another. The walls had many arched windows that must have been beautiful once, but with age and decay they now only accentuated the overall mystique of the ruins. A closer inspection of the main keep revealed signs of fire damage, likely from the conflagration where, as per the town legend, my grandmother and father had allegedly died (we know they did not). The walls here were suffering from a brutal onslaught of nature, as thick vines snaked their way through and over these walls in an attempt to subjugate them. The walls, however, still stood firm, fighting back the invasion, not ready to give in just yet.

It was almost dark by then and true to Werner's warning about the weather, the temperature had dropped significantly since we left my hotel, while the wind had picked up in intensity, causing me to shiver even though I had a jacket on. "When will this man arrive?" I asked Werner.

"He should already be here, waiting for us inside," replied Werner, as he indicated that we should enter the main keep. I looked at the yawning darkness that lay beyond the windows of the main keep and wondered if I was crazy to have agreed to come along to this desolate place with one and perhaps two men about whom I knew next to nothing? I stood there for an instant, torn with indecision and ready to bolt at the first sign of trouble, but no trouble came and there was just the wind, a patiently waiting Werner, and the approaching night. Finally, I decided that if something did indeed lurk within the shadows inside the main keep, it couldn't be any worse than the slow death that I was dying from as my body continued to betray me. 'Hey, you only die once,' I said to myself as I stepped through the door of the main keep and into the darkness within.

I stood in what must have once been the great hall of the castle. The roof had partially collapsed, exposing the night sky and letting in a tiny amount of light from stars shimmering far above. A large staircase began in the center of the room, its upward flight arrested midway where a portion of the upper wing of the castle had collapsed, leaving the staircase seemingly suspended in air, leading to nowhere. Werner had a torch in his hand and with it he made large sweeping arcs all around as if looking for something. I asked him for the torch so I could better see what lay around me and he seemed reluctant at first, but finally acquiesced. With the torch in my hand, I started examining the ruins of my family's former abode, though there wasn't really much to see. Any object of value had long since been removed from the premises and all that remained were crumbling walls and rubble.

I realized that it would perhaps be better for me to return during the daytime to get a better look around and I turned to Werner to voice these thoughts, but he had disappeared! Suppressing the sudden panic bubbling inside my mind, I swung the torch all around me, fully expecting (hoping really) to find Werner standing in another corner of the room, but the arcs of light only revealed the fact that I was all alone, or so I thought, until I finally shined my light onto the staircase and saw the figure of a man standing at the very edge where the stairs ended in mid-air, quietly observing me.

At first, I thought it was Werner, trying to pull off a silly prank to scare me, but I quickly realized that it couldn't be him. Werner was stocky and of medium height and had been wearing a blue jacket. The man on the stairs was trim, quite tall, and clad all in black. "Hello?" I called out to the man standing on the stairs, my voice sounding weak and quivering as it echoed through the dead silence surrounding me.

The man waved his hand at me without saying anything and then he started descending the stairs. To my eyes that struggled to pierce through the gloom, it seemed that he didn't walk but simply glided down the steps until he was standing a few feet away from me. His face was partially covered in shadows but I could still make out his youthful appearance and guessed him to be in his thirties. The man seemed oddly familiar, though I was sure I had never met him before. "*Guten Abend,*" he said in a rich baritone as he towered above me, "I have been waiting for you."

A shiver ran down my spine for no explicable reason and I responded "Thank you. I did not catch your name?"

The man smiled, revealing for an instant his extremely white teeth. "That's because I have not told you my name yet, Fräulein," he said smugly.

I waited for him to tell me his name, as any normal person would have at this point, but he remained silent, studying me. Embarrassed, I cleared my throat and said "Well, Thank you for agreeing to meet me. Herr Huber said that you know a lot about the von Greifswald family?"

The man nodded and said, "Herr Hubert was right. You could say that I am sort of an expert on the subject." He paused for a moment and asked "What is your interest in the von Greifswald family?"

"Albert and Katherine von Greifswald were my grandparents. I am the only daughter of their son Albert Junior," I replied.

Hearing this, the man's lips seemed to curl up as if in a silent snarl, and again I caught a glimpse of the abnormally white teeth and the sharp canines protruding from each corner of his lips. "Graf Albert von Greifswald was a very wealthy man," he said in his rich baritone, now tinged with a hint of anger. "Legends of his buried treasure have abounded for years and you won't be the first fraud to show up here staking a claim, though I must admit your story to be an actual descendant is quite unique."

At this time, the normal course of action for me would have been to beat a hasty retreat from this dark and desolate place and the stranger who gave me nothing but a sense of great unease, yet my heart told me to stand firm so I said "Look sir, I can understand your skepticism, for I too have heard the stories about the fire in which my grandmother and my father supposedly perished. However, I can assure you that they didn't and instead fled to America as refugees."

With those words, I dug into my bag and fished out my grandmother's German ID card and her pictures, which I proceeded to offer to this enigmatic man. He looked at the items in my outstretched hands for a moment and then gingerly took them from me. He first opened the kennkarte and studied it with great interest, then he examined the photographs which seemed to give him some pause.

Finally, he looked back at me and said "This kennkarte is authentic—I can tell from the stamps placed by the Nazi swine."

"So you believe me then?" I asked.

"*Nein,* Fräulein," he said shaking his head, "Not really. You see, there is a black market for such documents and you may have procured the kennkarte from such means. I have also heard that photographs can be doctored using modern technology."

I was now getting angry at this man who on one hand refused to tell me his name and on the other hand dared to call me a fraud to my face and seemed to stand in judgment on my bonafides. I put my hands on my hips (my standard pose when I meant to be defiant, my grandmother used to say) and said with as much sarcasm as I could muster "Well this is rich, from a man who won't even tell me his name, and who appears far too young to really know anything about my grandparents. What exactly makes you such an expert on the von Greifswald family, may I ask?"

The man gave another of his toothsome smiles. "Please excuse me, Fräulein, for I seem to have forgotten my manners," he said in a tone dripping with malice. "I am the Graf Albert von Greifswald, at your service," he finished as he stepped closer to me and I finally saw the red eyes, the bared fangs and the hungry expression on that terrifying face, not too different from that of the cat who is about to pounce on the canary. What kept me from screaming was the simple fact that despite its terrible visage, the face belonged to the man in the picture that I had carried with me, all the way from America.

The vampire grabbed my throat in a steely grip and I managed to croak "Grandfather?" still more stunned than scared.

"Enough of this farce!" he yelled in a voice filled with rage. "How dare you come here and desecrate the memory of my wife and child?" With those words, he forcefully turned my head so as to expose my throat and brought it closer to his waiting fangs, as I stood powerless to resist. There was a sharp pain as his teeth pierced my skin and then the world began to dissolve all around me, as I felt my very life starting to drain out of my body.

Suddenly his head jerked up and he staggered back, his lips painted crimson with my blood, and a look of intense confusion on his face. "Flesh of my flesh? Blood of my blood? How can this be?" he whispered to himself as he looked at me with wonder. I felt dizzy in my head and stumbled and he caught me in his arms but at his touch, I instinctively shrank back. "No *Liebling,* don't be scared," he said gently, "Blood does not lie. I am indeed your *opa* (grandfather); do not ever be afraid of me, child." He led me to a block of stone that lay nearby and we both sat down, my warm hands held between his own that were cold to the touch. "Tell me everything, child," he said looking at me.

I had by now caught my breath and looking at him I replied, "Perhaps you should start, Grandpa. How are you still alive, and how have you not aged a day since this photo was taken?" I handed him the only picture that I had of him and he took it from my hands and studied it with a rueful smile on his face.

"I remember the day this picture was taken, for I left to fight the very next day," he said, "I knew Germany was going to lose but my honor as a German demanded that I fight in defense of my country, so off I went to war, only to die an ignominious death in a foreign land, far from the family that I loved and adored."

At this point, we were interrupted by Werner Huber, who strolled in with a shovel over his shoulder, while whistling a catchy tune. He didn't notice us sitting on the rock nearby, for his eyes were still adjusting to the gloom. "Mein herr? Mein Herr?" he called out softly, "I am back to dispose of the body." Then his eyes dilated enough to spot us and a cry escaped from his lips.

My grandfather said to him "Werner, there won't be a need to dispose of any bodies tonight. This lady here is indeed my granddaughter. Her story is true."

The shovel fell from Werner's hands as he sank trembling to his knees. "Please forgive me mein herr, I had no way of knowing."

My grandfather stood up and walked over to Werner and grasping his shoulders gently, he helped Werber stand up. "You must never fear me, old friend, for you have done me a great service today and I am eternally in your debt. Go back to your family now," he said. Werner looked relieved as he grabbed the shovel and made a quick exit, leaving us alone again.

"I don't remember much about the moment of my death," my grandfather said, "One minute I was alive, then there was an explosion and everything went dark. I don't know for how long I lay there in that field strewn with the bodies of my dead comrades, but at some point during the night, I awoke and found that I had somehow cheated death, although it sometimes seems that it was really death that cheated me, of peace and rest." He paused for a moment in silent reflection and continued "When I awoke as one of the undead, my newborn eyes saw the world differently. I could see the tiny insects crawling within the dirt beneath my feet just as clearly as I could see the eagle flying high above in the sky. I noticed the movement of every blade of grass that stirred and every leaf that shivered. Mysteries of the night, hitherto hidden from my former human self, were now laid bare for I can see as clearly at night as you can during daytime," he said before wiping a tear that had escaped from my eye and traveled onto my cheek, as if to illustrate this last point. "I found that even my hearing had improved dramatically, for I could hear sounds from quite a distance away as if the source of these were placed right next to me. I also noticed the increased strength, speed, and agility that I was now able to command," he concluded with a sigh.

"Why did this happen to you?" I asked the question that had naturally come to my mind.

"To this day I do not know the reason, Liebling. At first, I thought that these were gifts that God had bestowed on me so I could protect my people. This was before I discovered that I could not abide sunlight and could only venture out once the sun went down. Then, there was the hunger, the deep and terrible thirst that could only be sated with human blood.

Try as I might, I could not resist it, for the need raged through my body like a burning inferno. It wasn't until I finally gave in and drained my very first victim that I realized that God had indeed forsaken me and I was cursed to forever haunt this earth as a creature of the night," replied grandfather.

"Did you go back home once you awoke...errr...came back from the dead?" I asked.

"Yes I did," said my grandfather unhappily. "I made it back home under cover of darkness and I revealed myself to your grandmother, showed her what had happened to me and what I'd become."

"What did she say? Was she scared?" I asked.

"No child, your grandmother was made of sterner stuff than that," he said while smiling at the memory. 'My poor Albert' is all she said as she held me, while I sobbed in her arms, shedding tears of red." Grandpa Albert paused for a moment, reliving the painful memories before he continued. "However, she absolutely refused to let me see little Albert, and try as I might, I could not convince her. She sent me away saying that all this was too much for her and that she needed some time to think." His voice caught in his throat as Grandpa continued his tale. "I told myself that she would eventually come around, for regardless of what else I may have become, I was still the man she loved and I loved them both the same, my wife and my son, so I went away and hid in the forest, preying on the Nazis that I encountered as they fled the Red Army that was marching closer and closer to our little town. However, little did I know that it was to be the last time I would see my Katharina and little Albert.

"Otto, Werner's father, still worked at the castle and I revealed my secret to him. His family has faithfully served the von Greifswalds for generations and Otto proved every bit the loyal servant. It was he who brought me the news of the fire at the castle and showed me the charred remains of my wife and son. Although I wonder now if he staged it all, as a final act of loyalty to my wife," said my Grandfather. "It's all starting to make sense now, the sudden and unexplained fire at the castle, the equally sudden and unexplained fire at the site where the town documents had been stored for safekeeping. She must have orchestrated both events to remove all traces of her existence, prior to fleeing to America.

"Had I paid more attention, I perhaps would have seen the signs, but my mind was occupied with another pressing problem, which was the Red Army that was drawing ever closer. There were dark rumors of rape and plunder that the Russians unleashed on every town and village they passed through and I had to protect my town and its people, just as my ancestors had done for generations past. So one night, while the Red Army lay encamped less than 50 kilometers away, a stroll in the park for a creature that I had become, I paid the Russian Commander a visit. I drained both of his bodyguards in front of him, as he watched with wide-eyed horror. Then I told him that if he left Greifswald alone, I would not prey on his men, but if the Russians harmed even a hair on any of my townsfolk, I would rip him and his apart from limb to limb, and bathe in their blood. He readily agreed and as history is my witness, Greifswald was spared the Russian's depredations," said my grandfather.

I told him then about my grandmother's arrival in America with my father, about the life she built in Texas, about my parents and their passing. Grandfather Albert listened with rapturous attention while I spoke and then for a while, he cried pitifully. "I wish I had known!" he sobbed. "I would have followed her to the ends of this earth. Perhaps that's why she left the way she did; she didn't want Albert Junior to witness the evil thing that his papa had become." He took pictures of my parents that I had also brought with me, for he could apparently see them clearly in the dark. "My boy!" he wailed as he caressed my father's face in the picture, "forever lost to me!" I found myself crying as well for I could feel that his pain and grief were genuine and I hugged him as we both shed tears together for a long while. Finally, composing himself, my grandfather spoke. "Child, I sensed something else in your blood, a sickness that tastes of death. Do you know about it?"

"Yup," I replied with a weak smile. "Pancreatic cancer, Stage 4 which is considered terminal. As per the doctor, I have just a few months left to live."

Upon hearing this, my grandfather shot up from the stone and yelled in a thunderous voice, as if speaking to God himself. "No! I will not let that happen. Not again!" Then turning towards me, he said in a gentler voice "My child, I thought I was forever alone in this world, all my family died but then by a miracle, you appeared. The flesh of my flesh, the blood of my blood, and yet God still conspires to deprive me of your company as well."

Grandfather Albert knelt down and gently took my face in his hands as he said: "Liebling, I can offer you life eternal, free from sickness, death, and ravages of old age. We can travel the world and experience all its wonders, unlike any human ever could. But I will not force it upon you for the choice has to be yours."

"Will I have to kill innocent people for their blood?" I asked. "You don't have to," said Grandfather. "You can only choose the evildoers, and there are many of them in this world—in fact, too many." We sat in silence as I considered his offer and its implications. If I turned it down, I would be dead in a few months; however, if I accepted it, it would literally be a decision set in stone as there would be no going back.

If truth be told, I kind of liked the idea, and I imagined myself as a vampire *fem fatale,* an undead angel possessed with the strength to protect the weak, strength that I could never muster in life. The more I thought about it, the more the idea appealed to me. So when my Grandfather asked me again if I wanted to join him in the eternal night, I agreed.

Later, much later, as I opened my newborn eyes to a world pulsating with color, I realized that I was forever free.

DEATH COMES IN THREES

Eddie Rollins finally showed up for work. It wasn't like he rushed in or even strolled in, though he was quite late. One minute he wasn't there and the next minute he was, standing near a pile of rubble and surveying the scene of devastation before him, caused by the depredations of the Luftwaffe bombers that snuck across the English channel each night to drop their deadly loads over London.

"Oye Eddie," I shouted, "Welcome to the party mate. If your lordship is done surveying his jurisdiction, perhaps you would care to join us commoners and lend a hand in removing these bodies?" Eddie just stood there, looking at us sadly, so Bernie, the foreman finally said "Eddie, get your butt over here right now! You think these poor sods will move by themselves, eh?" The entire crew roared with laughter at the grim humor as we stood amongst the stiff corpses of the unlucky victims of last night's raid. The country was in the middle of a war, and the only way one could go on doing this morbid sort of work without going insane was to pretend that the dead were just part of the rubble.

Humor was therefore where the crew often found solace during working hours.

Eddie, however, continued to look at us sadly which was unusual for two reasons. First, Eddie had always been eager to show up for work, so his tardiness today was out of character. Secondly, Eddie was a bit of a clown, with a seemingly bottomless repertoire of jokes and funny anecdotes, so him standing there now with that hangdog look gave the crew some pause. "What's wrong, Eddie?" I asked.

Eddie responded by pointing in the direction of some buildings in the distance. "Death comes in threes," he said.

"What did he say?" asked Bernie, the foreman, then in his sixties and getting a little hard of hearing. "I think he said death comes in threes, Guv," I replied. "Now what the heck does that mean?" asked Bernie, frowning.

"I have no idea, Guv, but he sure looks sad," I replied.

Bernie turned towards Eddie and said in a gentler tone "Eddie, come down here son, and tell us what is bothering you?" Eddie didn't respond and instead starting walking off towards the buildings that he had previously pointed towards.

"Ralph," said the chief addressing me, "You better go after him and see what this is all about," he commanded. "If this turns out to be one of Eddie's usual pranks, I want you to yank the bugger back by his ears so we can give him a sound thrashing."

"Roger that Guv," I said and then motioning to one of the other lads, a chap called Harry, to come along, we both took off after Eddie.

We found Eddie standing in front of a building that had been partially destroyed in last night's bombings. While the lower level of the building was still intact, the upper portion had taken a partial hit by a stray bomb and half of it had been reduced to rubble while the walls of the other half stood precariously, with the roof ready to fall down at any moment. I recognized the building immediately and exclaimed "Christ, Eddie, isn't this where you live?"

Eddie nodded sadly while he looked at the building. "Death comes in threes," he said again. I knew that Eddie had shared a flat with his best friend Mike, Mike's wife (whose name I could not remember), and their two-year-old daughter.

"Eddie, were your flatmates at home when this happened?" I asked him. Eddie nodded sadly again and pointed towards the now demolished second level of his building. I felt sorry for Eddie and told him so. "We will find them, Eddie, don't you worry," I said as we climbed the stairs, which were thankfully still intact, in order to reach Eddie's flat.

The corridor was dark and littered with rubble. Dust hung in the air barring our way, as if in silent protest to the cruel manner in which we humans treat each other. There had been only two flats on the upper level and only one (presumably Eddie's) had been destroyed while the other had escaped only with minor damage, though it was still unsafe due to the danger of the roof collapsing. Harry and I knocked on the door of the second apartment which was opened by a wizened old lady in her petticoat. She peered at us across ancient glasses that had seen better days. "Ma'am, this place is not safe anymore, do you have somewhere else to go?" I asked. She shook her head so we gently led her downstairs, and after collecting the tenants in the downstairs flat, we took everybody to the building next door where another tenant graciously accepted them to wait over tea while we telephoned the fire marshall to come and assess the building. "It may be a few hours before the fire marshall makes his way here, sir," I said to the tenant, a retired colonel.

"Not an issue, young man," he replied, "Thank you for your service." Harry and I went back to Eddie's flat where we found Eddie standing near the door, looking sadly inside.

The flat had once been home to living, breathing human beings, but a cruel twist of fate had reduced it to dust and ashes. We started removing the rubble in one corner of the flat and worked our way around methodically as Eddie stood in the doorway watching us. "Here!" shouted Harry suddenly and as I walked over to him, I saw a hand sticking out from beneath the debris. We dug out the body beneath and it turned out to be that of Mike. I looked over to Eddie, trying to convey my silent condolences but he kept staring elsewhere. We resumed our search and soon discovered another body, this time of a woman, whom I assumed to be Mike's wife. This left only the child and the prospect of finding her corpse was not something either Harry or I was looking forward to. Children were difficult, always difficult and no amount of jokes and grim humor helped with the horror of seeing a little hand or feet sticking out from the rubble. Steeling ourselves, we resumed our search.

I had just cleared a large section of the wall that had collapsed when I discovered the crib and the child sleeping within it. By some miracle, the wall had collapsed at an angle where it had lodged itself against another wall, thereby sheltering the crib from other debris that had rained down. The child had been trapped in this safe space and must have cried all night before falling asleep from exhaustion. Tears came into my eyes as I stood watching her little chest rise and fall and when I turned towards Harry, I could see his eyes wet with moisture too. Gently picking up the little girl so as not to wake her up, I turned towards Eddie and whispered "She is alive mate! She is alive! It's a miracle."

Eddie looked at us with a sad smile. "Death comes in threes," he said again while pointing towards a doorway that led to another room that we had not yet explored. I wondered aloud if there had been other occupants in the flat that we didn't know of and told Harry to go look while I cradled the sleeping child in my arms.

Harry must have been digging for a minute or two when suddenly I heard an exclamation and the sound of him falling. I rushed through the doorway and saw Harry kneeling on the floor, unhurt and staring towards a spot he had been digging at, his eyes wide open with shock and fright. I walked closer to this spot and saw for myself the dead face of one Edward Rollins, known as Eddie to his friends, his broken body buried between a pile of rubble, even as somehow he also stood in the doorway behind me, looking as sad as one can be.

THE BEAST WITHIN

Andrei Yegorov had never been comfortable in his skin. He hated his long, matted hair, black as a raven; he hated his ice-blue eyes, cold as the Siberian hinterland in which he was born. He hated his large hands and the way the nails grew on them, pointed and sharp. He hated his ears, long with pointed tips, quite like those of the *chukcha,* the Siberian Husky dogs that people

in these parts used for pulling their sleighs. He hated everything about himself.

"You are a handsome boy," said Albina, Andrei's old *babushka,* with whom he lived in a small hut in a forest near the village of Tomsk. "Pay no mind to the villagers. They are just scared of you," she told him often.

"I hate the lot," growled Andrei. "Whenever I pass through the village, the men spit on me, the women avert their eyes and the children run alongside taunting me. I feel like ripping the heads off their little bodies," he said getting angrier and angrier at the memory of the insults.

"You will soon turn sixteen, Andrei, and you must learn to control your temper," cautioned Albina. "Remember what I told you. Our family has a curse upon it and we must therefore never take the life of another."

"Yes, yes, I know," snorted Andrei. "Next you will tell me how papa didn't listen to you after mama died and therefore had to run away into the forest, never to return." Albina didn't respond and just looked sad which made Andrei sad too.

"I'm sorry babushka," he said gently. "I will try harder to not get so angry." Albina smiled at this and kissed him on his cheek and then sent him out to fetch more firewood.

Andrei's birthday was just a few weeks away, not that it would be any different from the rest of the days, for they were too poor to celebrate anything. Still, he looked forward to it, for it would mean that he would be old enough to join the Cossack regiment that was stationed near the village. He figured that he would make a passable living in the service of the czar and therefore ensure that his babushka did not want for anything in her old age. Besides, as a soldier, he would be immune to the villager's taunts and insults. "Let them try messing with me once I am a Cossack riding my horse," he said aloud as he play-acted a sword fight with a stick from his bundle of firewood.

Life continued at its normal pace in Andrei's little world. A day before his birthday, he managed to shoot a small roe deer with his bow, much to Albina's delight. "We will eat a little of it tonight and have a feast for your birthday tomorrow," she said.

That night, a new moon rose and bathed the countryside in its silvery brilliance. Andrei sat outside their little hut with Albina, roasting a leg of deer on a small fire as she told him stories about their family history, tales that never lost their magic even after countless retellings. A wolf howled in the distance, sending a shiver of nervous excitement down Andrei's spine.

Albina paused for a moment, listening as the wolf howled again. "Pay him no mind," she said to Andrei. "He is just lonely."

The next morning dawned bright and clear and Albina woke Andrei with a soft kiss on his forehead. "Happy birthday, child," she said, "Today my little boy has grown up to be a man." Andrei smiled and let loose a huge yawn as he tried to rise, only to fall back onto the bed. "What's wrong?" asked Albina as she put her hand on his forehead, "Why you are burning up!" she exclaimed after feeling Andrei's hot skin. "Don't try to get up, I will go and get some medicine."

"How?" croaked Andrei. "We have no money for medicine."

"Don't you worry, boy," said Albina, "I will trade what remains of the deer." Albina packed up the deer carcass into a bag and stepped out of the hut. She paused for a moment and observed the ground around the hut, on which the pawprints of a large wolf were visible in the snow. Breaking off a branch from a nearby tree, she quickly used the leaves to eliminate the pawprints and then hurried off in the direction of the village.

Morning slowly turned to afternoon, but Albina didn't return. Andrei tossed and turned on the bed, his mind engulfed in feverish dreams in which he saw himself running across the moonlit Siberian plains alongside a large black wolf. Together they chased their prey, blood pumping in their hearts and rushing through their minds, consumed by the thrill of the hunt, their paws barely touching the snow as they ran, faster and faster, until they were almost upon their quarry, which turned out be a man. The black wolf urged Andrei to attack, and Andrei surged forward and was upon the hapless victim in an instant, his vicious jaws tearing at the man's throat as the taste of the man's sweet blood filled Andrei's senses. Only then did he realize that the victim's face was Andrei's own, and at that moment he woke up from the nightmare with his heart thudding against his chest, and a scream caught within his throat.

As he slowly calmed down, Andrei realized two things. One, his fever had broken and he no longer felt sick. Second, the evening was fast approaching and his babushka had still not returned from the village. A couple of miles of dense forest lay between their hut and the village and even though there would be a full moon tonight, it wasn't safe for her to traverse the forest alone once the sun went down. Grabbing his bow and some arrows, Andrei started towards the village, walking as quickly as possible to take advantage of the light that remained.

Andrei was nearing the edge of the forest when he heard loud voices on the other side. His natural wariness of the village people caused him to immediately drop down on his haunches and crawl forward slowly so as not to give away his presence. Peering through the trees, he saw the most terrible scene imaginable. In the clearing next to the forest, a wooden scaffold had been set up, along with what appeared to be a pyre made of firewood. On the scaffold, naked and with her hands tied behind her back stood Albina, her face livid with bruises that were starting to turn blue. Next to her stood Yevgeny Popovich, the richest man in the village and perhaps also the cruelest.

Yevgeny addressed the crowd of villagers gathered around and Andrei caught snippets of what was being said: "Killed all my sheep...at night...mother of that accursed wolf...soon that young pup will turn too... they will hunt our children next...burn them all." At the mention of burning, the villagers cheered and Andrei gritted his teeth as Yevgeny dragged his babushka down from the scaffold and threw her onto the pyre. Somebody handed him a burning torch and Yevgeny turned towards the small figure of Albina that lay prone over the pyre. He gave her a vicious kick to rouse her, but she didn't respond and so he spit on her. Then with a sadistic smile, he picked up a lit torch and proceeded to set the pyre on fire. As the flames ate through the firewood and started licking her legs, Albina began to scream.

Andrei watched all of this, his eyes burning with tears of rage and frustration. He knew that he could not save his babushka, for there were too many of the villagers present. He could, however, surely save her from excruciating pain and so drawing an arrow on his bow, he took careful aim for her heart. Years of hunting in the wild had made Andrei an excellent marksman and when he let the arrow fly, it swiftly found its mark as Albina's screams were suddenly cut short. Ignoring

Albina's previous warnings that ran through his mind, Andrei quickly let a second arrow fly, which embedded itself in Yevgeny's left eye, who pitched forward like a felled tree, dead before his corpse hit the ground. There was quite a commotion amongst the villagers at this new and sudden development, but Andrei didn't stay to watch. Casting his bow and arrows aside, he ran off into the wild, neither knowing nor caring where he went as the air was rent by his screams of rage, and which were answered by the howls of a lone wolf.

Andrei ran for a long time, and finally exhausted, he stopped in a moonlit clearing and dropped to his knees. His fever was back and his body burnt as if on fire. There was strange music in the air, music not from any instruments but something that emanated from the silvery light of the moon that called out to him. Instinct told him to shed all of his clothes and doing so brought him some relief. He noticed that the sounds of the forest all around him had become amplified. His bones cracked and turned and his spine twisted, forcing him onto all fours, just as his hand and feet swiveled and his nails elongated, tearing the soft skin. His vision too changed, becoming sharper and better suited for the night and he could now see the creatures of the forest that stood and watched from the edge of the clearing as if to bear witness to the change that was overcoming him. He could feel their heartbeat, even smell their fear, for he could tell that they were all terrified of him.

All except one.

He sensed that there was another who watched him and yet did not fear him. Turning his head towards a particularly dark patch of the forest that surrounded the clearing, Andrei let loose a growl from deep within his throat. A shape detached itself from the darkness and walked towards Andrei. The light of the moon revealed a large black wolf, who now stood close to Andrei watching him with baleful eyes, ice blue just like his own, eyes that Andrei had never forgotten even after all these years. "Papa?" he whispered, though the words came out as a growl. Hearing this, the other wolf let loose a mournful howl, and Andrei joined in, feeling comfortable in his skin for the first time in his life.

Made in the USA
Middletown, DE
13 June 2021